S0-AQC-465

MIRACLE MyX

REVIEW

In the Massachusetts town of Miracle lives Myx Amens, only 14 years old but a key player in the Miracle police force. Heck, Myx has already died twice, so what's a little danger in the line of duty? His first death (by lightning) left him with a photographic memory. His second death (at the hands of a bully) left him unable to sleep and his senses discombobulated: he can smell sounds, feel tastes, and hear feelings. This unusal affliction is called synesthesia, and with a doctor's help, Myx has learned to live with it. When corpses start turning up with odd parts missing, the cops reluctantly call on bionic Myx to use his particular skills to help investigate the crimes (hearing feelings comes in pretty handy when you're asking questions). Myx, whose sleepless nights allow him ample time for sleuthing, proves especially adept at drawing people out, especially the beautiful, grieving mother of one of the victims.

What makes this debut novel exceptional is Diotalevi's clever use of Myx's sense-mingling; more than a mere plot device, the character's synesthetic gift enables the author to wax poetic one minute ("her hand smelled pink with carved curls of green") and comic the next ("her breasts talked to me, but I'm keeping their conversation private"). A wickedly funny, surprisingly moving genre-bending tale of small-town secrets, lies, and revenge.

— Mary Frances Wilkens, *Booklist* starred review

A NOVEL

DAVE DIOTALEVI

LARGO, USA

MIRACLE MYX

Copyright © 2008 by Dave Diotalevi.

All Rights Reserved. Published and printed in the United States of America by Kunati
Inc. (USA) and simultaneously printed and published in Canada by Kunati Inc. (Canada)
No part of this book may be reproduced, copied or used in any form
or manner whatsoever without written permission,
except in the case of brief quotations in reviews and critical articles.

For information, contact Kunati Inc., Book Publishers in both USA and Canada.
In USA: 6901 Bryan Dairy Road, Suite 150, Largo, FL 33777 USA
In Canada: 75 First Street, Suite 128, Orangeville, ON L9W 5B6 CANADA,
or e-mail to info@kunati.com.

FIRST EDITION

Designed by Kam Wai Yu
Persona Corp. I www.personaco.com

ISBN-13: 978-1-60164-155-7 I EAN 9781601641557 I FIC000000 FICTION/General

Published by Kunati Inc. (USA) and Kunati Inc. (Canada).
Provocative. Bold. Controversial.™

http://www.kunati.com

TM—Kunati and Kunati Trailer are trademarks
owned by Kunati Inc. Persona is a trademark owned by Persona Corp.
All other trademarks are the property of their respective owners.

Disclaimer: This is a work of fiction. All events described herein are imaginary, including
settings and characters. Any similarity to real persons, entities, or companies is purely
coincidental and not intended to represent real places or living persons. Real brand names,
company names, names of public personalities or real people may be employed for credibility
because they are part of our culture and everyday lives. Regardless of context, their use is
meant neither as endorsement nor criticism: such names are used fictitiously without intent to
describe their actual conduct or value. All other names, products or brands are inventions of the
author's imagination. Kunati Inc. and its directors, employees, distributors, retailers, wholesalers
and assigns disclaims any liability or responsibility for the author's statements, words, ideas,
criticisms or observations. Kunati assumes no responsibility for errors, inaccuracies, or omissions.

Library of Congress Cataloging-in-Publication Data

Diotalevi, David A., 1951-
  Miracle Myx : a novel / Dave Diotalevi. -- 1st ed.
      p. cm.
  Summary: "Twice dead, and equipped with a synesthetic brain -- he can smell
colors among other abilities -- Myx Amens is a unique fictional "detective"
who can't leave any mystery unsolved in Miracle, Massachusetts"--Provided by
publisher.
  ISBN 978-1-60164-155-7
  1. Cyborgs--Fiction. 2. Massachusetts--Fiction. I. Title.
  PS3604.I58M57 2008
  813'.6--dc22

                          2008001056

Dedication

In memory of

Dr. Michael Aronoff,

Myx's first fan.

Chapter One

I've died twice.

So far.

But, then again, I'm only fourteen.

Lemons. The moonlight tasted like lemons. Kind of sour and felt yellow with points. It came through Mrs. Walker's bedroom blinds, painting bright strips between the shadows. In the moon's spotlight, I ran my right thumb over the blue tattoo on my left bicep: M Y X. Myx is what everyone called me, even though that wasn't my real name (which hardly anyone knew anymore). Where the tattoo came from, I didn't know.

Mrs. Walker's bedroom smelt of stale breath and farts on the fade. She was messier than I would have guessed. I really didn't guess much; I liked to be surprised by people's personal lives. She looked much neater in school, though. Piles of clothes thrown on the furniture and floor, magazines, and scraps of notepaper with a few words scratched at odd angles covered a lot of the available area.

I looked into the mirror above the dresser. There she was with Mr. Walker, a few feet away, both sleeping as peacefully as if they were alone. I'd rather not get this close, but my search of the rest of the house hadn't turned up my key, the one she took from me in class today. Getting the key in the first place had been hard enough (although fun and interesting). I couldn't let a little thing like an authoritarian trying to teach me a lesson in classroom procedure—

no deliveries during Math, I guess—keep me from my hard-earned prize.

The top of the dresser was as cluttered with past importance as the rest of the room. But there, where she must have emptied her pockets, was the blue twine that looped through the key's bowhole. The key itself was hidden under the litter. Instead of pulling the twine, I carefully uncovered it, moving the bits of trouser trash until I could haul it silently free. I looked at it, a shiny, short barrel key. Then, I slid it into my right pants pocket.

I smiled at the mirror. I felt good, good to be alive. Her hairbrush, lying there on the dresser, was full of long blonde strands. This hadn't been cleaned for months. I pulled out the tangle in two rips and threw the hair on the floor. A clean brush—no charge.

I brushed my hair straight back. Perfect. I wondered if she'd notice any black strands I left.

That's when Mrs. Walker turned over, thankfully away from me and towards her husband, draping her left leg over the top sheet that covered them.

Hey, she slept naked.

I watched in the mirror for any other movement. Nothing. But there was a dark spot on her ass, left cheek.

I had what I wanted: the key.

This is the time I should just quickly leave.

I walked to the bed to get a closer look at that ass spot. It was a tattoo. Who would have thought Mrs. Walker had a tattoo? An indigo butterfly with a red outline stroke. Nice work. Dragon's work. It had a low bull fiddle sound to it.

She turned over quickly and half sat up, bracing herself on her elbows. I had sensed her breathing change and dropped silently to the floor beside the bed. It would be easier for me if she didn't look down. They usually don't. I was beginning to think women had more senses than I did, especially on their asses.

My face was close to the mound of clothes she had shucked off before bed. *Hey, she wore a thong.* Who would have … ?

"Harold, wake up," she whispered. "There's someone in the house." A repeated shake of the bed told me she must be jabbing the poor guy.

I envied the place he was coming from: that deep, oblivious time out of life—sleep. I hadn't slept since the Indian killed me. Three long, continuous years.

Harold—Mr. Walker—gurgled and groaned and cleared his throat. This is where the husband tells his wife she's either crazy or imagining things.

"I got my gun in the nightstand here. I'll get up right now and check the whole house top to bottom and shoot the creep."

Huh!

"Ginny, you do this three times a week." His voice had a bit of a whine to it now. "Quit it. There's nobody here. There was nobody here last night and there was nobody here last week. There's no reason for anybody to come here every night and watch you sleep."

Except tonight.

That's better. More of what I was used to. Ginny, eh? Virginia, Ginny. Made sense.

Mr. Walker's voice changed, lost some of the jagged edges it made me see and became curvier. "What you need, Baby, is some vitamin H. C'mere." It sounded like he shifted closer to Mrs. Walker.

Uh-oh. Please, not that.

"Harold, go to sleep for God's sake. You have an early morning."

She made a quick flip to her stomach and hung her right hand over the side of the bed, an inch from my nose. I sniffed twice, taking care not to make any windy sounds.

Her hand smelled pink with carved curls of green, surprisingly like her thong. No wonder poor Mr. W was on his own. I surmised "Ginny" had let her fingers do the "walking" earlier in the evening. I grinned at my use of her name, Walker.

Then my stomach rumbled. It sounded loud to me, and I hoped she hadn't heard. No response, so I was still an unknown guest. As soon as their breathing became regular, I got up and made it to the hardwood floor of the hallway. I stepped around the board that had squeaked on the way in.

Their bathroom was at the top of the stairs. My stomach churnings told me it was time to leave a deposit. Wadded toilet paper dropped in first made for a silent business transaction. Of course, flushing would have been foolish.

I was hungry. I was always hungry. Maybe it was because of not sleeping and constantly being on the move. I didn't remember this hunger before the Indian.

Since the Walker's kitchen was right there on the way out, I decided to partake of their unspoken hospitality. I had the time, like always when your whole twenty-four hours needed filling. Bread, peanut butter and grape jelly were fine; I didn't feel like cooking anyway. It was safe to open the refrigerator—a swinging door shielded the kitchen from the stairs.

I had finished my second sandwich and was about done with the glass of milk when I heard heavy footsteps in the hall upstairs. They stopped in the bathroom.

"Jesus Christ, Ginny!"

Time to go. I put my glass in the sink and, after wiping my mouth with it, crumpled the paper towel on which I had made the sandwiches and tossed it with a banking set shot into the trash.

I locked the back door on my way out. The Walkers were again safe—and alone.

It would take about a half hour to walk from Catalpa Street to the center of Miracle. The moon was lower now, and had a few clouds drifting by it, filtering its light. The taste had changed to tangerines, and the points weren't as sharp. I could hear spring peepers calling far off, so I stopped walking just to listen for a minute. They sounded balloon-light and soft green. Their song made me smile.

Not a lot of traffic at 3:37 A.M. Every once in a while I saw headlights in the distance ahead or behind me. If a car got close, I drifted into the cover of a backyard or bush until it passed. I had found it was never a good idea to be too noticeable or memorable. I didn't mind the cruising perverts; it was the busybody do-gooders who usually caused annoyances.

A big white van hugged the corner of Hollow and Maize ahead. It sounded like it would stall (but never did) and the headlights made two buzzing cylinders that faded down the street. Large blue letters spelled *Miracle Daily News* on its side. A skinny, ugly guy was filling the sidewalk newspaper dispenser feet away. His khaki shorts and gray T-shirt with a badly stretched breast pocket were cinched together by a thin black leather belt pulled to its tightest hole. The long loose end of it flopped limply with each of his movements and left hissing swirls.

"Any extras?" I said when I got close.

He turned, a bit startled, and swallowed before saying, "Myx! What are you doing up so early?"

I laughed.

"Just taking a nice walk, Bindy."

Bindy was one of my nighttime regulars. We intersected a few times a month. At the beginning of the school year, he had complained to me that his daughter, Miriam, a senior at Miracle High, was being blackballed and generally harassed by Shelly Powell, resident school bitch queen. All I can say is that if you don't want your diary read, you shouldn't leave it in a locked box in the back of your bedroom closet at the bottom of your clothes hamper where everyone can get at it. It only took a little pinching (I think "blackmail" is such an ugly word) to get Miriam into Shelly's good graces.

Miriam was happy. Bindy was happy. I was happy. Shelly was scared. It always works out right.

"Going my way?" I asked.

"If the center's your way. I'm heading for Main Street."

I got in the locked-open sliding door of the van and stood beside him as he drove, swaying and balancing on the turns. The smell of the ink on the piles of papers stacked in the back felt oily and smooth with a bitter taste. The plastic ties squeezing the papers into bundles showed slightly blue and translucent. They had disharmonious high pitches.

There was another smell, green and sharp and sour: blood. My reaction was always fierce, almost mean.

"Accident, Bindy?" I said touching the back of his hand. There was blood, fresh and caked on his scarred knuckles. He had boxed when younger and told me he still had a heavy bag hanging at home.

"Part of the deal, kid. When you're in a hurry, these things are sharks ready to eat you up."

I knew he meant the newspaper stands, but his words looked

gray. Not black, a total lie; not white, the complete truth. I found gray could mean confusion, nervousness, evasion, deception, or bluff. Something was up, but I didn't care.

My synesthesia at first had seemed like a disease—now it was my tool, my shield, and sometimes, my weapon. I still didn't know how to read all the impressions I got from my senses. My life since my first death had been one of calibration; since my second death, adjustment.

Not being able to legally drive sucked. Of course, I knew *how* to drive and did so when I had to, like last year when I followed Malik, the arsonist, up the Mass Pike to 128 in Waltham. (He really shouldn't have played with matches.) Still, who wants to be pulled over? I like to stay in the shadows, which is not on the roads and highways while under age.

We passed maybe a dozen cars. I looked at all of them. I looked at everything, and remembered everything. It was habit now that I could handle it.

"This is good," I said as we got to East Main Street. I didn't want him to know where I was going. I never wanted anyone to know too much about what I did, who I knew, and how I did things. I wasn't trying to be mysterious, but I found that if people thought they knew you, they'd use you. And finally, if the circumstances were right, they'd justify turning on you, no matter how nice they seemed. I liked to do what interested me, what was fun or gave me a thrill or taught me something.

I'd learned that prying into others' troubles seemed to be a good way to stay busy and interested. Although sometimes it taught me things no one should know.

The van slowed near Dunkin' Donuts. "You want something?" I

asked as I hopped and trotted out of the moving vehicle.

"Next time, Myx. Lots to do," he said as he speeded up again, never fully stopping. His red taillights stabbed my fingertips a bit as I watched them get smaller. I snuffed air out of my nose a few times, purging the blood smell.

The fluorescent lights sounded blue and flat in Dunkin's. They were just opening, and Amy gave me two glazed donuts, soft and fresh. I was her first "customer."

Time to deliver the key. I ate the donuts as I walked up East Main to Main, and resisted the urge to lick my fingers. I hadn't washed my hands since I used the facilities at Mrs. Walker's. Running water gets attention in a silent house. I had found that out through experience.

A squat granite building sat in the middle of town. The flood light near the front steps shined hot and white on two perfectly centered words carved in what looked like Engravers Bold over the door: Miracle Police.

Out of habit, I circled once and took in the details. Something was going on; there were cruisers, the Chief's car, and several private vehicles parked in front and on the side, Birch Street. This wasn't the time and this wasn't the place for me. All the signs told me to go home.

I climbed the stairs and walked into the station.

Chapter Two

"You're a polymodal synesthete," Dr. Zylodic had told me three years before without looking up from his notes. I was only eleven then.

"I thought I was Catholic," I said, smiling at my joke.

Dr. Zylodic raised his eyes over the thick black plastic frames of his glasses and then focused back on his notebook, scribbling, "Subject maintains what he deems to be a sense of humor in the midst of personal tragedy, turmoil, and readjustment."

"I'm a subject now?" I asked.

"You can read my handwriting upside down?"

Back then, I was still showing off. I hadn't learned that most people weren't impressed or amused—but annoyed, frightened, or secretly planning how to use my new-found talents for their own benefit.

"Sure," I said leaning over the table and grabbing the pen from his hand, "and that's not all. Watch this!"

With my left hand I wrote on the same line he had just finished: "Why do you call me subject when you know my name is Myx?"

He stared at my writing for a moment without expression then nodded to himself. "I've never seen this before … Myx, you've just written upside down. But, the interesting facet is, you've written in my own handwriting. I can't tell *the* difference between my script and yours."

"I just have to match the sounds and colors of your words on the paper. My hand knows how to do it. Easy."

Dr. Zylodic's posture never changed. Neither did his expression. "This is very exciting," he said with the same monotone he had been using all day. But to me, the shape of his voice was sharper, and he smelled a slightly different color too. He really *was* excited.

It had been six months since I had died the first time. This was all still new to me, but I was learning fast—how to deal with the strange way I experienced the world, that is. At first, everything piled onto me at once. I couldn't fight off all the ways the light, heat, pressure, and sounds came at me. It was too much, too fast, too hard. I would squeeze my eyes closed and press my hands over my ears to try and shut out the relentless confusion.

Back then I wished every day that I had stayed dead and just kept feeling what I had felt in that room, the glow room. The endless attack on my senses made me want to run away from my life.

Instead, I ran, just literally and physically ran as fast and far and as long as I could whenever I could. It made me feel better and more in control. Running made things fit. I think running let me catch up with myself. It left a space to let all of me agree on who I was now and how to be my new self better. Climbing was an offshoot of running. A rock, a tree, a rope—a building. The strain of pulling, the height, the danger all consumed the raw fuel of my confusion and anger. I wanted to exhaust my senses. I only exhausted my body, condensed and hardened it.

Any release exhaustion brought ended after the Indian sent me for my second visit to the glow room. No more sleep, no more tiredness, no more reprieves.

The habit of running and climbing remained, though.

Gradually I could see how to use my new perceptions, and how my

senses blended into something useful. I didn't fight the impressions any more. I let them come and found I could choose how to control my attention. It started to be fun. It started to be interesting. I started to get nosey!

Other people's lives began to open up to me. The way they looked and smelled and moved and talked told me more than before. More about what they felt and what they meant. Also, more about their secrets—and where they hid them.

Dr. Zylodic was from the Harvard Psychology Department's Cognition, Brain, and Behavior Group. Mary Milloy, a former neighbor, worked for the Massachusetts Department of Social Services. It was through her I started a long series of examinations, testing, and head scratching among doctors trying to figure out why I couldn't understand the world any more after my grandmother and I died. She finally got Dr. Zylodic involved. Before entering private psychiatric practice in his Belmont home, he had headed the Harvard group.

Mrs. Milloy was really concerned and helpful. I still almost feel a little guilty for having to pinch her later when I wanted to get adopted. Almost.

"Do you know what synesthesia is, Myx?" Dr. Zylodic asked.

"Spell it," I said. He did. "Synesthesia is a non-objective sensation or image of a sense other than the one being stimulated," I said proudly. (I found out later that synesthesia meant my senses talked to each other, making me hear colors, taste shapes, smells sounds, and all sorts of other combinations. No wonder I was scared and confused.)

Dr. Zylodic was staring at me and tapping the point of his pen, fast and lightly, on the table. Something had excited him, although

the thought didn't tell his face. That remained expressionless.

"You were looking up and to your left. You were remembering. You were seeing it, weren't you?" He asked me, but nodded to himself like he had already made his mind up.

"I looked all the way through a dictionary once while I was waiting in a doctor's office," I said.

He reached down beside him and fumbled a big book out of his briefcase. On the spine, I saw the title was *Psychological Methods, Assessments, Research & Statistics*. Dr. Zylodic randomly opened it to about the middle, banged it perpendicular to the table, its open pages facing me. The sound was purple, but had smooth edges because the binding was soft against the wood of the table.

In what seemed less than a second, he clapped the book shut. "What did you see?" His voice now had a redness and little points of yellow light on it.

"You didn't give me time to …"

"What did you see?" He was louder.

I got to my knees on the chair, reached across the table for his pad, and flipped to a clean page. With a pencil from the table, I started to print words from my head with my left hand. After about a minute, I picked up another pencil in my right hand and drew what Dr. Zylodic later told me was a bar chart. I drew while I was still writing.

"That's enough, Myx," he said after another minute. I handed him the pad. He pressed the fingertips of his left hand to his forehead and shook his head slightly from side to side. He looked at my writing for a long time, then opened the book again and laid my efforts on top of it. "I'm lucky you wrote the page number down," he said as a matter of fact. "This is exact—down to the size of the lettering and

the serifs."

He crossed his arms, took a deep breath and said, "You have an eidetic memory."

"Spell it," I said.

He actually laughed.

Chapter Three

The stone steps felt uneven as I climbed toward the police station door. I could hear popping, like packing material bursting, as my feet read the irregular surface.

Inside shined too brightly, and pressed on me with a hard redness. Sgt. Wayne stood at the front desk and ran a hand over his mouth repeatedly, pinching his lips each time. His eyes caught mine and he shook his head from side to side in little quick motions.

"Not a good time, Myx," he said, leaning closer and almost whispering. He looked toward the Chief's closed door, back at me, and tilted his head toward the exit, "Better go now."

"Please let me have an envelope, and I'll be out of here," I said, putting my hand out. I'd come here with the intention of finishing this key business, and I wasn't leaving it undone no matter what was going on.

Sgt. Wayne handed me a small A-6 envelope with a clear window. I handed it back and asked, "Could I have a business envelope instead, Sgt. Wayne?" He looked toward the Chief's door, let out a breath and gave me a long, white envelope. "And a piece of paper, please."

"Hurry it up, Myx. Get out of here."

I turned away from him and took the key on the string from my pocket. It was shiny in the bright light, and the string had frayed ends near the knot. I folded it into the paper, making several layers so you couldn't feel it, slipped it neatly into the envelope, licked the glued flap, and sealed it by running a finger along the edge several times. The glue tasted slightly sweet, yellow, and cool. I took a pen from the counter and wrote: Chief Maldonato. I didn't use my own handwriting, but a beautiful script I had recently seen. My hand sang the music of its curves as I wrote.

"Will you give this to the Chief for me, Sergeant?" The Chief and I had an understanding: I provided certain things he needed, on occasion, and he ignored certain things I did, on occasion. We both didn't like it, but it was a relationship that worked. The Sergeant took the envelope while looking again at the Chief's door. Three voices: the Chief, a female, and another male. They felt rough and jagged. Each voice sank a weight into my stomach. I never liked that feeling, but I'd gotten used to it. Trouble. I knew it was trouble.

The door handle jiggled—a hand on it wanting to get out. It stopped and then jiggled again. It sounded like a small bell to me. The voices got louder and the door was yanked open by one of the most beautiful women I had ever seen. Tall, blonde, tight jeans, loose-fitting pullover silk blue blouse, no bra. What's not to like?

Her face burned red with emotion and her jaw bulged with applied force. She looked at me, squinted, and I wished I had left a moment earlier. She pointed and whispered through clenched teeth, "What's this little shit doing here?"

Little?

"Hi, Mrs. Powell," I said in my cheeriest voice. Why let her affect my night? On the other hand, I hated coincidence. This was Shelly's mother, and I had just finished thinking about Shelly for the first time in months not a half hour ago.

"Angelo, I want to know why he's here." Her eyes never left me, never blinked. They were a soft blue, a slight peppermint taste with a "ssshhhh" sound. Anyone could tell that she had been crying. Me especially; I could smell her tears, cobalt and cold.

Chief Angelo Maldonato lurched behind her, then saw me. I waved. His eyes widened and his face hardened. "Get out, Amens." The Chief always sounded like he had to clear his throat. It looked like bubbles to me when he talked. I suppressed the urge to clear my own throat. He had on his usual spotless white shirt, blue tie, and gleaming gold badge. The combination always pleased me if I ignored how the shirt stretched over his rounded belly until it was bounded by the latitude of his black belt.

I turned to go but stopped when Mrs. Powell shrieked, "Amens? Myx Amens? Angie, arrest this little bastard!"

She lunged and clawed for my eyes with her right hand. Her long nails shone with a desaturated purple polish. Not a chip—they were perfect. Of course I had easily read her movements: the change in the air currents, her breathing, the tightening of her muscles. These, along with the slight sheen of perspiration that appears when people attack me, gave plenty of warning. So I sidestepped and caught her as she plunged past in the awkward and failed attempt to do poor, innocent me some harm. (Innocent this time, anyway.)

I readjusted my right hand, which had at first rested directly on her full, rounded, all-natural left breast. I held tight as she struggled so neither of us would get hurt. I was stronger than I looked. Much stronger. She tried stamping my instep, but that didn't work either.

I inhaled deeply and resisted putting my nose against the nape of her neck to get a better whiff. Mrs. Powell had a faint spice smell to her. I would bet she had used *Omnia* by Bulgari the day before. I rarely lose a bet. Well, okay, if I bet, I never lose. I had smelled many perfumes at the mall and could identify any of them easily and even draw the bottles and packages if I needed to (which, I understand, I never would). Another sniff told me she had her period. No menopause here.

"Patty, take it easy." A small, balding man with rimless glasses rushed out of the office and pulled her from my reluctant release. Sam Powell, an engineer for Zaytheon. He was also Chairman of Miracle's Board of Selectmen. She shook herself free and turned on me again, pointing and scowling.

"This little bastard scared her to death. She told me he knew things and was a creep. And now he's here. He did it, Angelo. He killed Shelly!"

I don't think I'm that little: I weigh 163 and am a good five foot nine. But, no matter. *Shelly, dead?* This wasn't just any ordinary night in Miracle, Massachusetts.

Mrs. Powell, her face distorted by anger and sorrow, started another assault. Sgt. Wayne, without anyone but me noticing, had come between us.

He considered the police station his property, his domain, his charge; the Chief let him run it the way he wanted. The way he wanted, as long as I had seen, was orderly, with no waves. Without Sgt. Wayne's intervention, Patty Powell was about to make waves.

The Sergeant held up his thick, short-fingered hands, a palm facing each of us. He did it as if he were stopping traffic on Main Street. I looked at his callused hand, and remembered how casually he had broken Terry Kincaid's forearm with a grab and twist when Terry tried to slap Karen Baker's already-bloodied mouth one last time at the Silver Cloud Lounge on East Main Street. Terry was Miracle's self-proclaimed "toughest man." He was the toughest drunk, but, in my opinion, would become a quick collection of contusions, bruises,

and splinterings if left alone with Sgt. Wayne for a few minutes. I
had been there to give Karen some Polaroids that had been stolen by
her ex. It was me who called Sgt. Wayne when I saw Terry start to
play rougher with every drink.

Mrs. Powell leaned forward in one last furious charge toward me,
only to be restrained without any perceptible effort by the Sergeant.
I, at the same time, had remained motionless, inches away from that
human vise. The Sergeant gave off a low, purple hum with rounded
edges. Constrained power was my impression.

"Enough," was all the Sergeant said. And that was enough.

Chief Maldonato walked forward and put a hand on Sgt.
Wayne's shoulder. "It's okay, Freddy. Everyone is going to behave.
Right, Patty?" He angled his tired-looking face down and sighed as
he looked into her eyes. She breathed deeply and stepped back. The
Chief looked at me, widening his glare and pressing his lips tightly
together, showing his discontent at my intrusion. I shrugged and
raised my eyebrows. After a slow shake of his head, Chief Maldonato
explained further: "Patty, it's unfortunate that Amens is here, but it's
because of something I asked him to deliver. And I know he had
nothing to do with Shelly's death—he was here at that approximate
time. So, let's just calm down and put all our energy where it should
be ... in finding out what really happened."

Then he turned to me, lowered his head and mumbled, while
almost looking through his bushy brows, "Myx, stay out of the way
for now; later, I want to know if you saw anything tonight."

Sgt. Wayne inched to the front desk and with a last look at Patty
Powell, eased behind it. Order restored.

This left me and Mrs. Powell with nothing between us but the
silence that now filled the station.

"I'll leave, Chief," I said. I didn't want to become involved in another murder. Next to my own deaths, others' were my least favorites.

"No!" said the Chief and Mrs. Powell at the same time.

Drat! I never say that out loud, but I seem to think it often enough.

While all attention redirected itself away from me, I moved to the desk, took a sheet of paper and quickly listed a column of 27 alphanumeric sequences on it. I wrote in a plain, legible Ariel font, which gave off a satisfying whirr with each stroke.

I offered it to Chief Maldonato and said, "License plates I saw tonight, if it's any help." I had left off two: one was Bindy's, the other I couldn't remember.

That bothered me.

He took it and snuffed a little air out of his nose, not quite disbelieving like he used to. He raised his voice. "Mike."

A young officer came out one of the four doorways along the short corridor behind the Sergeant. He had a buzz cut, his scalp showing pale through the head stubble. His uniform was new and every bit of the shiny leather creaked with not-yet-worn-in stiffness. It gave me a sharp itch around my middle.

"Run these," the Chief said.

This was Mike Benvenuto, Miracle's newest policeman.

He took the paper, glanced at it, looked at the rest of us nervously, and said, "Right." He retreated to the same office, pausing at the doorway to look at our group one last time. This was the first big thing to happen since he had been on the force, and he seemed to be half excited and half sick.

Mrs. Powell spoke first, "I want to know where Fuckless here *was* tonight." She pointed at me with that superbly manicured right forefinger.

Fuckless? Although this was no time for humor, I looked over my right shoulder, as if she were pointing at someone behind me. I knew the Chief wouldn't want *anybody* to know where I had been tonight, or any night that I did *errands* for him.

"Myx," the Chief said tiredly. "Are you going to help or hurt here?" He didn't wait for an answer (I would have said, "Neither," if given the chance) before turning to Mrs. Powell. "He definitely wasn't involved, Patty. I know where he was when it happened. I told you that already."

"Shelly's dead. She hated him. She was scared to death of him. And here he is. You're telling me this is all by luck? Dumb fuckin' luck?" She took a deep breath, those breasts levitating against the fabric, and then let it out. Mrs. Powell was remapping her position—and my role; there's dozens of tells a body makes when it happens, and I seldom miss any of them. The dull hum of the room's tension changed tone for me, became softer, with a more pleasing frequency.

"He's here a lot." Sgt. Wayne seemed as surprised as anyone in the room that he had spoken. He looked down and pretended to scribble on a report.

The Chief gave a fierce look toward the Sergeant and then said, "He's right. Amens is here way too much. But he has his uses."

"I want to talk to him—alone—now." She pointed to the Chief's office.

"Patty ..." her husband started to say with a long-trained look of resignation.

"I don't think ..." the Chief was cut off by a definite, "Now!" from Mrs. Powell.

She turned and walked to the Chief's office. I knew I was expected to follow, and I did.

What did she have to say, or ask, that had to be kept private?

She was taller, so I straightened as much as I could as I paced behind her. Her faded jeans stretched taut with each step and showed off one great ass.

Chapter Four

I closed the door behind me. It was heavy, but the hinges were well-oiled. The smooth, old-fashioned doorknob had once been painted, but hands and turns had worn away most traces, leaving a brown/green patina of varying grimy shades on the brass patches. It felt cool in my right hand, leaving me with a bitter taste. The door's yellowish pane of pebbled glass showed only vague shadows, some moving, of the outer room we had just left.

A reassuring loud click signaled docking the door to frame. I spun to view the Chief's office.

Don't look at her tits. Don't look at her tits. Don't look at her tits. I thought one more time would definitely program me. *Don't look at her tits.*

Her breasts swayed gently and heavily under her blouse as she turned. They sagged perfectly, just enough to suggest a "worn-in" comfort that would welcome gentle cupping and weighing.

I love my ability to read people and I know it gives me an advantage. Teaching me to look at synesthesia as an asset was the best thing Dr. Zylodic had done for me. He said that he had merely "reframed" my thinking. I had used my edge many times to anticipate actions and to avoid, let's say, unpleasant outcomes. Right now I had let Mrs. Powell read me and anticipate my fantasy actions. I wondered if she had the wiles, the nerve, and the determination to press for an edge.

She waited until I raised my eyes to hers before saying, "I don't like you." Her voice was white.

"I can live with that," I said, reasoning that a respectful and polite response. I think I'm a likable person, and most would like me a lot more if they could separate the real me from the intrusive, meddling, coercive, and plain scary things that I did to them when I got involved in their lives. I don't *not* like people just because they don't like me. That would be very limiting.

This was the first time I was ever left alone in Chief Maldonato's office. By *alone*, I mean without police presence that would take offense at what I was about to do. Mrs. Powell should pose no problem, and I would be disappointed in myself if she even suspected anything, even though she would be watching me the whole time.

A grey metal desk piled with stacks of folders, some open and at angles, most closed and neatly lying on top of each other. Phone, light, framed photos, 15-inch LCD flat-panel computer screen, keyboard, mouse, Rolodex, a half cup of coffee (light), and a butternut donut missing one mouthful.

Rolodex.

"I'm sorry about Shelly, Mrs. Powell," I said as I walked around the desk and sat in the Chief's green vinyl swivel chair. My weight compressed the cushion beneath me, squeezing out a stream of air. It smelled of sweat and a bit like ass too.

"She hated you. She told me you were mean and weird."

Mean?

"Shelly just didn't get a chance to really know me. We met in a kind of funny situation," I said. I definitely didn't want to get into specifics here. (Specifics are only good for pinching.)

As I said this, I idly opened the curved cover of the black Rolodex, and turned one of the large twin knobs, the right one. Soft clicks came in succession as it fanned the alphabetically sorted white, slotted cards in front of me. They were all typed—some with handwritten notes. Turn, turn, turn says the Bible ... or was it the Byrds?

"Shelly said you could find out anything, and that scared her. What did you know about Shelly or about our family?"

I hoped I looked like a kid playing with something to avoid eye contact because of nervousness. *Contact.* The word made me almost smile. Contacts: names, addresses, phone numbers, and other personal information was what I was "borrowing" as fast as I could flip. Like anything I looked at, I could see it all again later when I wanted. It only took seconds before I was done and closed the cover. Mrs. Powell, standing in front of the desk with her hands on her hips didn't suspect anything. How could she?

Why was she asking? Where was she going with this? What did I have to gain by answering?

I decided that it was best to say "Nothing" and get out of this as soon as possible.

"A lot," I heard myself say.

I hit a key on the keyboard to wake up the computer.

"I wonder if there are any cool games on here?" I hoped I sounded convincing. I, of course, was playing a different game, a game I played often with others' information. I called it "Hide 'n Sneak." You hide, I sneak until I find it.

The screen lit up and waited for a password. So, everything isn't always easy. Why couldn't the Chief be more trusting? Dr. Zylodic would have called that a rhetorical question.

"I know that Mr. Powell molested Shelly for over a year when she was thirteen. You did the right thing when you found out. You put a stop to it and got Mr. Powell to go to therapy."

I could guess at a password all day long and never be right. But

I had found that lots of people forget their passwords so often that they write them down and keep them handy. I stared at the desk for a second, and then up at Mrs. Powell.

I'm lucky that I can see a mental picture while I'm looking at the scene actually before me. She was leaning toward me, bracing herself with both hands on the desk. The front of her loose blouse fell away and gave me a view of everything but her nipples. The soft, blurred edges of her dark tan marked the masking effect her swimsuit had left. Her breasts, pale and pendulous, showed even whiter in the tiny stretch marks at their bases, caused, I concluded with a nod, by their weight. They talked to me, but I'm keeping their conversation private.

"How dare you lie like this, you little prick! Especially tonight."

My mental picture showed no Postits (a favorite memory jogger) or other out-of-place words, checkmarks, or handwritten arrows. But, while still appreciating Mrs. Powell's pose, I noticed two smeared letters written in blue ballpoint on the glass of the Maldonato family portrait. Mrs. Maldonato could lose both quite a few pounds and lots of makeup. The kids, a boy and three girls, had her big teeth in their small mouths. Still, they did look happy, and I hoped looking at this gave the Chief a sense of pride, stability, and love.

"You know I'm not lying." I had found Mrs. Powell's diary also during my "visit" to the Powell residence months ago. I had never bothered to read it after looking through it, but flipped to a page now in my mind that had some heavy underlining. "And you, you fucked Scrappy Burnett, the oil burner guy. Mr. Powell doesn't know … yet." This was a rumor Scrappy told a few people who were too scared of Mrs. Powell and her "venerable" Chairman husband to spread. Mrs. Powell's diary blistered two pages of hatred toward Scrappy for his lies, and I knew it wasn't true. I bet there was some unfortunate outcome for Scrappy but never found out for sure.

The letters *td* were scratched on the Chief's 8-year-old daughter Kerri's dress.

Touchdownkerri, kerritouchdown. Neither of these got me into the computer. Kerrimaldonatotouchdown. Nope.

"Are you threatening me?" Mrs. Powell whispered. Her daughter murdered, and now me. I could sympathize with the strain she was under.

Kerripatriots. Patriotskerri. Nope.

"I guess I'm answering your question, so you know I'm not daring anything, but telling the truth. I know lots, but I know how to keep my mouth shut. I have to admit, though, I can be a real blabbermouth if somebody doesn't play fair." I found it more effective to sound like a vague, immature twit—something I hoped I wasn't because *that* would eventually lead to serious (aka deadly) consequences for me sooner than later, considering the type of people I seemed to be constantly meeting.

"I see how you've been watching me. Are you looking to fuck me, you little asshole? Because that's not going to happen—no matter what." Her voice was light gray.

And I thought my glances so subtle. Her previous experiences with males must have tainted her assessment of me.

Kerri7points. Kerrisevenpoints. Kerri6points (leaving the extra point off). Nope.

Why do women always think that men have one motivation?

Never mind.

"Your secrets are safe with me—no charge. Besides, I'm only fourteen and you must be thirty-one or thirty-two. I ... I wouldn't know what to do," I said, trying to sound hesitant, shy, and flustered.

It was transparent fibbing. Transparent unless you were vain, off balance because of mental trauma, and willing to believe I was just another stupid kid. Tonight, these all applied to her. I knew, in fact, that Mrs. Patricia Powell was forty-two extremely kind years old.

She straightened, her face softened, and her palms absentmindedly slid, smoothing from her waist back over her buttocks and ending on the front of her thighs. The friction caused a slight blue "sssssss."

I had looked through a book on body language once ....

That donut reminded me I was hungry. I picked it up and took a bite. A sip of coffee softened it before I swallowed. I liked my coffee sweeter. This had dark fissures filled with brown sharp spirals.

I abandoned my football strategies. *Td, td, td.* Could it mean "today"? I tried combinations of today's date and Kerri. Nope. I tried combinations of Saturday and Kerri. Nope.

Wait a second. It was still early morning. Maybe the Chief hadn't changed yesterday's password yet.

FridayKerri—I was in!

The computer welcomed me into the Chief's private world of Windows. His wallpaper was another photo of his family, obviously taken during the same session as the one on his desk. Their teeth seemed even bigger.

I looked up into Mrs. Powell's stare. Her short blonde hair was blunt cut with a relaxed body wave. Several loose, broad commas formed bangs hiding parts of her forehead. She seemed about to speak, but I said, "People usually want to talk to me alone when they want something." I didn't mention the other reasons they wanted me alone: threats or violence. "What do you want?"

To her it must have seemed I was scratching my ankle. I had really slipped my SanDisk 4 gigabyte flashdrive from my pocket and was inserting it into the USB port on the front on the Chief's computer near my right leg under his desk. The portable drive was smaller than a stick of gum. Perfect for my purposes.

It slid in easily and the computer recognized it with no problems. I had used this many times to copy information from and to install small eavesdropping programs onto others' computers. I installed a keylogger, a little thing that takes notice of every keystroke and emails the results to me periodically. In this way, I could tell whatever a person typed: emails, websites, passwords—everything. I also installed a screen capture program that would allow me to see what was on the Chief's screen any time I wanted, and a Trojan which would actually make it possible to control this machine from another computer.

These were small programs, took almost no time to install, and were virtually unnoticeable, except if you ran a sophisticated spyware detector. I didn't think Chief Maldonato was that computer savvy. A quick check showed he hadn't run an antivirus scan or updated his virus definitions for six months. Tsk, tsk.

Over the past few years, I had installed variations of these programs on dozens of personal and business computers in Miracle and surrounding towns. Tons of useless and boring information, but littered with those occasional little glittering gems. By that I mean something I could use to my benefit or against someone else.

Another bite of donut. More coffee.

"My baby was murdered tonight," Mrs. Powell started, her voice shaking a bit. "I want the bastard that did it dead. I don't want him caught. I don't want him tried. I don't want him convicted … I want him dead." The shake was gone; her voice was white.

I had started copying folders and files from the Chief's computer onto my flashdrive. The green light at its tip was fluttering quickly, and I was thankful that it was hidden from Mrs. Powell's view. I hoped I was just appearing to be aimlessly dicking around. A kid, playing. I never looked at the screen for more than a moment, being able to see it in my mind, and let my hands flow over the keyboard and move the mouse for all the required maneuvers while I kept my eyes on the lovely lady in front of me.

She seemed all business now. She wanted to use me. Who didn't? This was no surprise. Use me, control me; turn me on, turn me off. They always got more than they bargained for, though. Once you let me in, I found out everything, and the end results seldom matched their expectations. Maybe because I made up the results as I went along. Sometimes they exceeded anticipations. Lots of times, bad things happened.

Picture going to a doctor for a zit, and he tells you it's cancer. You just wanted your complexion cleared up, and suddenly your life was fucked. If people knew this analogy and applied it to me, would they still be so greedy in using me? Probably!

Sixty-two percent. That's what the dialog box on the computer screen showed along with a dotted green line slowly filling in from left to right. All the files I wanted were being copied. I didn't take the "hidden" porn. Foot fetishes weren't my thing. *I wonder what Mrs. Powell's feet look like. I bet she paints her toenails, and maybe has a toe ring.*

A shadow appeared on the door's translucent glass. The handle jiggled, its light clack, clack felt heavy and slow, but sent a prickly surge through me. This seemed to happen whenever there was a real threat of being caught at something.

Seventy-eight percent. I might have to pull it if—

A muffled voice deep in the outer office sounded and the shadow leaned against the door, as if needing to rest his belly there while listening; a white shirt and blue tie pressed flat against the glass. The Chief.

He answered, "Okay, lemme see," and left the door.

Eighty-eight percent.

"Dead? The Chief doesn't let me kill anybody anymore." I wanted to sound like a wiseass punk so she would decide against involving me.

One hundred percent. Finished—and the dialog box disappeared. I had copied what I thought could be interesting or valuable to me in the future. We'll see. I reached down again and pulled the flash drive from the computer, capped its USB slot, and slid it into my pocket.

I logged off the computer and sent it back to sleep while taking a last bite of donut. The Chief had a little left for his interrupted coffee break later.

Mrs. Powell wasn't fazed by my reply. She had a strong will that wasn't about to be thwarted by some dumb-ass kid. "You're going to find out who did this. And you're going to find out before," she nodded toward the door and outer office, "Scotland Yard figures it out."

If I wasn't so naïve, I would have begun to think she didn't have much respect for the Miracle Police Department.

I stood up and rounded the desk until I was facing her, hands in pockets, ready to say "no" to any of her requests now that I had what I wanted.

"I'll pay you. After you give me the name and where I can find him." Her voice was direct, hard, and made me visualize dull gray triangles.

"I don't want your money," I said. Did I just take a small step backwards? I needed to get out of here without having to worry about Shelly Powell's death. I felt confident that my experience and indomitable will would easily outmatch Mrs. Powell's determination.

She made an instantaneous change of strategy. With a deep breath, everything about her relaxed, softened. She looked down a bit and then back up with a slight smile as she stepped close to me. Her arms came up, and she placed her forearms on my shoulders, her wrists limply crossed behind my head. One hand pulled gently at the back of my hair, grasping a lock between thumb and forefinger close to my scalp and then sliding its length until it pulled free. She repeated this, so it became a pleasant pattern.

I could feel the heat from her body. Her face was less than a foot from mine. Her blue eyes, an inch higher than mine, were no longer fully open. I looked at her lips, slightly red from yesterday's gloss. When she spoke, barely above a whisper, I could see reflected specks of the bright lights on the wetness of her tongue.

"Well," she said, "what *do* you want?"

I felt a bit off balance with my hands in my pockets, so I slipped them out and onto Mrs. Powell's hips, feeling the rims of her front pockets with my thumbs. The corners of her mouth turned into a slight smile.

Her mouth started to float closer to mine as her eyes drowsed shut.

Poor Scrappy. What chance …?

"Cookies," I heard myself say.

She stopped, opened her eyes, and then crinkled them half shut again in puzzlement. "What?"

"Lemon cookies. Shelly would bring them to school once in a

while. I smelled them when I passed by her in the cafeteria. I heard her say you made them together. They were yellow with a white glaze."

Mrs. Powell stared at me, her eyes starting to glisten, then film. "Lemon butter wafers," she said.

"I'll help and when this is done, invite me over for some lemon butter wafers."

She leaned forward, kissed my cheek, and eased her face into my neck and shoulder. I held her close as she cried for a long time.

Chapter Five

I was filled with her scent. It clung and hovered as I opened the Chief's door and watched Mrs. Powell step past me.

She hesitated, grasped the edge of the door, and looked at me as if she had something else to say—but didn't. There were thin, red jagged lines in the whites of her eyes. The strain of tears.

With a visible intake of air, she regained herself and announced, "Myx is working for me on this."

Not us—me.

"Patty ..."

A single look stopped her husband. He might be Chairman of the Board of Selectmen, but she was clearly his chair ... person.

I had only taken one step out of the office when the Chief slapped the top of the front desk with a crack (an unpretty brown sound), "Amens. Pockets," he said.

Should I react with righteous indignation and protest such lack of trust? Naaww.

Front left pocket: change, a little cash, a paperclip. Front right pocket: Bic lighter, Swiss Army Knife (Deluxe Tinker model). Watch pocket: round toothpick, one end chewed. Back right pocket: empty. Back left pocket: cell phone, a pair of latex gloves (I liked the Microflex Diamond Grip powder-free type). My sorry little collection lay on the desk looking lonely. I wanted them all safely back in my pockets.

"Freddy," the Chief said, then lifted one of the gloves and shook his head.

Sgt. Wayne nodded to me, "Touch and go, Myx."

I spread my legs and braced against the desk while he quickly, but thoroughly, patted me down. There was that dull hum again, louder when he touched me. "Right," he said toward the Chief. I restocked my pockets.

"My donut?" The Chief looked almost hopeful for a second.

"Sorry."

You could hardly hear the Chief's "Damn."

"Sam," said Mrs. Powell. It reminded me of calling a dog you expect to behave. She turned toward the exit and he fell in step behind her.

"Mrs. Powell?" I jogged the few steps across the room to her, reached out, and put my left hand on her hip, steadying myself to a stop as she turned toward me. I felt the rivet and rough rim of her front pocket. The metal and cloth colluded with slight sounds and curved shapes.

"I'll need to see her body and her room. Shelly's." I hoped I sounded respectful and hesitant enough.

Sam Powell raised his voice, "I won't let ..."

"Sam! I don't care if he has to eat her a forkful at a time to find out what happened. And we're going to find out quick. Right, Amens?" She looked at me. I shrugged. "Got that, Chief?" Her voice was white, but with red edges. "This afternoon, Amens," she called back over her left shoulder as she pushed open the door.

While everyone was watching the Powells leave, I slid my SanDisk flash drive into my back right pocket. I made sure to shield the action with my body. Mrs. Powell never noticed when I slipped it into her pants in the Chief's office or retrieved it just now. Maybe the Chief should have searched us both.

That thought made me smile a bit. Just a little bit.

Now the Chief was smiling. "You know where the morgue is?"

He knew I had "awoken" there twice.

"Cold, white room with bright lights in the basement of Miracle Regional Hospital?" Eh, let him have his fun. I can take a joke.

"I don't like this at all, Amens. As far as I'm concerned, you're just for show. You saw Patty Powell. She's a handful, and can only fuck things up if she gets involved. But she did just lose her only child. We'll bend her way—for now. As long as it doesn't fuck up my investigation. Which means you won't fuck up my investigation. You got any questions about that part of it, and I'll straighten out your thinking in five or six ways. Most of them not pleasant. Got it?"

"All for show, Chief. All for show." My voice was grey, but he couldn't see that. Even I was surprised that I was only half telling the truth. "Better look for Hector Ramone, her boyfriend. At least he was last I knew. He's older, almost thirty, and Shelly kept him a secret from her parents. And he has a mean streak ... thinks he's a tough guy."

"I know Ramone," the Chief said.

Sgt. Wayne was writing, and needed only a nod from the Chief to put that on his short list of things to do.

"Want to tell me what happened?" I asked, knowing that information usually flowed in one direction here.

"Sgt. Wayne." The Chief pointed to the door.

My first solid deduction in this murder: that meant "no."

All Sgt. Wayne said was, "Myx, leave"

I left.

The few low, long hazy clouds tasted faintly like cinnamon candy.

They were stained pink by the imminent sun, which would probably bob over the Eastern horizon before I got to the hospital. Still early.

Never sleeping makes it always early, or always late for me. Still, I judged relative time by "normal" standards. Time had finally become a string of "now." At first, without the punctuation of sleep, I had felt an anxiety, a weight of alwaysness. A Hell of eternity, right here, all at once.

Dr. Zylodic had again used reframing of an idea by training me to focus on one moment at a time, and living in that moment totally. He helped me by not only pointing out the idea, but also by experimenting with hypnosis. I don't think I was ever hypnotized, but I tried any time he wanted to practice on me. The latest was just last week. He really was pretty vain about his Ericksonian hypnosis skills. I never saw any evidence that it worked, though.

I do give him credit for showing me how to make my life livable in small segments, even though the Indian took away my snoozes. I don't know what I would have done without Dr. Zylodic since my grandmother died, and I had all these new problems to cope with.

A black 2002 Dodge Ram truck was parked across the street, running. Third time I had seen it this week; this time its plate was visible.

I started to cross the street. Why not introduce myself? It pulled away and drove under the banner.

Next time.

A white vinyl banner stretched high across Main Street. On it, bright blue letters (a minty Nadienne font creased by gentle sag ripples) proclaimed for all traffic: Founder's Day—May 17th. Under that headline, it read: Witness The Opening Of Sonnet's Box Live

At Noon—Town Common.

Live? I hope so.

To say Elbridge Sonnet had been a woodworker would be like saying Einstein was a cipherer. Sonnet's house on Oak Street, which he built alone and with precision 250 years ago, was a Massachusetts Historic Site visited by thousands of craftsmen every year. Each, I'm sure, wanted to rub against his genius and take a little along. I wonder if any did?

Brass Harkins, Sonnet House's night security guard, was another of my regulars. He was the blackest man I knew, up from Mississippi where he had played jazz in the 60s and 70s. Brass loved jazz (I found his trumpet, its shine gone—clouded by grime, fingerprints, and spills, in a worn case left open on his kitchen table in his untidy apartment; I had dropped by once while he was on duty); he loved Wendy's Chili (and, occasionally the Spicy Chicken Sandwich); he loved whiskey. He also loved to visit Elmira Westage, who lived a few streets over. Her husband worked nights too.

Brass told me lots of times, "A woman is like music, just like music." Maybe he had his own synesthetic thing going.

On many nights, I supplied the Wendy's. Occasionally, I was left "in charge" of Sonnet House while Brass made one of his visits.

He would reach out his big, black hands—his palms lighter and pinker—and put them on my shoulders, "Anything happens ... I mean anything ... you call me and I be right back quicker than a gal can change her mind." In the dim light, his eyes would almost shine against his black face. The chili never hid the whiskey on his breath. On the one night I followed him, I found that the bottoms of his feet were as pink as his palms. Hers too.

I'd been through Sonnet house dozens of times and all I can say is, "Wood, wood, wood." Highly polished wood. It was nice, I mean it was beautiful, but nothing that special to me. What I was missing was the joints. Mr. Sonnet had perfected some sort of sliding and locking joint that made it impossible to take apart without destroying. All his work was a kind of seamless Chinese puzzle. This amazed and fascinated those who could appreciate the innovation and skill needed to construct it. To me, it was just pretty.

The only thing that amazed me was the West Room at sunset. Ol' Elbridge had created a large inlaid map on the East wall. The brochure said it was about fourteen feet wide by seven feet tall. Each of the over 14,000 wooden parquet tiles measured a little over one inch square. The thing is, it was a map of no place on earth that anyone could figure. Inside a thick border of filigree design (which wasn't even symmetrical, a mistake to me) there was an island, complete with rivers and mountains.

Experts said it didn't match any known location. I had looked through every page of a thick world atlas once and later tried to match the island, but didn't have any better luck. I had also looked through every book on the wooden (what else?) bookshelves in the Sonnet library room. No matches. No hints. Just lots of ramblings handwritten in Sonnet's journals.

A neat thing about the map was that it looked different at sunset. When the sunlight coming in the large windows hit the map, some of the tiles got duller, and some took on a rosier (raspberry-tasting) shade. As far as I could see, this was random. Maybe Sonnet used different batches of wood and didn't notice. Seems like he should have, because it looked uneven for about an hour every day. Another strange thing is no one noticed this but me. Either I was seeing things, or my senses told me something that others' couldn't compute.

The story is Sonnet left England in shame, came to Massachusetts, had a revelation that changed his life, and founded Miracle in 1755 with a bunch of followers.

Of course there were hints of a fabulous treasure that Sonnet had either brought with him or amassed when he got here. Since not a pound of it had ever been seen, I considered this to be legend, apocrypha.

Just before he disappeared in 1763, he built a box. Wood, of course. Seamless parquet. A one-foot cube. Sonnet said it was to be opened 250 years to the day after the founding of Miracle. That was this Tuesday.

The box had been examined by each succeeding generation, and ceremonial ownership had been handed down from Town Leader to Town Leader. Each year, for one week in May, it was put on display in the West Room at Sonnet House along with its "key." No one had ever been able to open it without the key, which consisted of two flat, grooved pieces of wood (naturally), their edges sealed with wax imprinted by a signet ring (presumably Elbridge Sonnet's).

Other than that week in May, both key and box endured the gloom of a safety deposit box at the bank.

Finally, on Tuesday, Elbridge Sonnet would reach out that callused hand (I'm assuming a woodworker's hands would be toughened) and pass his last secrets.

Chapter Six

I hadn't been here for a while. Here being the Autopsy Room at Miracle Regional, just a fifteen-minute walk from the Police Station.

"Welcome home, Myx!" Always cheerful, always loud: Dr. Fabrizio, Miracle's Medical Examiner. He had a graying clump of tangled hair clinging to the very bottom of his pointed chin. Other than that and some eyebrows and eyelashes, his head was follicleless. It reflected the bright lights in slightly blue bubbles. His goatee sounded like static.

"Here's my only mistake," he said waving his hand in a large arc towards me.

"Really?"

He repeated his hand wave. "Here's my only mistake that can be proved and was documented!" He then tapped a piece of paper taped to the wall beside his desk.

"A reminder—to be careful, to be sure." He threw both hands up to a little above shoulder height, wrists flicking back. He smiled. It reminded me of a magician finishing a trick and encouraging his audience's approval.

My Death Certificate. My first death: June 21, 2001.

My grandmother had made a happy home for me since my mother's death in 1996. She flew to Indiana for the funeral, took me back to Miracle with her, and never let me doubt for a second I was wanted or loved.

It's funny that I remember so little of my mother. And now I wished I could remember and relive more of my life back then with my grandmother. It's only funny because my whole life has become memory.

But that loving time was before the glow room.

"Here just to see me?" He stood up and walked toward the real reason for my visit. "You were colder and stiller than she is. Then you coughed and scared the shit out of me." He looked down. "I don't think she's going to scare anybody like that today."

Shelly Powell lay naked on the autopsy table. I had always thought she was pretty and sexy. What remained here didn't remind me of that.

"I hear you're pretty good, Myx. Want to take a guess at the cause of death?" Dr. Fabrizio had come up behind me and draped his chin over my left shoulder. Out of the corner of my eye, the static was louder.

"Gunshot to the chest?" I tried to sound unsure and hesitant, like it wasn't obvious. The moist gray edges of the dark pit slightly Northwest of Shelly's left nipple (small, pink, and flaccid) made slurring brown sounds—not steady, but fluctuating. Peppering and branding told me it was a close shot.

He whispered, "You got bingo."

I walked to a box of latex gloves on a low, rolling cart and pulled a pair on. Why waste mine? I may need them someplace my prints shouldn't be.

"After she was dead, I hope?"

"Yeah, not much bleeding," he answered.

I was pointing to her lower lip. More specifically, to where her lower lip used to be. It had been cut away in a broad rectangle, leaving her bottom teeth and gums exposed, edges clotted and dried of saliva.

"Kitchen shears, maybe?" There were several small cuts in the perimeter, making me visualize changing directions in successive snips. I didn't like the vision.

"I have taught you well," said Dr. Fabrizio.

"When did you ever teach me anything?"

"This is where you were supposed to play along to make it more fun."

Fun.

"They find it?"

Dr. Fabrizio looked around the room and then theatrically checked his pockets. "Nope. Didn't come with the body. A memento?"

This was his first serious question. Maybe death had become so routine that the laws of mortal gravity didn't apply here … to him. Maybe his joking was his armor against death's constant presence. Maybe he just didn't give a shit.

"Don't think so. If it wasn't for this," I said pointing, "I could've thought it was a warning or a trophy. This makes me believe he was looking for something … and found it."

"He?"

"Sorry, Master. Mustn't jump to conclusions."

I had been pointing to Shelly's crotch. She had trimmed her pubic hair to a tight triangle. That landing strip had been carelessly dry shaved, leaving abrasions. The few hairs that had been left were light auburn.

I shouldn't have been wondering if Mrs. Powell's pubic hair was the same color, or if she trimmed hers too.

"And, class, what does one look for in this manner?"

Following his previous suggestion, I played along with his lecturing tone.

"Something that is indigenous to the skin, or something that was put there?" I said after raising my right hand.

He nodded and said, "And the thing most likely to have been put there is a …" He drew out the "a" as a cue.

We both said, "Tattoo."

This brought out a frightening reaction from me, totally unexpected. I stared blankly. I don't know how long. Something was telling me I should have known this. I just couldn't remember why.

I couldn't remember.

This had started happening this week. I tried to remember and there were no sensations: no sounds, no tastes, no pressures, no images—nothing but a soft fog. It scared me. I hadn't been scared for a long time.

I was upset because I had finally become familiar and confident with the person I had been forced to become since I had died. If holes were being ripped in that, how could I trust myself?

Even worse, if I was returning to "normal," how could I live that way after seeing how rich the world was when you were able to eat it all up?

"Myx? You okay, Myx?" Dr. Fabrizio had his hand on my shoulder and shook it a little. "You're not going spongy on me, are you?"

"Just thinking." My voice was gray. "Okay if I do my thing here and take a good look?"

"Are you planning to plant, obscure, change, or destroy any official evidence?"

"Not yet."

With a casual sweep of his left hand in Shelly's direction, he said,

"All yours. She's not going anywhere."

There was a smooth, short, shiny metal parabola under her neck, tilting her face up as if for a last lipless kiss goodbye.

I brought my face close to her scalp and inhaled. Shampoos and cigarette smoke mostly. Yellows and greens. Mostly sharp edges. At least my senses were recording as usual and with the same efficiency. Maybe my "forgetting" was just one glitch somewhere.

I felt a little better after thinking that.

Her mouth had the smell of blood and onions and cigarettes. Her underarms, a salty brown aroma. Probably a surge of fear. Poor Shelly. I had grown to accept death more than I could accept suffering.

A rubber body block, essentially a brick, was under her, presenting her upper body at an exaggerated angle. Her chest was full of gunshot. Burnt gunpowder dominated all else.

In death, her breasts, which I had on occasion watched bouncing as she walked, weren't breasts anymore. They were just things, objects having lost their personality.

They were definitely smaller than her Mother's. I'd guess 34B to Mrs. Powell's 36C. This was all by eye, of course.

Shelly's abdomen had nothing to offer. I bent low to her crotch and inhaled. Remnants of the usual womanly secretions and blood from the brutal shave were all I could detect.

"No semen," I said out loud.

"Bet that's not the first time you've said that," came from Dr. Fabrizio's desk. I let it go.

Down the hairless legs to her feet, which smelled only vaguely like feet. They were pink and lotioned and pedicured. Perfect.

She had put on Dolce & Gabbana Light Blue sometime the day

before. I liked it. Spray probably.

Her arms had an almost white fuzz, much lighter than the blonde of the hair on her head.

Why hadn't he shaved her head?

"He didn't shave her head," I said straightening up.

"Well, a tattoo there wouldn't have been much of a secret, would it? Big shaved spot showing after it's done."

He didn't even look up.

Yeah, the tattoo on the inside of the lip was a secret. That sick feeling of not remembering was back. And it got stronger when I sniffed at the fingers of her right hand. Cigarettes, sure—but there was something else, something that should be familiar. But I couldn't remember. Instead of the shapes and tastes and all the other clues my senses usually gave each other, I got a darkness: unmovable, impenetrable. This was new to me and I wasn't coping well.

"Fingernails?"

"Didn't look like anything foreign underneath. We'll see," said the distracted doctor. The *Miracle Daily News* was taking most of his attention now.

I moved back up to her face; traces of perfect makeup were still intact. Always perfect, never overdone.

I slid her right eyelid up gently with my left thumb. Blue and dilated.

Did you see the glow room, Shelly? Are you there now?

The Solstice Jamboree was to have been my first Cub Scout campout. I had been excited about every bit of it, although a little embarrassed that my grandmother was helping me put up my tent. Other kids had their dads.

There had been just a few clouds, none especially large or dark. I might have felt the hair on my arms and the back of my neck rise a little before the lightning hit, but I'm not sure.

I never saw it or heard it. We were putting up the tent, and then I was holding her hand in the glow room.

It had side walls, a back wall, and a ceiling. I never saw if it had a floor or a wall behind me. I never looked. None of the corners or seams were hard, they just merged and melded. They looked like they were made of soft pearls that constantly changed if you looked for a while. A dim light glimmered from every inch.

I felt wonderful. Happy. Peaceful.

My grandmother let go of my hand and walked forward, toward the back wall, and then right through it. She never turned her face toward me. I thought, without concern, "Where are you going, Grandma?" I wondered if she had forgotten to take me.

Once she was through, I became aware of another figure in the room. He/she (I couldn't tell which) was pointing to the left wall. I looked and she walked over and pushed. A door-like opening showed black through it. He repeated this until there were six openings. Then she pointed behind me.

I had coughed and opened my eyes on this same table I leaned against now. The glow room was gone.

My grandmother had died. I hadn't.

"Can we turn her over?" I closed her eye.

"Sox won again," he said as he got up. "You know, I'm not ashamed to admit that they made me bawl last October. You know—when they won it all."

I didn't think anything could make him shed a tear. But the Red

Sox were different, different for a lot of people.

"I suppose you want nice, nice," he said after taking away her supports. I could imagine how rough he could be normally, having to do this alone all the time.

"Yeah, let's go easy."

We rolled Shelly to her side. She was facing me. Then, with one more rocking motion, we got her prone, her breasts mashed against the hard surface.

"There's something you missed," I said pointing to an obvious red blotch on her right buttock.

He looked closer, exaggerating the body language. "Well, I'll be. You're right."

"What's the technical term for that?" I asked.

"Zit—or pimple, if you prefer. I'll be over here, keeping current." He returned to his paper.

I didn't learn anything new from the rest of my examination. The phone on Dr. Fabrizio's desk rang just as I made that conclusion. It sounded extra loud in this place.

"Dr. Fabrizio. Yeah. Okay, bring him in. He's still here." He listened a little more, held the mouthpiece to his shoulder, muffling it, and said, "Chief says he's got Hector Ramone."

"Is he talking?" I asked.

Dr. Fabrizio didn't bother to relay my question. Instead, he said, "I'd bet not since the gunshot to the chest."

I nodded. "Anything missing?"

This time he asked, then matter-of-factly replied, "Only his penis."

That sick feeling again.

His penis. I should know this. Somehow.

"Dragon at Skin Sins. Tell the Chief to find him fast." I didn't have to remember much to deduce this because Dragon was the owner of Miracle's only tattoo studio. Myron "Dragon" Steinsaltz was the only tattoo artist *in* Miracle.

Chapter Seven

The air outside smelled good, devoid of red strings and green, sharp-edged disks—hospital smells. The black Dodge truck sat across the street; it wasn't running. The driver had circled around after I saw him on Main Street and followed me to the hospital. I let him and acted like I wasn't noticing his amateurish efforts. I had been followed by pros and always knew where they were almost at once.

I crossed the street at an angle that would take me slightly in front of the truck, looking both ways, just like I had no place special to go, or hadn't just seen a murdered classmate.

He wasn't a good actor and pretended to read the newspaper in his lap. He glanced sideways repeatedly, keeping track of me the whole time it took me to cover the forty or so feet. Each movement of his eyes sounded like a sharp click in my right ear.

When I got close enough, I said, "Wow! Nice truck, Mister." I had to admit: it was spotless. I tried to sound thoroughly impressed and enthused. I know I did because my voice looked almost white and had graceful arcs. Enough to fool someone who really wants to believe. It never takes much to deceive the deceitful, even though they think they're too wise to be fooled by the same tricks they use.

Hmmm. Did I think that too?

The truck bed was neatly filled with lumber, some large tools, an immaculate blue toolbox, and another hand-made box about six feet long. It had three clasps to hold it shut. There was also a yellow rectangular magnetic sign, I assume meant for the driver's side door. It read: Miracle Carpentry & Woodworking in large arced green letters. Under that in much smaller letters, not arced: Divine Work—Down-To-Earth Prices. Across the bottom was a big phone number. A local number.

I mentally flipped through the Miracle phone book. The business listing showed 247 Beverley Street. I could have taken the time to look through the rest of the residential listings for 247 Beverley Street and gotten his name if he lived there also (and if it wasn't private).

Instead, I stuck out my hand when I was close enough and said, "Hi. I'm Myx Amens. Your truck is super. What's your name?"

He pretended to be somewhat startled by the interruption but said in a breathy whispered voice, "Sarge Halpern." Purple and oily. He shook my hand; his was hard and strong from manual labor. I matched the pressure of his grasp perfectly. The shake vibrated his long hair. When I let go, he stroked his Fu Manchu mustache a few times. I bet that was a habit.

Back to the phone book for the alphabetical listing. He did live at the same address. Listed as "Brian," not "Sarge."

"Mix? That's a funny name." He was warming up. Probably pleased at his luck. I just fell right into his plan here. That is, if he did have a plan and wasn't just interested in watching my ass as I walked, fuel for a masturbatory marathon later while locked in the bathroom at 247 Beverley Street.

I lifted my arm and showed him my left bicep. My tattoo was surrounded by irregular Lichtenberg figure remnants which looked like purple flames. Dr. Fabrizio had told me Lichtenberg figures, or captured lightning on the skin, faded away with time. Most of them had faded, but I was left with these reinforcing my name. Baptism by lightning.

"M-Y-X," I spelled. I smiled, trying to look my friendliest. I wanted to see if "Sarge" was involved in Shelly's death, was out to seduce and molest poor little me, had a totally different agenda in mind, or was just coincidentally innocent. Okay, I didn't believe the innocent option at all.

"That a tattoo?" he asked, genuinely interested.

Tattoo.

"Yeah, but the outline was an accident that happened later. My friends Shelly and Hector have tattoos."

He didn't react. Not a flinch or a flutter. Not even I could detect any recognition in his face or body movements. The odds of his being the tattoo harvester just decreased. Maybe he simply didn't know their names, but I was already crossing him off my list. That is, if I had a list.

"Wow. You look pretty strong," he said, seeing an opportunity to gain my favor.

I could go with that.

"Oh yeah. You should see me work out all the time. I think it's really important to be in good shape. Wanna feel?" I flexed and stuck my bicep close to the open window.

The interior smelled clean and new. Smooth greens in long swerves. He had a new blue Red Sox T-shirt on. Ironed. No wedding ring. He did the ironing himself.

His scalp showed grayish through the part running down the middle of his head as he reached his right hand across and gave a rough squeeze to my muscle. Not a caress, just enough contact to fulfill an obligation. He wasn't after my ass.

"That's something. I respect a guy who likes PT," he said, lifting himself in the seat to shift toward me. "We should work out together sometime. I got a nice gym set up at the house."

"Eh. Maybe." I didn't want to seem too easy.

"And I just got some video games from my nephew along with his old system. I don't know anything about them and need some help. You any good?"

"Oh yeah! I play all the time. I think I got the record on one game." Enough hard-to-get. I wanted to see where this was going.

"Get in. Home's not far." Although he tried to keep the excitement out of his voice, he didn't. It rippled, telling me he was very, very pleased.

"Awww. Sorry, Sarge. I told my Mom I'd be home soon. She gets worried easy. How about tonight?" I really had to get to Skin Sins, or I would have taken care of Sarge right now.

"Custom jobs; I've got to give some estimates tonight. No good for me. I won't be home."

Then you won't see me visit while you're gone.

"Tomorrow, then. I'll pick you up right here. About ten o'clock. What do you like better, cake or donuts?"

Cake? Donuts?

Maybe I had this guy all wrong.

"Donuts, for sure!" My voice was very white. I pointed to the Dunkin's bag on the seat beside him. "That smells like a biscuit sausage, egg & cheese sandwich. Man, that smells good!"

I wasn't fooling.

"Myx, you're amazing. Close your eyes."

I did, and heard him uncrinkle the bag near the window. "What else," he asked.

"Lemon poppyseed muffin," I said, my voice rising in anticipated victory.

"You win!" His laugh was genuine. "And here's your prize." He handed me the bag, sealing the deal, of course. "See you here tomorrow. Okay?"

"That's great. I'll be right here."

I took my first bite as he drove off. It was as tasty as it smelled. I ate slowly as I walked.

Skin Sins: I pictured the storefront in my mind.

There was a blur in the front window, down in the left corner. I couldn't remember what was there.

I tried to taste it, feel it, hear it, smell it, and sight it back into my consciousness. Nothing helped. I got that feeling again. That sick feeling. Not enough to stop eating, though.

Maybe I needed to die again to tune up. I grinned.

That's a bad idea.

When I got there, flashing cruiser lights and radio squawks filled the street in front of Dragon's narrow studio. The red and blue neon sign, usually on only in the evening, still glimmered: Skin Sins.

I looked in the window at where the blur had been in my mind. What was there definitely didn't match what I was trying to remember. It was empty.

The yellow crime scene tape fluttered in the easterly breeze, making a pleasing stutter sound. Officer Sturtz, a tired-looking veteran, nodded to the entrance. "Chief wants you inside."

Maybe this was better than being shooed away, like usual. Maybe not. The two wooden steps up had shallow valleys, a record of scuffing and weight. They still felt steady and solid. The sign buzzed a bit above me.

Myron had a beautiful midnight blue and orchid dragon on his left shoulder. Its head breathed fire at an angle; its serpentine body wound and coiled to his elbow. Many tattoos covered his torso, but this was the most prominent. I had always assumed it was the basis for his nickname. You never know.

Dragon knew lots of people. Lots of the kinds of people who were interesting and important in the types of things I meddled with. We had helped each other several times. He wasn't afraid to take risks. I also didn't trust him much. But, who did I trust?

When I saw him sitting there at the stained roll-top desk in the corner, I concluded he didn't need that final body decoration: the bullet hole in his chest. Maybe he didn't deserve it either.

The Chief saw me and pointed to all the tattoos. "I guess he didn't read Leviticus."

I had looked at the Bible once. I scanned Leviticus now, searching for the Chief's allusion. One of the "Ye shall nots" prohibited printing marks on the body. Dragon had definitely "bent" that rule. He had told me that "art" was his religion now.

"Myron could read?" I asked.

We both laughed before turning back to the body.

He looked peaceful. In life, he was jittery, jumpy, agitated—except when he had that electric pen in his hand. Then he was a concentrated economy of precision, an artist. I had watched him work, especially late at night.

"I don't see any other wounds. Nothing?" I looked to the Chief while slipping my left latex glove on. He knew I was asking if any body parts were missing. I didn't have to see the body to know there weren't.

"No. Not like the other two. You know why?"

Before he could protest, I leaned in and lifted Myron's left eyelid. I looked deep. I did this now whenever someone had recently vacated the flesh.

The glow room?

I never expected an answer. Maybe because some part of me already knew it.

The brown, dilated eye stared in return.

"Don't fuck with the evidence," the Chief sighed. I lowered the eyelid.

"Same gun is my guess, Myx. You walk right in and point us to two more victims. Want to tell me what else you know—and why you know it?"

Chief Maldonato had a suspicious mind. He had a right to be, but I didn't want to be part of some let's-go-over-this-one-more-time interrogation that ate up my day. I had to make my involvement seem simple and logical. Antiseptic kibitzing.

"I knew Hector was Shelly's boyfriend. I thought he probably killed her. I was wrong since he's dead too. Dr. Fabrizio said Shelly probably had a tattoo that was cut out and taken. When you called and said Ramone's dick was gone (I resisted saying "prick was plucked" since I didn't want to distract the Chief), we assumed he had a tattoo. Since Myron is the only show in town, he seemed like a suspect or a target."

I jerked my ungloved thumb towards the body. "Bull's-eye."

He nodded unconsciously while smoothing back his thick eyebrows with the thumb and forefinger of his right hand. I hoped that meant he accepted everything I had said.

"What else you know?"

"It's what he knew," I said and looked toward Myron. "He inked the tattoos, and died because of it."

I pointed to a thick three-ring binder open on the desk. It held tattoo flash, the designs an artist works from, in plastic sleeves. The rings were pulled apart.

"Maybe the bad guy took something." I knew he did.

Myron used to work hard designing his flash and took pride in featuring it in the front window. Why couldn't I remember what had been in the window? This was getting on my ass, and I liked my ass free of freight.

"You're good at looking at stuff. You know what it was?"

"No." My voice was white. "Can I look around?" I asked.

"Yeah, but …" He pointed at me. I knew that was his "Don't fuck with the evidence" point. I put on my other glove.

I looked closely at the body but learned nothing more. Same small-caliber gun, I assumed. Same shooter, I assumed. I hated assuming. I liked knowing.

At the rear of the shop, a beaded curtain covered a doorway. The acrylic beads were strung to show a pale yellow lightning bolt on a field of blue. It separated the business from Myron's living space, and sounded like a waterfall when I passed through it. Windy and free.

This was barely a space. Just room for a bed, a dresser, and a wooden crate, sitting on its end, which served as a night table. The bed was a simple metal frame with no headboard. It was neatly made with a tight blue blanket, but the pillowcase had yellowed with use in the center.

The crate had a small lamp on it, the bottom of its green shade tilting toward the bed a bit. A blue leather-bound book lay there closed. MATCHZOR showed in raised letters on the cover along with some Hebrew.

A dusty white doily covered the top of the dresser. Bristles down, a hairbrush sat at the right side. A half roll of Lifesavers (peppermint by the smell) had lost its blue paper cover, leaving just the shiny foil. Back, almost against the pale green wall, was a small metal menorah. The nine candles had burnt down close to the holders. A framed picture rested on top of a light-colored yarmulke. It showed Myron when he was a little younger than me. He was in a jacket and tie and yarmulke between two well-dressed adults. His parents, I bet. They looked happy, all of them.

Myron, shalom.

Chapter Eight

I ran home. Three miles from Skin Sins to Farno Avenue. Maybe six-minute miles (I wasn't pushing at all). I found a certain peace while running, maybe the kind I used to absorb in sleep.

I couldn't be sure.

I could be sure that a 2005 black Lincoln Town Car was waiting in front of Benny and Bunny's shop slash residence. My residence, too. A short, wide man, his black suit stretching to contain all of him, leaned with his back against the driver's door. His thick arms strained into a fold, and it looked like an effort to hold them there. Wraparound black sunglasses hid his eyes. The sun glinted off them when he turned his head the right way. I didn't think he could have buttoned his white dress-shirt around that chunky neck if he tried. He had no tie.

The tinted rear window was half-open, and whoever sat there wasn't visible.

If I had a dread reflex, it would have been flexing right now. This couldn't be good. But I hadn't been seen yet and could easily have turned around and gotten away.

"Hey! It says no parking to the corner," I said pointing to the sign as I crossed the street.

The short man (as I got closer, I found he wasn't short at all—just very, very wide) leaned to the open back window and said something. A thin man, in his thirties, got out in one easy and graceful motion. The door slammed shut with that heavy and satisfying thud of a well-made product. The sound was a rounded blue.

"We got a special permit," shorty said, way too loudly. He was slightly hoarse. I bet he was always slightly hoarse.

"Oh. Then I guess it's okay. Park here as long as you want while I go into my house and shower (I had sweat through my shirt while running) and have something to eat." I might as well pick a part and play it. Since dying, I'd learned to enjoy playing at life.

Shorty spoke again, "Maybe you'll just come along with us right now instead."

"I'm not psychic or anything, but I thought you might say something like that." I'm sure Shorty wasn't appreciating anything I said.

The thin man finally spoke. He wore a black suit also; it was perfectly tailored and complemented by a brilliantly white shirt and gray striped tie. His eyes were also concealed.

"This is Guy," he said, pointing to Shorty. "I'm Rico."

"Gaetano and Federico, maybe?" I said.

"Kid thinks it's a game, Rico." Then to me, "How'd you do that?"

To a person like Guy, guessing someone's real name was probably a neat trick. I figured I'd show off a bit and explain. "There are only a few—"

Rico interrupted, "Mr. Damianzo expects you to accompany us. He gets what he expects."

"I don't think my parents would like that." My voice was very dark.

"Benny?" Guy laughed. "He thinks a little ride will do you good. Hey, kid, your mother has a nice ass."

"And how about that rack? ... I mean ... you can't talk about my Mommy like that!" I said in mock outrage. Bunny had a body that rivaled Mrs. Powell's.

Guy was fun to play with. His mouth formed a silent "Whaaaa?"

Rico was efficient. All business. "This is the part where you get in the car." His voice had a controlled melody, like he could easily sing his words if he wanted to. Apparently, he didn't want to.

"I know the Police Chief, you know," I said as Guy put one hand on my left shoulder and opened the back door with the other. I knew that hand could push me into the pavement or crush skin and bone and blood and muscle. He wasn't workout strong; he was animal strong.

"Say 'Hi' to Angie for me," he said. "Watch your head. You get hurt, I want to do it on purpose." Now *he* was playing—playing a game of intimidation that was pretty effective.

I got in and slid across the smooth, dark gray leather bench seat. It smelled good in there, new car good. Rico got in beside me, and Guy shut his door before falling into the driver's seat.

Rico was wearing *Dreamer* cologne by Versace. Just enough. Guy had on a little splash of the CVS knockoff of Mennon aftershave. It helped mask his bulky sweating. A little, anyway.

"Windows open or air conditioning?" he called back.

"I like the windows open," I leaned forward as I spoke.

"Wasn't talking to you."

I knew that but wanted to seem part of the team.

"Open them up once we leave town. No use anyone seeing our little guest," Rico said, looking straight ahead.

Little!

"You going to sexually molest me?" I wanted to see if I could throw him a little.

Rico waited, unmoving, and then pointed forward with his chin,

"No. That's his job." He looked kind of pleased with himself.

"Come on, Rico. The kid's going to get the wrong idea about me." Guy was serious. I surmised he was limited and specific in his uses, which I'm sure were very effective when needed.

"Armani?" I asked. I already knew, but …

"Sears," Guy laughed, and made a big deal about dusting his right sleeve off with his big left hand. He shook his head, said "Sears" again softly to himself and chuckled.

"You plan on talking all the way?" Rico liked to look straight ahead.

I shrugged, eloquently I hoped.

"Armani?" Rico straightened his right arm and tugged twice on the coat sleeve, hiding the white cuff of his dress shirt. "You tell me, smart guy."

At first I wondered if he was testing me, but there were small signals: the yellow highlights in his voice, the lyrical squeak of the turn of his lips—he was playing with me. I knew then he liked me; they both did. This was good because I was used to the opposite. I willingly played along.

"Suit: three-button single-breasted, vented back, mid-weight wool with flat front pants," I read off in my mind from a catalog I had seen once. "Slim fit, tailored in Boston."

"New York City."

"Over a grand."

He held up his right hand, palm down, and tilted it from side to side.

"The sunglasses are Armani too, the 155S model. Two hundred bucks. Can I try them on?" I took Rico's silence to mean "no."

"How much did my suit cost?" Guy asked, looking at me in the rearview mirror.

"Nothing. You tore it off a poor slob just before something horrible happened to him."

Guy shook his head and said, "Kid's good!" He sang the last word.

I almost laughed. Was Guy kidding me back or reacting honestly? His voice was a murky shade and hard to decipher.

We were passing a McDonald's. "I'm hungry, How about buying me breakfast?"

I got the silent "no" again.

"What are you carrying?" This time I used *my* chin to point towards Rico's right armpit.

"How do you know I'm carrying anything? That's why I went to New York City."

He was right about the suit's fit. It didn't show a sag or a bulge where his gun rested.

"It's the way you move. You dance with it. You lead, it follows, and doesn't slop around on its own." I didn't bother to mention that I could hear a harmony on the gun side of his body and not a subtle single note like his right side was playing.

His right hand reached under his arm and pulled out a small gray gun. It shrilled with minor variations. The harmony remained in his hand and his gun.

"Guy, pull over and stop the car."

"Rico, don't do this. You know I hate when you do this."

But Guy pulled over, and he didn't look back—not by turning or by glancing in the mirror. We were on a wooded road. I hadn't seen a house for a while.

The gun was small, about five inches long and four inches high. I read Kahr MK40 on its side. Worcester, Mass.

Rico made sure I saw him flick the safety off with his thumb.

"Here, Kid. What are you going to do now?" He handed me the gun, butt first. His eyes, I could see them dimly through the glasses, never left mine. He was reading me.

As I reached for it, he asked, "Do you know why I had Guy stop the car?"

"So I have the choice of shooting him without crashing."

He smiled. "What other choices do you have?"

The gun felt warm and light. It was narrow, less than an inch. I could tell it liked me from the sound it gave off and the sweet taste in my mouth.

Guy sighed, "Oh boy," in the front.

Was Rico testing me, testing himself, or just getting a thrill fix? Other than his increased concentration, his body sounded and looked much the same, even to me. I decided this was my test, to see if I was worthy in some value system he believed in. All his body movements, or lack thereof, showed me he was more confident in controlling it than Guy, who squirmed and started to sweat a bit, seemed to be.

"I can give the gun back, shoot out the window and try to get some attention, shoot you ... or this ..."

I raised the gun with one fluid motion and leveled the barrel hard against my own right temple while squeezing my eyes tightly shut and pressing my lips together.

I heard Rico shift forward and reach. He was quick. Not as quick as the Indian, not as quick as I was, but third in my experience. Which meant pretty good.

As soon as I heard his move, which I had guessed, I lunged

forward, snaked the gun under his coat and into the leather holster. It had "DeSantis" imprinted on it.

Rico had closed his hand on the empty air vacated by my own. Even though I had startled him, something that probably hadn't happened for a while, he was almost fully recovered by the time he pulled the Kahr again from his holster.

He shook his head. "You put the safety back on."

"Accidents can happen," I sang.

Guy seemed relieved. "That's a new one, huh, Rico?"

"Drive, Guy." Apparently I had passed the test.

After a while I stated, "I don't know why Mr. Damianzo wants to see *me*." I tried to sound innocent.

Guy looked in the mirror again. "Christ! You kidnapped his daughter."

Chapter Nine

Less than a half hour East on Route 9 got us to Wellesley, a wealthy neighborhood another half hour outside of Boston.

I would call the Damianzo home an estate because the large, white two-story house lay in the middle of about six acres of manicured lawn. It was fronted by a low stone wall—a pleasure to look at because of its craftsmanship. No mortar. The stones told me why they fit and how the top got to be so flat and even. It sounded like a long pull on a cello.

Guy slowed and veered off the road onto the driveway up to the house, which swerved gently to the front door and circled back. There was an offshoot to the three-car garage at the right of the main structure. The wall broke with a stone column about eight feet high on either side of the drive. A man wearing a zippered blue nylon jacket and blue baseball cap (no logos) stood just inside the left stone column. There was a small white kiosk behind him. Inside it, a radio played a sports-talk station. It wasn't very loud.

He leaned down and looked in Guy's open window. His right hand rested on the sidearm strapped to his waist and creaked the leather a bit. He looked at me.

"Hi. Nice morning," I said with a big smile. I could see myself in the guard's mirrored sunglasses; I looked good.

"The visitor," he said to Guy.

"Yeah. We'll watch him this time," Guy said, stabbing his right thumb in my general direction.

"You know he made trouble for me last time."

"I've learned my lesson," I said, leaning forward and down to look up at the guard, who had straightened. Rico pulled me back and shook his head silently "no."

Guy changed the subject and asked, "How's Mama today?"

"One of her bad days. She just sits there, looking. Crying sometimes."

"We can only pray for her," Guy said.

"I'll let them know you're here." He pulled a radio from his belt as Guy drove forward.

"What's the matter with Mama?" I had leaned forward again, but Rico didn't pull me back this time.

"Tony, her son. Dana-Farber about three years ago. He didn't make it. He was about your age."

Dana-Farber was a cancer institute in Boston.

"I'm sorry." My voice was white, but it sounded puny to me. They didn't say anything. I didn't either the rest of the way up the drive.

Ten windows across the top floor. Six windows, one a bay window, on the bottom floor. I looked at rooms in my mind. I looked at the back yard, its large garden—all images from my last visit here. I had hoped it would be my last visit ever. Maybe, instead, *this* would be my last visit. Maybe my last anywhere.

Guy pulled up to the front door. A white-columned overhang shielded it. When the car stopped, Rico got out and said, "Get out my side," and waited for me to slide over. When I got out, he shut the door and leaned close to me, "Remember, Kid … respect."

"You know why you came with us today?" he asked

"Because you never would stop," I said.

He nodded and echoed, "Because we never would stop."

Guy pulled away to park in front of the garages. Rico took my elbow and ushered me into the front door.

The interior was bright, colorful, and tastefully expensive. Possibly a few things too ornately "old country." Lots of glass and marble. It felt open and alive.

I hoped I did after today.

"We're going upstairs. The back staircase," Rico pointed along the hallway.

We passed a large room on the right, the kitchen. The sunlight showed in streams through the large windows, dust dancing in windless swirls. It felt like harp strings at the ends of their notes. I could hear birds through the open side door. A woman sat silhouetted at the kitchen table, her back to us. She was motionless, and her hands rested folded on the table. I slowed and Rico's immediate pull on my elbow told me no delays were tolerated.

The narrow back stairs showed polished wood on either side of the runner. Nothing squeaked.

Mr. Damianzo was a balding, thin man, maybe in his late fifties, dressed conservatively in yet another expensive dark suit. He was seated at a large oak desk almost against the back wall. There were two windows behind him, measuring about knee-high to as far as I could reach. They had six large panes each and didn't open. A large bust of Julius Caesar stared at him from the desk. I wondered how heavy it was.

He looked up over the tops of his reading glasses as we entered his home office, then clapped his hands together loudly and laughed a "Ha-hey!" I could tell he wasn't really happy to see me in the conventional way. His voice had red-edged anger in it.

"I finally get to meet our little friend."

Little.

He got up and walked over to me, took my other elbow and in an exaggerated show of hospitality said, "Sit, sit." He guided me to a high-backed green leather chair near Julius.

I sat. It was comfy.

Rico remained standing behind me. Guy had just walked in.

I still didn't have a feel if this was supposed to just scare me, or if I was going to be made an example. Example was bad.

He sat back down at his desk, took his glasses off, and tossed them onto the papers lying on the black blotter.

"I bet you thought I'd forget about you. I bet you thought I couldn't find out who you were or where you lived."

"A boy can hope." I said this just before Guy's big hand slapped against the back of my head. I heard it coming, but like all of this, avoidance seemed like the wrong thing to do. I'd hate to feel if Guy really wound up and let go.

"No, no, Guy. We want to know what Mr. Amens has to say. It's Myx Amens, right?" Mr. Damianzo's voice was a soothing gray.

"He's a talker, Boss," Guy said.

"Good, good. I like to listen so I learn a lot. But, first, Myx, I talk, and you listen."

I nodded. I had a feeling this was going to be long, but maybe not too informative.

"Business is business. We all know we have to do certain things to make things work right. Some of these things are not pleasant, but we are forced to do them. We all understand, and accept it."

He went on (I knew he was going to go on), "Everybody has his job. You had the pleasure of meeting Rico and Guy. You saw Bobby at the entrance, down near the street. You remember him? He's down there and not in the house anymore until he learns not to let people like you come and go whenever they please. He's not happy with you. Can you see why?"

Mr. Damianzo swept his hand in a wide and graceful arc. "You see what they do? Mario, here," he looked around then he yelled, "Mario." A small man in a short-sleeved white shirt quickly came in from a side door. "Mario knows all the business, everything. Small details I could never keep in my head. You see how this works?"

"Three people were executed last night in Miracle because of tattoos. Does he know that?" I said and ducked, but Guy wasn't swinging.

Mr. Damianzo looked at me and blinked, then pointed at Mario with his chin. He left.

"And even in Miracle, there's an associate who deals in gold, only gold. Where it comes from, we don't care. Who it comes from, we don't care. You see how specialized business can get? It all works together because the rules are there and we work by the rules."

I knew there was more.

"Family and home are outside those rules. Someone fucks with that," he held both hands at shoulder height, palms up, "you have to make an example."

I had said example was *bad*.

"My daughter, God bless her soul, is my whole life. Mine and Mama's. She just was married last month. A happy day, a celebration."

"I bet she had a lovely gown," I said. I didn't know if I was going to be allowed any explanation of my *perceived* offense, but saw this as a slight opening. Guy moved behind me, and I braced.

To my relief, Mr. Damianzo held up his hand and no jolt came.

"Her gown was a one-of-a-kind. An original from Florentina's in Boston. Florentina designed it just for my Christina. My girl, and she got it on her own. Even her Papa couldn't get her this gown. She beat out all the other girls. She won it."

He was full of pride now, smiles and nods as he spoke. The wisest thing for me to do was to shut up completely and let him go on to tell about Christina's triumph.

"I helped," I interrupted.

"What?" he asked, as if he couldn't believe such a bizarre statement.

I figured this was my chance, my only chance. So, I spoke quickly.

"Florentina Benedica held a lottery for a gown, and your daughter won."

I felt Guy's hand on my shoulder. I bet it was a gentle squeeze in his estimation, but it sent jagged purple sawtooths through my arm and down my back. My mouth tasted sour.

Mr. Damianzo said, "Tell, tell." Maybe he wanted to hear of her glory from another.

I rubbed my shoulder when Guy let go. "Over seventy-five thousand brides-to-be entered. One hundred of those got to be in the final drawing in Boston. Each finalist received a bearer ticket that would get them in the door. Christina wasn't one of those final one hundred. Not originally, anyway."

"She was disappointed, cried and carried on for days when she didn't get one of those goddammed tickets. I don't like seeing my daughter disappointed, but there are some things even her Papa can't do. But she showed her papa—she won the whole fuckin' thing on her own! My little girl takes after her papa, eh?" Damianzo made a grand gesture to the room. Everyone knew their part and made some vague affirmation that sounded like a happy "Ha-hey!"

"That's where I came in. Mr. Damianzo, you must have many friends, but you also must have those who wish you harm. I found out your daughter was going to be kidnapped in Miracle. They were using a winning Florentina ticket as bait."

He looked more interested now, folded his hands, leaned forward. He tilted his chin slightly in my direction. I took this as a cue to keep going.

"Long story short: I stole the ticket from the kidnappers (I thought he would like the 'stole' part; I don't think of what I do as stealing, but it seemed to be a good use of the word here), intercepted Christina, went to Boston with her, and won the drawing."

He shook his head, disbelieving. "And how did you do *that?*"

He wanted more. Okay.

"Each ticket holder could bring one person with them. They all brought their mothers or girlfriends. From all over the country they came. One hundred and ninety-nine excited women were outside Florentina's salon on Newbury Street at ten o'clock, waiting for the doors to open and let them in. The other person was me. Christina can be very persuasive, and insisted I come with her."

Mr. Damianzo let out a sigh and nodded.

"We exchanged the bearer's ticket for a numbered lottery ticket at the door. I was wishing all the women good luck and telling them how pretty they would look in Florentina's gown."

I left out my impressions of how musky and funky it smelled and felt in there with all those excited women packed into a small area.

"Florentina herself finally climbed up on a riser in the front of the room and said, 'Who shall I choose to draw the winner?' and looked through the crowd. You see, I was the only male in the room, and I can be very cute."

I turned and smiled an overly toothy grin at Guy and Rico. Rico shook his head. Guy just tried to keep his thick arms barely folded over his chest.

"The women, lots of them, pointed to me. I looked all red-faced and embarrassed. Of course, I *wanted* to pick the winner. And I didn't want to ride back with Christina if she lost. It was easy for me to crease Christina's ticket before she put half of it in the fishbowl. I made a big show of swirling my hand around in it, making it look like I was mixing it up good before I finally felt hers." I didn't tell them the slight fold I made had its own sound and color. Her ticket talked to me, called to me. It was so easy, but they all didn't know that.

"Christina screamed and cried when she found out she'd won. I stayed away from her so it didn't seem like something was up. I spent my time consoling the other women. Some of them were good sports, others, real bitches."

"So, you're trying to tell me that you're some big hero instead of being in on this?" Mr. Damianzo didn't get to where he was by being very trusting, I guess.

"My mistake was letting Christina take me back here with her. She was ecstatic, and wanted to tell you and her Mama what she had done. When she saw how angry you were at her because she had been missing, she changed her story."

Mr. Damianzo slapped his palm hard and loudly on the desk. "Now you tell me my daughter lied to me about everything—winning the dress, outsmarting those fuckin' scum who tried to catch her with the ticket, and lying about you? How dumb do you think I am?"

"Mr. Damianzo, I lie for only two reasons: to save someone's feelings, and to save my ass. I think Christina lied mostly to make her Papa proud of her. Her lie let you think I was in on the kidnapping. You see, it's all just a mistake that we can forget."

I smiled hopefully. It was false hope, but the smile felt good anyway.

"Bobby locked you in my study down the hall when you got here with Christina. That's my safe room. No windows, no way in or out except through the door to the hall, and Bobby says he never left outside the door after he locked you in. Explain that."

"You ever read *The Count of Monte Cristo* by Dumas?" I knew this was going to make him angry, but he asked for it.

He looked at Rico and Guy. "Kid thinks I'm a fancy reader like him." Then he looked at me and said, "Maybe I'm tired of you now."

I talked fast. "The Count escaped from prison by hiding in his cell until they left the door open and he walked out, free. I did the same thing."

"You telling me you hid from Bobby when he came in to get you. There's no place to hide in there. He looked."

"You know your big red leather couch?"

"I love that couch. Tell me you didn't touch my couch."

I figured telling him the truth was the cooler of the hot waters I could be in. "I cut a slit in the bottom of the long cushion, spread the stuffing evenly under the Oriental rug, and hid inside the cushion for about an hour and a half until Bobby came looking for me. He looked around for a while, swearing all the time, and ran out, leaving the door open. I got out of the cushion, repacked it with the stuffing, and left."

"That couch used to be a little lumpy," Mr. Damianzo said, mostly to himself. "So, you think you can come and go like you want here and make us fools?" It really wasn't a question.

"I didn't steal anything. Look." I leaned forward, picked up a pencil and wrote 5-17-27-41-64-33 on a Post-it. I handed it to him.

He read it and yelled, "Mario!" Mario rushed in and took the post-it from Mr. Damianzo's outstretched hand. "Change that fuckin' number."

It was the combination to his hidden safe in the study. I had played around with it while waiting in there, just before I thought of hiding in the couch.

"You're something, kid, you're something. But you can't make a fool out of me."

"I left you the names of the man and woman who were going to kidnap Christina. Doesn't that count for me?" I had taped a note to the door of the study.

"That only proves you would rat out your friends to save yourself. Nobody likes a rat, right Rico?"

I turned and saw Rico shrug. "Maybe he's telling the truth."

"So, he's got you fooled too." He waved a hand toward Guy. "What do you think?" I knew this wasn't going to be a vote, just a way of dominating the situation.

"I kinda like the kid, Boss. That doesn't mean that business isn't just business if you say so."

"See," Mr. Damianzo said, smiling with satisfaction, "nobody believes you."

Huh?

"You think you're so smart with your reading and acting cute that you can get out of anything."

This was exactly the time to remain silent and let him talk himself into a decision to let me go.

"I can always see a way out," I heard myself say.

He took this as a challenge, and his smile hardened. "And what's your way out now?"

I nodded to the side door where Mario had been making his appearances. "See that?"

When they all looked, I shot up, grabbed the bust of Caesar (it was even heavier than it appeared), and heaved it through the window to the right of the desk. I followed it. I crossed my arms in front of my face and raised my knees to present as small an area as I could. Julius had taken a good section of glass and panes with it. I didn't feel any cuts. I did feel that tingle of anticipation in my back. I thought Rico might be quick enough ...

The fresh air felt good, warmer than inside and smelling like the garden in the distance and the grass below. I guessed it had been cut the day before. Out of the house's shadow, dew shone in little beads on it. Green and bright, oversaturated color with dots of sunlight.

I liked falling. It gave me that fun feeling in my stomach. If this wasn't as serious a situation, I would have liked it more. I dropped only about fourteen feet. I had jumped much farther and not broken anything—yet. I didn't break anything this time, either.

The grass was soft. Julius had landed before me, about ten feet from the house. He lay head-down, half sunk. I had jumped with only enough forward motion to get me through the window completely. I didn't want to be too far from the house in case Rico leaned out and fired immediately. He would have to lean more to aim at me near the house. I looked at the image of the broken window my eyes had snapped as I passed through it. There was jagged glass left at the bottom. This would make it harder to get a good shot at me if I stayed close to the building.

I landed with less of a thud than Julius, cushioning with my legs and rolling as gracefully as I could in one fluid motion. That part went well, and I had to smile. I pulled a handful of change from my pocket—it felt like four dimes, two quarters, and five pennies—turned counterclockwise and threw it against the house toward its west end. The change made dull, gray sounds against the siding. They were a bit louder than the excited voices above. Mr. Damianzo offered a vibrato as he held some long notes in his angry outburst.

I continued my rotation until I was facing east, and ran to the corner in the house's slim shadow. I knew where I was headed, and it wasn't going to be sprinting across the open lawn; I was going into the house again.

Mama was still sitting there motionless, staring at a yellowed piece of paper on the table. Overused folds had torn apart pieces, leaving them attached by short edges or corners. I reached out as I sat down in the chair beside her. The paper was soft, its fibers polished by hands over the years. She also had a clean white sheet of paper in front of her. And a pencil. Just a few words were written. "Gnocchi" was fairly centered near the top. The handwriting was faint and shaky. It sounded weak and full of sharps, disharmonious. Very different from the joyous musical script of the worn original.

Mama didn't look at me. Maybe she didn't see, or was looking somewhere inside that blocked out my presence.

I picked up the pencil and pulled the almost blank piece of paper in front of me. I wrote as I spoke. My hand followed the song.

I started, "I had some frozen gnocchi about a month ago. From the store. They had no taste at all." I had cooked some at the Hendersons' home on Fruit Street while they were at work. But I didn't think Mama would want to hear those details.

"Mama, I made Papa mad at me. I did some things. I tried to help Christina and her wedding dress, but Papa thinks I did some bad things. He thinks I was disrespectful, but I didn't mean it that way. I think he wants to punish me."

She didn't move. Her eyes blinked once in a while and her chest moved with her slow breathing, but that was it. She stared at the paper in front of her.

My hand stopped moving, the song ended. It was a recipe, in Italian.

Sounds were louder now from the rest of the house. Guy's voice called loudly from the kitchen door opening onto the hallway, "Here's the little shit!"

Yeah, yeah.

Rico pushed past Guy and asked, "Did he bother you, Mama?" He didn't have his gun out. I wondered if he had pulled it at all.

She didn't move.

All he said was, "Come on, kid," and pointed to the door. I slid the paper toward mama as I got up. Then I walked in front of Rico. Guy was just inside the doorway, flexing his hands slowly. They wanted me, and not in any good way, either.

As I passed him, he said, "You did it this time, kid." I ducked and Guy's hand passed through the space where the back of my head would have been. I figured this was the time for avoidance. In a non-threatening way, of course.

I continued my forced march—all the way back to the office I had just left minutes before through the new exit I had created. A light, refreshing breeze came in the broken window.

Mr. Damianzo leaned against the front of his desk, arms folded.

There was a bad look on his face. I bet not many that didn't work for him had seen that look more than once.

I didn't look at the window, but, since it was now open …

Guy walked over and stood in front of it. Rico stayed behind me.

"You took my daughter, ripped my couch, broke my window. And I still don't know how my statue is." He was building up pressure. It wouldn't take long until he blew up in my direction.

I didn't have to look toward Mario's door to know I would never make it there before bad things happened.

"You come in my house and you do this?" He waved all around him, not just at the window. I took it to mean the whole mess. Then, to Rico and Guy, "He thinks he can bust up my home. My home! And come and go with my family." His voice was rising. It was a very light shade with red, irregular zigzags through it. They kept silent; they knew he wasn't looking for a response.

"I didn't mean any disrespect," I said. I hoped I sounded respectful. It occurred to me then that I didn't mind dying, but I wasn't a big fan of suffering. It looked more and more like he was aiming for teaching me a lesson, and a lesson usually meant pain.

My words sounded puny, even to me.

"Shaddap! You said all you're gonna say. Now you hafta learn a lesson."

See? A lesson. I would rather have been wrong here, and didn't feel any triumph in my successful prediction.

"Look how skinny he is."

The voice came from the doorway behind me, behind Rico. It was almost as loud as Mr. Damianzo's.

Mama stood there, the paper in her right hand.

"Mama!" Mr. Damianzo seemed to forget me for a moment. There was a little joy in that one word.

"You letting flies in my house?" Her eyes were wide and she put one hand on her hip as she waved the paper toward the broken window. "I keep a clean house. And you want to let the flies in. Fix that. Fix that now."

"Mama. We have business here. You know business. We'll talk later." He had pointed at me when he said "here."

"You got no business. He's just a boy. You never broke a window when you were a boy?" She walked up to me and shook the paper a bit. "That's my mama's handwriting. Look! It's like she wrote it this morning. I can see her back at the old table making a big deal of writing this down. I was just a girl. It's like her talking to me again, after all the years she's been gone."

"He cut my couch and took Christina, too."

Mama paid no attention and pinched my cheek hard. "He doesn't eat good. I can tell." She tapped under her left eye a few times. "Look at him."

"He broke my window." Mr. Damianzo was losing volume quickly.

"We're having homemade gnocchi, not that store stuff. That's not gnocchi. Two kinds, garlic and basil, and marinara. Two kinds." Then, to me while making little karate chops in the air with her hand, "You know how much work this is?"

She walked to the doorway and leaned out, calling loudly, "Maria, tomatoes and basilica and *prezzemolo*. And ripe ones. Not hard. I want them soft like your sister's ass. We're making gnocchi."

Mama leaned back in and motioned to me to follow. "You know how much work you're making me do? You're helping. Come."

I turned and followed. Rico looked like he wanted to smile, but didn't.

When I got to the hall, I heard Mr. Damianzo mutter, "My statue."

Mama heard too and sang, "The flies. Stop those flies."

Chapter Ten

Only Guy ate more than I did.

I sat next to Mama, who kept asking me how it was, and when I came up with another way to say "the best I ever ate," would pinch my cheeks again.

Mr. Damianzo presided at the head of the table and grumbled until Mama pointed out I didn't have any wine.

He grabbed a Waterford crystal carafe to his left, leaned toward me past Mama, and poured my glass full.

"I have this made special. Wait till you taste it. Not too dry, not too sweet. Perfect for this. Perfect." He had an obvious pride about it. "A little wine is good for you. Good for the blood."

I took a sip, all bright corners with strings of dashed, low whistles. "*Abbondanza* and health," I said as I raised my glass. I thought they would like that. They did. After cries of "Aayy," they all raised their glasses and repeated my toast.

I had helped Mama make and roll the little potato dumplings. She used a worn gnocchi comb, and I used a fork. After watching her hand-roll a few, I could follow the tune of the motion perfectly. She was amazed at how fast I could make them.

After the meal, Mr. Damianzo walked me to the front door. Guy was getting the car.

"You're a big pain in the ass, kid. But, Mama's happy, so I'm happy. It's been a long time."

Big!

We faced each other, close to one of the grooved white pillars in front. I could see the black Lincoln backing up from the garage.

"You're what I call a loose end. I don't like loose ends. But ..." He shook his head. "Mario tells me we had nothing to do with the business in Miracle last night. This important to you?"

"My classmate was shot and killed. They cut her face. I promised her mother I would find things out." My voice was white.

Mr. Damianzo let out a breath. "Sooner or later, you mess with stuff like this, and you get hurt, maybe hurt bad. I hear anything, I tell you."

He seemed to be making a decision, and folded his arms before speaking. "Now, you can help me too. In Miracle, a few months ago, some property of mine got lost. Disappeared. An old leather suitcase. Louis Vuitton. You understand?"

Oh no! Not my suitcase!

I nodded. "Little LVs all over it? That's their symbol, right? What was in it?" My voice looked dark since I already knew the answers.

"Now that's the pain in the ass in you trying to get out. You just keep your eyes open. You see something, you tell me. See, we help each other. Now go." He waved towards the car, which had just pulled in behind me.

Guy called through the open passenger window, "Get in front with me, Kid. I'm not going to look like your chauffeur."

I got in.

As we were about to pull away, Rico came out the front door. He leaned down and handed me a paper bag. "Mama wanted you to have some cannoli for home."

We had also made those.

I asked him as he straightened up, "Did you have a shot?"

"Does it matter?"

He knew I was talking about that one moment when I crashed through the window. I didn't know if he had decided not to shoot, or didn't have time.

I shrugged. "Nice to know."

"You ever want to learn to shoot, we'll get together." He wasn't going to tell me.

"I got a good aim," I said with a somewhat prideful smile.

"Lots of good aimers don't aim so good any more. More to it. You'll see." He tapped the top of the car and Guy started around the circle and out the drive.

I waved at Bobby on the way out. He didn't wave back.

I opened the bag. On top of a white cardboard box tied with thin, green-striped string sat a hard-sided black glass case. A new pair of Armani 155S sunglasses rested inside along with a card with a phone number. I put the glasses on.

"Cannoli smell pretty good," Guy said. I agreed.

The suitcase contained $4,800,000. Or, it used to before I spent some if it.

Its leather might have been green at one point; it was brownish now, and the brass edges were nicked and tarnished. The suitcase wasn't quite square anymore, either. It leaned a bit to the back and to the right side. Been through a lot, I had guessed.

One evening in late March, just when the weather was starting to turn, I had noticed that lights were on all night and the back door was wide open at the only house on Orchard Street. It was a dead end and had a convenient shortcut beaten in a winding path through the woods. It led to East Main Street; I used it a lot, especially at night.

Nobody noticed the lights and door but me, and being a good citizen, I took the responsibility on the second night to see if everything was okay inside.

It wasn't.

The man with the thin black mustache had been knifed twice— once in the shoulder (that didn't look too bad) and once just above the right clavicle, near his throat (that looked deadly). He had almost made it to the front door with the suitcase before he fell. Before he fell and bled his life out on the cheap brown carpet.

The other man had taken two gunshots at close range: one to the stomach and one higher. He lay on his back in the middle of the living room, a butcher's knife with a black handle a few feet from his bloodied right hand. The TV was on. A rerun of *The Andy Griffith Show* where Barney catches the bank robber.

The boys probably had an argument over the suitcase, like maybe who should own it. Mustache won, at least for a while.

I had put on my latex gloves when I saw the result of the bickering in front of me. No use getting officially involved here. The suitcase was heavy, and locked. Mustache's pockets had no key that would fit it.

I lifted his left eyelid and looked. I wondered my usual question of the dead, "The glow room?" The gun was still in his right hand.

The knife man had the key in his front pants pocket. It was alone on a loop made out of a red twist tie. I looked in his eye too. I never get any answer, but I ask. I don't know what I'm really looking for there, but it feels like the right thing to do.

I pulled the suitcase handle out of Mustache's fingers. It wasn't hard. The key fit and each suitcase clasp made a loud sound as it clattered open. I said a big "Ohhh!" when I saw all those Ben

Franklins lined up inside. Full of hundreds. Each pack had a broad green bill band around it. I had counted 250 bills in a pack: $25,000 each. There were eight packs across, three down, and three deep. That's a lot of hundreds, almost five million dollars worth. All old, worn, dirty bills—but still in good enough shape for what I had in mind, like spending them. I checked to make sure the serial numbers weren't in any order. They weren't. This wasn't bank money; this was good money.

It's not money that is the root of all evil, it's the love of money. I had to admit: it was love at first sight. Evil, evil that would take offense at my claiming the suitcase, was certainly going to come looking for it. I thought it was a good plan not to be there when it came.

I took Mustache's car keys, watched the end of Andy, shut off the TV and lights, and closed the back door behind me. I left the suitcase behind the house and made a quick check of the street. Deserted and quiet, just right for getting away with millions of dollars.

Not having a driver's license sucks. But there was no license that covered taking a dead man's car and his bagful of cash, so I didn't feel deprived when I opted for a cool ride in the 2003 silver PT Cruiser parked in front. It stank of cigarettes and was full of Roy Orbison CDs.

I took back roads to Miracle Self-Storage. Karen Baker—Karen of the stolen polaroids—owned it and let me have a small outside unit free of charge. A boy needs a little privacy, and I had it filled with things that might prove "embarrassing" if linked to me. They might be embarrassing to others, too.

The plain, shiny Master Lock combination padlock had felt cold in my hands. It took only a minute to hide the suitcase in the back right corner and lock the unit again. I had taken a couple hundred-dollar bills. All I had to do was return the car.

It was easy enough. Just to be cautious, I first parked a half-mile from the house, walked there through the back yards and fields, and saw it was still undisturbed and unoccupied by living beings. I drove up, parked, put Mustache's keys back, turned the lights and TV back on (must have been an Andy marathon), and left.

Two days later, I had read that the rented house had burned completely to the ground. The paper said it was deserted. Someone must have "cleaned" it before applying the torch. Police were looking for the last renter. Good luck.

"You want that last cannoli? Guy asked. The open box was on the seat between us.

"Let's split it," I said as I tore it in half. "You pick."

He took the bigger half.

As Guy pulled to the curb in front of my home, he said, "You know, kid, I took it real easy on you when I slapped you. Because I like you."

"Oh, I know, Guy. You see how I played along and pretended it hurt?" I hadn't pretended one bit.

I got out, but reached back in to shake his enveloping hand.

"Yeah. You did good." As he pulled away he said, "You need anything …" and left it at that. Just like that.

Chapter Eleven

Home was above Miracle's only pawn shop. It was also Miracle's only locksmith service.

Benny Fortuna was my dad, my adopted dad. He wasn't so bad: a second-rate locksmith, a third-rate businessman, a second-rate petty thief and con artist, and, at best, a very reluctant father.

Bunny Fortuna, the former Ludmila Pashakova, was Benny's mail-order, or more correctly, internet-order, bride of four years. She hated me. Maybe she didn't bargain on our little family when she moved here from Moscow. She ran the dance studio next to the pawn shop. Miracle Movement, the sign said in large magenta letters (Vivaldi font) written on a graceful curve. It was on a green background. Below that, in smaller letters: Ballet, Modern Dance, Tap, Aerobics.

Aerobics was right. I bet Bunny had the best body from here all the way back to her native Moscow. Her 5'11" figure was perfect. Perfect for normal society, but apparently not perfect for the emaciated world of Russian professional ballet. They had booted her for outgrowing her costumes. That and several indiscretions she would rather no one else in the world know about. But I knew.

Our apartments were above the storefronts. I have to give Bunny credit, she kept them immaculate. That's saying something because Benny was a real slob. I, on the other hand, was as neat as Bunny, and kept my one room, my bedroom, in order—and locked with another combination padlock. Benny could get in if he really concentrated and gambled that I wouldn't find out and then "leak" some pretty damning information about him. The lock was to keep the curious and lovely Bunny at bay.

Benny, head down, was cutting a key when I walked in. The vibration from the machine shook his balding head a bit.

"Hi, Dad! I'm home," I said with more enthusiasm than was needed or was to be appreciated.

Benny jumped and swore. "Look what you made me do." He took the key he had been cutting from the holder and held it up. It had a deep groove gouged out of it. He threw it disgustedly into a box beside the key maker. It had others in it. He didn't need me to make mistakes.

"You do it," he said, stepping away.

I felt like showing off a bit. The machine uses the key you're copying as a template, and forces the duplicate to be cut exactly. I took the original key from its holder and looked at the uneven edge. It spoke to me in its angles.

I tossed it to Benny and proceeded to cut the new key from memory. I could do this for any key I had ever seen. Sometimes I would pretend to be interested in someone's keychain and then just look at their keys and make one for myself later. Each edge, with its grooves and peaks, had a song that I played again as I cut.

I took the key out, blew on it and handed it to Benny. He put it together with the original and held them up; they matched.

"Mine would've been as good if you didn't screw me up."

"Miss me?" I asked, knowing his real answer no matter what he said. I hadn't been back since I left for school the day before.

This wasn't uncommon and was the main reason I chose Benny and Bunny as my adopted parents. I needed parents who didn't give a shit about me and my habits. Benny and Bunny fulfilled my every expectation.

After my grandmother died, I circulated through several foster homes. This was rather unpleasant, not so much because of the unloving and harsh treatment I encountered, but more because foster parents try to exert so much control. A normal kid might be forced to put up with that. After I died, I wasn't normal any more. After the Indian killed me, I knew I had to take control, because I didn't sleep. I needed freedom at night: freedom to move, freedom to search, freedom to learn, freedom to break and enter.

Mary Milloy had pushed through my adoption. She really didn't think the Fortunas would be good parents for me, but also didn't want certain "sensitive" things to get back to her office at the Massachusetts Department of Social Services.

Benny and Bunny had lots to lose if they didn't play along. That's one reason I picked them. The other was I got the use of Benny's shop. My part of the bargain was staying out of their way as much as possible. I kept my part.

It was an arrangement that suited me. It kept the local and state government out of my activities, gave me an address, a place to keep my clothes, and a place to shower. What more could I ask, except loving parents who marveled at all the wonderful things I did? But, I guess good parents would be constantly shocked and disapprove of my adventures. So the Fortuna household was probably the best place for me.

"I thought you were in real trouble, Myx. Trouble when Rico showed up here, you know?" He looked a little disappointed that I had made it home.

"Mr. Damianzo says hello, and wants me to keep an eye on you."

My voice was dark. I thought a quarter turn on his screws would have a lasting and beneficial effect on our familial arrangement.

Benny did a small double-take and said, "Christ." Then he recovered a bit and added, "Hey, Bunny's pissed at you. Try to go make nice, will you?"

"When do I not make nice? She's pissed more than anyone I know. What do you see in her?" I always enjoyed Benny's response to this question. It was like a reflex.

He held his hands up to shoulder height and turned completely around while saying, "Look at me."

Benny was a pudgy, paunchy five foot seven, forty-three-year-old with indifferent personal hygiene.

Now here comes the point.

He pointed next door toward Bunny's studio. "Then go look at her." This was to remind me that Bunny made Playboy models look like Brownies.

"Sure, Benny, but is it worth it?"

We both laughed.

I went next door to get my latest dose of pissiness.

Ludmila (she was never Bunny to me when she was moving, dancing) was leading an aerobics group of seventeen women. I stayed in the back as they tried to keep up with her. The loud music and eighteen female sweats and secretions made my senses dance in strange arrays.

Ludmila led and shouted and encouraged. She drove them, her voice melodic with that Russian accent. She was very good at this. It was no wonder they loved her, and her classes kept growing.

The music ended, and everyone applauded, me included. Ludmila pirouetted almost too quickly to follow, then bent low, extending her long left leg behind her and high in the air, toes pointed ruler-straight. Both arms made slow and graceful arcs to their final position extended in front of her. It felt perfect.

Her mesmerized cult let out little gasps and squeals of appreciation. I barely contained my own—she was that potent.

Then she straightened and clapped toward the ladies. "Good, good. You worked hard today."

They rushed up to her, talking, laughing, asking questions. I imagine they fantasized about having a body like hers and gliding across the floor with her ease and grace.

She was good for them. I have been hated by less worthy people.

They finally headed for their towels and bags. I waved to those I knew and gave nods and little "doing great" encouragements. Some came over to say goodbye before they left. All their faces were red and moist. I could feel their heat in little waves.

Bunny wore a kingfisher blue Nagano unitard with a halter neck. *Sans* stirrups. I gave it a lot of credit for accommodating her. She looked like a superheroine from a comic book.

She crooked a finger repeatedly in my direction, beckoning me to an audience at the front of the studio.

The last woman left through the glass door facing the street. Bunny went from smiling and waving to a murderous look while wagging her left index finger at me.

"You bring those men upon us. You know who they are? You know what they can do?" Her voice was contralto, and fit her, her face and form. It had just enough vibration to add richness without drawing attention to the fact.

"Guy said you have a nice ass," I said.

"The big one?"

I nodded.

"So obvious. He frightens me." She shuddered.

I knew what she meant, but didn't add that I thought Rico was the more dangerous.

"We don't need you and your trouble. Look. You saw those women. I'm building something here, something good. I don't need more worries from you or from anywhere."

Bunny's black, square-cut bangs shook a little as she talked. They always fell back perfectly into her Prince Valiant hairstyle.

"It was just a misunderstanding. I straightened it all up and now we're friends. They won't be back unless I call them." I hoped that the hint of threat would soften her a bit.

It mustn't have made much of an impression because she continued with her next grievance, "And I'm not your phone-answering machine. The police called. A Mrs. Powell called. Are you causing concerns for us?"

"Three people were shot and killed last night. One I went to school with. They want me to tell them if I hear anything about it." I didn't think it was necessary or productive to tell Bunny that I was going to be more creatively involved than that.

"Don't bring death here."

Her sweat didn't stink. She smelled a salty soap and water good.

"Death I'll leave far away from here." I smiled. "Anything in the refrigerator?"

"Go."

I did.

Chapter Twelve

Pellets. The water felt like pellets on my back as I stood in the shower, head down, eyes closed, my hands against the wall below the shower head, supporting me as I washed away all those hours. I liked it cool for the final rinse, and I indulged myself for ten minutes each day.

Dr. Zylodic had told me I needed a punctuation to take the place of sleep. I needed to divide my life so I wasn't swallowed by it. The shower worked; it worked as long as I didn't reminisce in it. I trained myself only to feel it and to be fully present in the cleansing.

I heard the washer cut in for its final cycle, and jerked out of the stream before it turned to ice. Shower over, I shut it off and dried myself with a big, rough, tan towel. The friction and pressure felt good on my skin, presenting me shapes and depositing pressures in my chest and abdomen that would have allowed me to recreate all my movements, even the tiniest, if need be. That would be silly, though.

I pulled on my black Nike running shorts and walked past the Fortunas' bedroom. (We had worked it out so I didn't become Myx Fortuna in the adoption.) The afternoon sun spotlighted the cream and rose colors that Bunny had chosen for bed coverings and bureau scarves. Bunny was a diligent and persevering housekeeper. Benny's heap of dirty clothes at the foot of the bed and his Dunkin' Donuts coffee cup left on the dresser meant ass-kicking later. I would say that Benny would never learn if "never" wasn't such a long time.

I transferred my clothes from the washer to the dryer in the small laundry room next to my bedroom. They felt cold and compact from the spin cycle. I raised a shirt to my nose to smell the residual perfume of the powdered detergent before tossing it into the front loading dryer. I did my laundry twice a week.

My bedroom was next to Benny and Bunny's. During sex, they may not be the loudest couple on the planet, but they have to be in the top five. I'm lucky my "embarrass" muscle got broken a long time ago.

My bed was in the right corner, against the outside wall, just beside one of the two windows. I had an eight-by-ten photograph hanging over it—the only thing on the light blue walls.

My pillow and sheets shone in the light, contrasting with the dark blue blanket that covered the bed. I had no bedspread, which irked Bunny's decorating tastes. (I left my door open when I was home and let Bunny think she was stealing peeks. I never wanted the room to become the "forbidden apple" of Farno Street to her.)

I shut my door behind me, and, like every day, I determined to give myself a chance to sleep. It was never that I felt tired; it was that I felt deprived.

After brushing my wet hair back, I settled on top of the bed, feeling the waffle-weave of the blanket beneath me. My head sank comfortably into the pillow. I began the relaxation exercises Dr. Zylodic had taught me, starting at my feet and working my way up. All I had to do was not think about the Indian, him killing me, and my ensuing years of wakefulness.

Johnny Bearcloud, of the Massaquidnec tribe, killed me.

The first time I died was an accident; the second time was on purpose—the Indian's purpose. Native American may be politically correct, but Johnny will always be "the Indian" to me.

Through intense sessions, Dr. Zylodic had taught me to use my synesthesia, the mingling of my senses, in a useful and non-confusing way. He made me look at it as a benefit, a power and not a burden. I started studying people, learning easily what their intentions were, how they were going to move and act, what they hid.

About a year after my lightning strike, I was getting pretty confident in my new abilities. I was in foster homes and tried to stay away as much as I could during the day, although all my foster parents were pretty controlling. I had started my habit of roaming Miracle. At least I could still sleep then and stay in one place at night.

John Roman owned a big software company in Boston. He also owned the most expensive home in Miracle. He also was the father of fifteen-year-old Sarah, who had been kidnapped. She had been missing for two days.

Roman was a hard-head who did things his own way. When a handwritten ransom note appeared, he had it printed in the newspaper against Chief Maldonato's protests. The article asked for leads and offered a reward. A reward sounded good since I had no money at all.

The note was printed in small shaky letters. One to another, they sounded strange to me, as if they didn't belong together. I had never felt that in writing before, so I was surprised to get that feeling again in the K-Mart parking lot.

I had been looking into all the parked cars (just curious) before walking through the store. A dirty clipboard was on the front seat of a 1993 Ford pickup. There were some penciled diagrams with dimensions and a few notes in script. But the music was the same as the ransom note's. Coincidences aren't always so coincidental. I looked in every car I saw back then. I still do. The more you look, the more chance of seeing something interesting.

One time I was walking by Veronica Sabine's candy apple–red Corvette convertible and ... but that's another story.

JB Landscaping was written in red letters on the side of the dented and dusty black truck. It had a phone number too. The smart thing to do would have been to go to the pay phone in front of the store and call the police.

I crawled under the dark green plastic tarp in the back of the truck. It covered some poly piping and fittings. I hoped the big lawnmower rig wouldn't roll too much when the truck started moving.

I waited maybe fifteen minutes, listening to shoppers drive in, then spit or fart before entering the store if they were alone, or complain to each other if they were a pair. Some came back to their cars, plastic bags crinkling in odd-angled green and purple polygons. I was still learning what all my senses meant back then. Calibration.

Then, steady and sure footsteps, quiet and precise—someone approached the driver's side of the truck. The driver hesitated; I could hear the slight ruffling of clothes as this person looked around. A little low grunt. It was a man. He must have had his hand on the door handle because his movements caused faint vibrations in the truck.

Then he did something that caused the hair on the back of my neck to prickle: he snuffed the air, breathing in and out quickly in short bursts. He was testing, sniffing like an animal.

After about thirty seconds of silence, he opened the door and started the truck. The door hadn't been locked.

We drove slowly. The exhaust of the truck nearly made me cough. I wasn't tempted to uncover myself to look and keep track of our route. I had seen a map of Miracle and could follow our progress and turns in my mind. When we stopped ten minutes later, I figured we were on Pond Mill Road.

Driver got out and let the truck run. All I could smell was the tarp and exhaust. I heard the clinking of a chain and the spring of a lock. Then he pulled a gate open, drove through and relocked the gate behind him. He drove on an unpaved, dusty road and took a turn to the right.

We stopped, the engine went dead, and Driver got out. He walked about twenty-five feet to the left of the truck. I heard him fumble past change in his pocket and extract something. I figured now was my chance to leave the truck, so I lifted an edge of the tarp and peeked— rusted derelict cars, a junkyard. This must be Mason's Auto Body, which had remained deserted since Albert Mason had gotten a heart attack while trying to tow a car from a No Parking zone downtown. The owner of the Camry had been arguing about the tow. Since his death, a newspaper article appeared every year stating that the junkyard had to be cleaned up and was an environmental hazard. Nothing was ever done, to my knowledge.

I slipped silently (I hoped) from the tarp and the truck. I exited to the right, letting the truck shield me in case Driver looked. I ran behind a '75 green Buick station wagon about a hundred feet from him. The right front side of the car had been caved in by a hideous impact; I wondered about the people in the crash.

Driver was wearing faded, dirty jeans and a tight, short-sleeved blue T-shirt—its breast pocket bulged with cigarettes. His suntanned arms flowed with stringy muscles and thick veins. He wore a red bandana rolled thin and tied around his neck, the two ends at angles as they spread from the tight knot.

His black and shiny hair was pulled back into a ponytail, and held by something hidden in the tangle. It was more than shoulder-length.

He was bent over the trunk of a blue Chevy. Then he stopped, waited motionless, and turned quickly. The second he started moving, I ducked behind the car. I held my breath until I heard him mutter something I couldn't understand and then return to his duties at the trunk.

This time, I looked through a cracked window on the driver's side and not over the car.

He reached in and effortlessly pulled Sarah Roman from the bottom of the trunk. Her hands and feet were tied behind her, held together by many turns of brown shipping twine. She had silver duct tape over her mouth.

Driver was an Indian. He had dark eyes and a nose that had been beaten flat. He looked mean, but sometimes first impressions can't be trusted. I had never seen him before.

He dropped Sarah from a few feet off the ground. She landed on her heels and then her butt. Her skinny butt—she was thin on the verge of frail.

Indian took a knife, it looked like a filet knife, from his belt and cut her bonds. Its blade was blackened except for the edge, which shone from a recent sharpening. Constant honing had narrowed the blade to less than one half of its original width.

"You try to run, I'll cut off your tits." He tapped the front of her blouse with the tip of the knife.

Indian made a motion across his mouth, signaling Sarah to take the tape off. She did.

"You make any noise and I'll cut out your tongue."

I could see a theme here: he *was* mean.

Sarah's face was dirty with streaks of clean. She had been crying.

"Piss." It was a command.

Sarah started to cry. "I can't. Not with you …"

"Piss. Now." His voice was low, almost a growl. It made me visualize rubbing my hand against sharp stones.

Sarah turned away from him, made a motion at her waist, and pulled her jeans and panties down to just past her knees in one motion. She grabbed the bumper as she half squatted and leaned back. A stream of urine puddled beneath her until the dusty earth drew it in, leaving a brown stain on the gray ground. It only took a few seconds.

She stood up and started to pull her clothes. There was blood on her panties.

"Wait," the Indian said and went to the front seat of the truck. I ducked until I heard the rustle of a plastic bag.

When I looked again, he had pulled a package of tampons from the K-Mart bag.

She hadn't turned around. He reached by her with the tampons and said, "Use this."

Her voice was full of notes, a musical whine, "Nooooo."

"You do it or I do it," he said as he fished again in the bag.

She did it and pulled her jeans and panties back into place.

He handed Sarah a large Snickers candy bar. She took it, not waiting for one of his short threats. He stood there watching her eat until it was half gone. Then he pulled out a bottle of Polar Spring water. He twisted the cap off and gave it to her. She took a long drink and ate the rest of the Snickers. She then finished the water.

"Please let me go," she pleaded and sobbed. That seemed to be the sign for him to tear a piece of duct tape. He pushed it hard across her mouth.

"Get in." He nodded to the trunk. She got in. It only took him a minute to retie her hands and feet. He gave her one rough shove down before he slammed the trunk. I heard it lock.

Indian started to look around again, and even took a few steps past his truck toward my hiding spot. I heard this, not saw it, because I had again crouched behind a tire so he couldn't see my feet if he looked under the car.

He muttered again and drove away.

I waited about five minutes, didn't hear anything and ran over to the trunk.

A junkyard presents a lot of makeshift tools. I found a long, flat metal bar. It took me a minute to use it as a pry bar and spring the trunk.

Her eyes were turned from me when I opened it, probably afraid that he had returned for some even more evil purpose.

"Sarah, we have to get out of here." I took the tape off her mouth and went searching for something sharp.

I found a foot-long piece of chrome trim. It was sharp enough to saw the twine loose.

I helped her out of the trunk and she almost screamed through her tears.

"If you don't stop that, I'm getting the tape," I joked.

She gave a sort of hysterical laugh and hugged me. I kind of returned it, patting her back lightly three times.

"Let's go." I led her to the west side of the yard, away from the street. I wanted to move through the woods until we reached a house we could call from.

Five minutes of dodging through rusted and demolished wrecks took us to a twelve-foot chain-link fence, topped with little twin-twined barbs every six inches. We walked along it until we found a spot where the top was bent over, probably by kids making their own entrance to the "playground."

"Up and over, Sarah," I said as I boosted her. She *did* have a bony ass.

"I felt your Spirit."

My hand rubbing against sharp rocks. That feeling again.

The Indian stood there, not twenty feet from the fence, from Sarah.

But the eleven-year-old version of me stood between them.

I hadn't heard him coming. I hadn't sensed him at all. That bothered me.

His hand was on the haft of the knife in his belt; that bothered me too. He didn't pull it as he started forward.

"Sarah, get to the road. A car, a car," I yelled not turning toward her. From the sounds, she was having a problem climbing. Maybe she was awkward, maybe she was still numb and stiff from her auto prison. Whatever the reason, she was taking too long to get over.

Since the lightning strike, I had been gaining confidence in reading people, how they moved. I could anticipate and outquick them. The Indian was different.

I wasn't sure of his movements. They were quiet and didn't speak to me, just flowed one to another spontaneously.

I wanted only to delay him enough for Sarah to make it over the fence and get a head start to the road. She was at the top and starting to swing her leg over.

The Indian ran over me without slowing. In one motion, he leaped for the fence, caught it, and grabbed Sarah's right ankle just before she pulled it over to the far side. She screamed.

He had her. What I had, after being knocked aside and to the ground by his flight, was the knife. I had pulled it from his belt in the collision.

Being eleven, and never having seen violence in person before, I could reasonably have stood there and maybe threatened him with his own knife—just to distract him—and then run away. That would have been smart.

Instead, I jumped as high as I could and drove the knife into hard muscle until it changed direction as it glanced off bone. The thin blade had flexed a bit as it entered and then sprung straight as its sharpness sliced deep into his flesh.

I had stabbed the Indian's ass, his left buttock.

He grunted a low animal sound, released Sarah and hit me with a backhand that I barely saw coming. I fell ten feet away from the fence, my arms flung back over my head sending the knife into the distance behind me.

My mouth tasted buttery bitter with rough fringes. It was full of blood. I looked up and saw Sarah fall to one side of the fence and the Indian land on the other, my side. As I tried to get up, he ran at me in a crouch while venting a high-pitched yell. My hair stood again.

I turned my head only enough to catch his open-handed slap on my forehead instead of my face. White shooting stars spun across a field of black in my vision. He lifted me by the hair. All was silence now except for his breathing. I brought my left hand up to the bandana around his neck, dug my fingers under it and pulled while bringing my feet up to his chest for leverage.

He grunted again as we both went to the ground. I turned and struggled to crawl away, but he jumped on top of me with his whole weight, squashing the air from my lungs.

His right arm encircled my chest, pinning my arms to my sides. His left arm did the same to my legs. With one smooth effort to balance himself, he stood and lifted me. He squeezed hard. I knew this was not for control, but to hurt me.

It did. I howled, using all my air. It didn't sound like me.

A lidless black fifty-five–gallon drum sat at a twenty-degree angle about thirty feet from the fence. It had one broad white stripe painted around its middle. An oil slick covered the surface of the rainwater filling it; there was a light green scum over some of it.

The Indian, never speaking, walked slowly toward the filled drum. I struggled with all my strength but only managed to move like a sluggish worm in his grip. I even tried to bash him with my head but never hit anything.

"No, noo, nooo!" I kept saying that one word.

The sunlight, at the low angle, penetrated only a few inches into the water, showing the orange rust on the dented rim and inner surface. The rest was blackness.

My arms were pinned. I was helpless. He was going to drown me.

He drove me headfirst into the water, releasing me only to quickly transfer his grasp to my legs to steer me straight to the bottom. My forehead scraped against the side all the way down until my head was crammed, neck bent back, against the bottom. He had my knees bent completely, one hand on each of my ankles.

Then he pushed down hard, compressing me. And he pushed for a long time.

The black water tasted sour. It burned my nose and sinuses when

I finally breathed it in.

It felt good not to struggle any more.

The blackness changed to that pearly light I had seen that one time before. I was in the room again and happy to be there.

The figure was there, looking down. I tried to look down too, but seemed to be only able to look at her. He pointed to the right wall, walked to it and pushed. A roughly rectangular black opening appeared.

She pointed behind me, and I vomited up the warm, sour water that had been filling me.

"I knew it!" Dr. Fabrizio sounded triumphant.

I was back at the morgue. Dr. Fabrizio tended to me, and before I was transferred to a bed upstairs, he confided while kind of gently brushing my hair back from my forehead, "I never filled out the certificate this time."

Sarah had made it to the road, flagged a car down and gotten help. The police found me, still in the water, over an hour later.

The Indian's name was Johnny Bearcloud. He had installed the Romans' sprinklers the year before. Who knows why he thought his kidnapping plan would work?

The State Police caught him on the Mass Pike, heading West. His truck was full of blood.

Of course, I got screwed out of the reward. First, Sarah's father reduced it through some pretext, and then my foster parents at the time, the Burnetts (yeah, the oil burner guy), spent it on themselves.

I learned that nothing is yours until it's yours, and that you make it yours by taking it, protecting it, and hiding it.

Another thing I learned was my sleeping nights were over. Even with medication in the hospital, I was constantly awake, never tired.

I did have a new appetite though, and had to eat as often as I could.

Even Dr. Zylodic hadn't found a method around my sleeplessness.

◎　◎　◎　◎　◎

I finished relaxing all of my body and still hadn't gotten any results. I opened my eyes and figured my clothes were ready in the dryer.

Time to return my phone calls, too. I never gave out my cell phone number (I changed phones too often), so I relied on Bunny and Benny. They always complained, but never caused trouble. I, in turn, never caused trouble for them. Never intentionally.

I called the Chief first. Sgt. Wayne put me through to him.

"Chief Maldonato." He sounded tired.

"How'd you know about Leviticus?" I asked.

The Chief sighed. "Rabbi Stein quoted it to me every time he wanted to shut down Skin Sins. Why do I answer your questions?"

"Because I'm a source of valuable information," I said cheerily.

"You have any?"

"No. You?" I wasn't hopeful, but you never know.

"No. Unless verifying that all three were killed with the same gun is valuable. You guessed that, I hope. It was a .32 caliber."

"It's good to know it's still *only* three."

"Damianzo's people called me, nosing around. Some nice fatherly advice would be for you not to fool with them. I'm not giving it for two reasons. One, because I know you wouldn't listen. And two, because part of me hopes they teach you a lesson."

"Thanks, Dad." He hung up. No goodbye.

Next, I called Mrs. Powell. On the third ring, Mr. Powell

answered.

"Hi, Mr. Powell, this is Myx Amens. Could I talk to Mrs. Powell?"

"She's not talking to anybody today."

I could hear a radio in the background. It was Miracle's tiny news station, WMCL, broadcasting. He didn't sound like he wanted to be talking to me, or anybody.

"But I'm returning her call." I was going to visit in a while, so I really didn't care if she came to the phone. Unless, that is, she had something to tell me. Something I didn't know.

A muffling sound—Mr. Powell had his hand over the mouthpiece and was talking in a loud voice. I couldn't make out the words, but the tune was familiar.

He took his hand away. "Wait a minute," he said.

I waited much less than a minute before one loud word blasted, "Amens."

"Returning your call, Mrs. Powell. I know this has to be a hard and long day for you."

"Cut the shit, Fuckless. Angie told me you knew about two other murders. I want to know what else you're not telling me."

Luckily, I was used to hostility. I didn't react to the verbal kind much any more. Stress brings it out, and I always seem to be around or cause stress. "I figure things out a little at a time. After I saw Shelly, I thought of a few possibilities and told the Chief."

"You saw my baby. You saw what that fuckin' nut did to her. I want his balls in a blender. You hear me?"

I didn't mention that the killer might not have balls.

"Shelly was a beautiful girl. She didn't deserve this." It's what I thought Mrs. Powell might want to hear.

She was quiet.

"Do you know if Shelly had a tattoo on the inside of her lip?" Might as well push ahead a bit.

"Tattoo? You think Shelly had a tattoo there?"

The Chief, for some reason, hadn't told Mrs. Powell about this development of the case. I didn't see any reason not to.

"I think so. And I think it may be important."

"When are you coming over here?"

"I can be there in fifteen minutes." I just had to slip into my freshly-washed clothes and grab something to eat.

"Make it an hour and a half. I have to shower and Sam will be meeting with the Chief again then."

"Okay."

"And why didn't you call back sooner? I expect you to keep me informed." She was really pushing. Her voice was getting louder and redder.

Did she always get her way? Probably yes. I could just get fed up and quit on her, but what fun would that be? And when I say I'll do something, I follow through on it. Usually no matter what.

"I had to be out of town for a while. It was important." I thought accepting Mr. Damianzo's "invitation" had been both important and fruitful.

"Nothing else is important until we find this guy, until we do this. You understand that?"

"Mrs. Powell ..."

Maybe she read something in my voice; maybe she could change direction quicker than a weathercock; maybe she had strategies and manipulations that worked well in the past. She interrupted me. I could hear her body position shift. Her tone altered and became almost a whisper, more intimate and private—just between us.

"Myx, I need you. When you held me this morning, it was the only time I felt I could get through this. You're different from everyone else. You understand things. You're good at finding out things that no one else can. I felt safe in your arms. You made me believe for the first time everything would work out all right. I need you now."

She trailed her last words off in a full-fledged quavering whisper.

She was good. Her voice was hardly clouded at all. But she really didn't expect this turnaround to work on me, did she? I'd been through too much to fall for this approach.

"You keep your chin up. I'll be there for you and we'll get through this," I heard myself giddily say. My voice was white.

"Bye," she said in that same vulnerable, breathy murmur.

"Bye," I said, smiling. I stood there with the phone to my ear a moment longer, looking blankly ahead. I wondered if she was smiling too.

I was hungry

I had left Bindy's truck off Chief Maldonato's list of license plates because I wanted him to myself. Before seeing Mrs. Powell, I had time to talk to Bindy ... and Miriam.

Chapter Thirteen

I threw the apple core over the top of a young poplar tree in the vacant lot across the street from Bindy's tenement on Fletcher. Nice throw. It just made it and continued on in a green arc. I could remember its flight as a line if I wanted to. I spit out the peach pit I had been sucking on. It hit the drain in the street and stopped on the grate. Stepping on it just wedged it tightly between the parallel metal slats. That was the last of the fruit I had taken from home: an apple, two peaches, and a plum.

Bindy lived on the third floor of the old building. It had been painted tan a long time ago, but a lot of that had flaked off, leaving grayish weathered wood showing, which looked like it was willing to give you splinters if you ran your hand up one of the railings. There were six parking spots in front, perpendicular to the street. Only two of them were filled. One was Bindy's 1989 Toyota Corolla. Faded red.

Good, he was home. This was the opposite of my usual reaction, because I preferred to wander through a house by myself. This time, I wanted to talk.

Each floor had a railed deck facing the street. Lots of the rails were missing or broken. Two sets of wooden stairs and landings brought me to the top floor. The stairs creaked, and on the second floor, I stopped and swayed from side to side until I got the staircase swinging pretty good. They needed repair, but in places like this, neglect was probably what they would get.

Downstairs, a dirty white piece of adhesive tape on the mailbox had said "Morton." A putty-colored button offered itself near the door handle. I pushed and a loud, harsh buzzer just inside nearly startled me. It tasted salty and yellow.

"I got it," said a bright female voice inside. Miriam. I hadn't really talked to her in school other than a "hi" and a nod since I stopped Shelly from bullying her. I had been here only once before, and that was to pick up some homemade brownies Miriam had promised me. She hadn't invited me in, so I just took the Saran-wrapped paper plateful at the door. Miriam had sprinkled their tops with powdered sugar.

Miriam's beauty didn't come from her features. Her face was a bit too thin, her brown eyes too close together, and her short hair a little too frizzy. But her smile and the tilt of her head told me who she really was. The music her voice always played reinforced my conclusions.

"Myx?" she said through the screen after opening the inner door. My name was a surprise and a question combined. Inside smelled like soup.

"Hi, Miriam. Is your dad home?" I knew he was, not only because of the car, but also because her mother had died several years before. There probably were only the two of them there, and she had called to someone else just a moment before.

"You want me to get him for you?" She wasn't inviting me in.

I shrugged. She called over her shoulder, "Dad, Myx Amens is here."

There was a moment or two, and then Bindy replied, "Tell him to wait a minute." She didn't say anything, but raised her eyebrows, opened her eyes wider, and barely wiggled her head. A reaction you give when you really don't know what to do.

She recovered with, "How did you like the brownies?"

"The best I ever had. Did you toast the walnuts?"

She laughed. "Yeah, that's my trick. My mother taught me." Then she pushed the screen door toward me. I stepped back. "Come on in, Myx. Sit at the table. Don't mind the place."

I've been in more homes than a real estate agent—invited sometimes, sometimes not. When you're invited, you can feel the pride or the vulnerability of your host.

I felt Miriam's vulnerability. The apartment was small, just a few rooms, and the furniture was old and worn. She kept it very clean and neat.

Instead of going to the table to the right of the door, I headed to a picture on the wall. It showed Miriam at about twelve years old between her parents.

I looked in my head at an old newspaper article I had seen. It was about the Miracle High School band.

"Your mother got the School Committee to pay for the band uniforms. That was something. Everybody was talking about that," I said while tapping her mother in the picture.

She smiled at me and then at the photo. "If it wasn't for Mum and the fundraisers and everything, we probably wouldn't have had a band that year."

There, a little bit of pride.

"Come, sit down."

I sat at the wooden kitchenette. The chair creaked and rocked a bit. Should glue the joints.

"You want something to eat?"

I looked at the little covered pan on the stove. Wisps of steam were escaping from the lid.

"Oh, no. I'm full 'cause I just ate." My voice wasn't all that gleaming.

Bindy opened a door, came out and closed it behind him. I guessed his bedroom. There was another room beside it with the door open. Miram's.

"What are you doing here, Myx." It wasn't all that friendly a tone.

"Bad business, Bindy." He didn't smile at my alliteration—not a good sign. "Shelly Powell and two other people were shot last night."

Miriam made a sharp sound with the quick intake of her breath. "Are they okay? Are they all right?" She squeezed my left arm as she bent to look into my eyes.

"No, Miriam. They're all gone." Instead of looking at her, I was watching Bindy. He wasn't looking at me. He didn't move. I picked up a set of keys that had been left on the table and jiggled them, as if idly playing and listening to them tinkle.

"Shelly? How could this happen? We're going to graduate next month." Miriam's eyes filled with tears; she put a hand to her mouth and pinched at her lips.

Maybe there's some kind of logic that you shouldn't die when you're close to a big milestone in life. Life had merely planned a bigger milestone for Shelly: her murder.

Bindy didn't talk much usually. He looked like he wasn't going to change his habits now. So I decided to start, and not with a question.

"Mrs. Powell wants me to ask around a little bit. You know how I do. Just to see what's what."

"Patty." It wasn't a statement or a question. Just an absentminded uttering while he looked ahead.

I gave an eloquent, "Yeah."

Miriam spoke first. "Who else, Myx? Not anybody in MHS?" She sat down in the chair opposite me, steadying herself with both hands on the table. There was a vinyl placemat in front of her; an array of pastel-colored fish covered it. Her bowl, napkin, and spoon waited there for soup.

"No. Dragon from Skin Sins and Hector Ramone. Did you know he was her boyfriend? Hector, that is."

She shook her head "no" and traced one of the fish with her right index finger. A tear from each eye fell when she squeezed her eyes shut. They reflected light from the placemat after making a pat-pat sound when they landed.

Bindy hadn't moved. He wasn't going to volunteer anything. That's okay with me. I was used to getting what I wanted by taking as well as receiving.

Maybe there wasn't even anything to take, but pressing always shows something.

"You cover a lot of area at night, Bindy. See anything?" He still wasn't looking at me. I never liked nor disliked that behavior; it was just what it was—another form of communication. He was communicating that he didn't want to answer.

So he asked instead, "Where did all this happen? And when?"

"I haven't gotten the details from the Chief yet." I didn't mention that I had been shown the exit at the police station when I wanted more information. And the Chief hadn't been in the mood for a briefing at Skin Sins. I was sure I could find out more now that I had led him to Myron and Ramone.

"Hard for me to pin anything down then. I don't look much unless something stands out." He made a backhanded tossing motion and frowned. "We gotta eat. Leave your number and I'll let you know if anything comes to me." Then he reached down and pushed at Miriam's shoulder, "Get him some paper."

Miriam took a white square of paper from a notepad magnetically stuck to the refrigerator and pulled a pen from its attached holder. Her hand was trembling a bit when I took them from her, and I gave it a little rub and shake before I let go and wrote my home number. I didn't expect Bunny to be angry because I didn't expect any calls from Bindy. I gave the paper and pen back to Miriam.

As I got up and put my hand on the doorknob to let myself out, I said, "I'm sure this will all be done in a day or two." I won't say how my voice looked to me.

Miriam was looking at the paper. When she looked up, her eyes glistened with remnant tears as she forced a small smile. I had drawn two fish from her placemat beside my number.

Chapter Fourteen

I was more than a half hour early when I got to the Powells' large split-level home on Lincoln Street. It was a ten-minute walk from Bindy's (at least for me because I took the direct route through parks, fields, and backyards).

It was a big house, bigger than an engineer should afford. That was because Mrs. Powell had money. Her family had money before she inherited it all. Maybe that's where she got her attitude and her control over Mr. Powell. Whatever the reason, she was used to getting her own way on her own terms.

There was one car in the driveway—her Lexus. Good. Mr. Powell was away. It would be easier to look around, so I circled once. The screened windows were open. I could hear the shower. Even easier. I would just use the back door to let myself in.

I kept a box of unmarked keys labeled "Mistakes" in Benny's shop. There, and not my room or my storage because they wouldn't look out of place and were easily available. They were my collection of tickets to the homes of Miracle. Benny knew not to mess with them, and he wouldn't have been able to tell where they went anyway. By the shape of each key's teeth, I could tell which lock and which house it fit. I had looked at Shelly's keys before my diary-reading visit. I used the keys I made then to get to it. I tried the back door. Locked. I pulled the same house key I had used then from my pocket and let myself in, locking the door again behind me. I stood still and listened. Just the shower.

There were two Jello puddings in the refrigerator: chocolate and banana. I ate them both and threw the empties in the trash under the sink. I didn't wash the spoon because that might cause a fluctuation in the shower temperature. I had made that mistake once. I licked the spoon clean, wiped it with the dishtowel hanging on the stove's oven handle, and put it back in the drawer. It had only taken a minute to eat them. The shower was still going.

On the way to Mrs. Powell's bedroom (I had learned last time that Mr. Powell slept in the guest room), I passed a card table set up in the den. It had a 2000-piece jigsaw puzzle barely started on it. The cover of the box, on display for reference, gave the title as Sky & Surf. It showed a strip of ocean receding to the horizon and the pale, blue sky above it. They were almost the same color. There was one tiny silhouetted seagull on the right. So far, they had completed about half the border and the seagull. The pieces were all spread out and speaking to me. Just their shapes and subtle color differences told me exactly where they belonged. I took a minute to put together about a hundred pieces, but could see where they all went.

I wondered if Shelly had done any.

Mrs. Powell's room had lots of soft yellows in the curtains, spread, and embroidered dresser scarves. The cheery atmosphere it created must be quite a contrast to her mood.

Her clothes from the morning lay on the floor: jeans, blouse, and panties. I picked the panties up. Victoria's Secret stretch mesh retro brief (I'd seen the catalog). They perfumed the air. Low rises, an oversaturated red lipstick color. One dark pubic hair had worked its way into the mesh and been trapped there. I put them back on the pile, exactly as they had been.

A triptych mirror stood at odd angles outside a large walk-in closet. Tasteful and expensive clothes and shoes were in neat rows.

A car was coming. I stopped and listened as it drove on by.

Then I entered the closet and felt the bottoms of several clothes travel bags. The third one had a hard rectangle in it—her diary. She hadn't moved it. I quietly unzipped the bag, took it out, and looked at it. I looked at only what was new since the last time I had seen it. I had a note from Bunny dismissing me from school for the afternoon that day. (At least it looked like a note from Bunny.) Afternoons usually mean deserted houses, welcoming and homey to a guest like me.

Mrs. Powell had written a long passage about the day's events. The script was elegantly graceful and sounded in long, greenish notes. It was full of genuine emotion, grief and anger mostly. She didn't have any insight into why or who, but vowed cruel and graphic revenge on Shelly's killer. These should be private thoughts, unseen by a stranger. I almost felt bad about trespassing on the intimate domain.

There were a few lines about me near the end. They hinted that I might be of help with my disgusting and rat-like methods. She also disdained how easily she could manipulate me.

I resolved to play harder to get and returned to some rat-like investigating when the shower stopped. I replaced the diary and headed for the living room.

After unlocking the front door, I rested on the beige overstuffed sofa in the combination living and dining room. It faced the three steps leading to the upper level which contained the bedrooms and bath. The two steps down to my left led to the kitchen, a less formal recreation room, the laundry, and the garage.

I debated whether to look uneasy or completely comfortable as the bathroom door opened, filling the hallway with artificial light.

"Mrs. Powell," I called, my voice shaky. I had decided to go with uneasy. Playing along with people's prejudices and preconceptions had always proved useful. Letting her think she was in control worked for me. "It's me, Myx Amens."

"Amens? You're early. How did you get in?"

"Front door was open."

Mrs. Powell left little wet footprints on each of the three highly polished wooden steps. They gleamed. She glided.

If she had been surprised by my presence, the effect had already passed. She had not dried herself at all after leaving the shower, but carelessly wrapped that thick burgundy-colored bath towel around her dripping body. One small corner tucked under her left armpit was all that held it on. The towel just covered her thighs' vertex.

She kept her eyes on me as she walked to the end of the couch. I stood up. No toe ring.

"Sam must have forgotten to lock it," she said as she gestured to the door with her head.

I wanted to tell her how gorgeous she looked without any makeup. Instead, I offered, "Yeah, I rang the bell, tried the door, and called. But I could hear the shower, so I just came in and sat down and waited. I hope that's all right?" I congratulated myself for sounding just off-balance enough.

She smiled and softened her blue eyes. "You could have stuck your head in and told me you were here, Myx."

"Oh, I didn't think it would be right to wander around. Besides, a bathroom's real private, Ma'am." I smiled, not only for appearances, but because I thought that was a nice, old-fashioned touch.

She reached up with her free right hand and lightly stroked my cheek once with a downward slide of her fingers. "Aren't you the sweet boy?" The musical tone was not dark. The scent was Safeguard soap, beige. I sniffed again—her period was over.

But, there was another odor: hate. I had been confused about it in the past because it had an oily sweetness mixed with a bitter tang. It took a long time to "calibrate" that combination, but finally I concluded that hate has some pleasure in it—some righteousness probably. That's the sweet part. The bitterness is the tortured desire for revenge.

Revenge was the strongest impression I got from Mrs. Powell, which is saying a lot with this gorgeous female, half-naked and dripping in front of me. All my senses told me revenge would fuel her, keep her together and directed until ... Until what? What would happen to her once she lost her lust for ruthless retribution?

I decided to concentrate on my own lust for now.

Her blonde hair was darkly wet. Water from it trickled in little drops down her face, their notes rising in pitch as they fell faster on their journey.

Mrs. Powell slowly brought the hand towel she had been carrying up to her head and with both hands brushed it back and forth hard over her hair. The bath towel surrounding her shook and strained, but held.

"Come," she glanced upstairs, "we'll talk."

Without waiting for my reply or reaction, she walked to the steps and climbed them. I admired her muscular calves as they flexed. I followed a bit behind and curbed my urge to bend a little to peek under the towel as she reached the top step.

I was surprised by my discipline and decorum. There would be time later to second-guess myself about the missed opportunity.

I followed her to the bedroom I had just left. With her back to me, she crouched low and scooped her discarded clothes in an armful. She turned and pushed them into my chest, higher than need be, so that her panties were just inches from my chin.

"Be a darling and throw these down in the laundry. It's just past the kitchen, all the way down." Her right index finger tapped at and then brushed across the bottom of my chin.

She was good at this. Very good. She was giving me a pheromone flood while training me to obey. She didn't really think this was going to work on me, did she?

On the way downstairs, I caught myself just before starting to hum a happy tune. I dropped her clothes in a blue nylon mesh hamper next to the washer. It was about half filled with some more of her things. A green version of the hamper held Mr. Powell's laundry. I knew, from my previous visit, that Shelly kept hers in her closet.

On the way back, I looked toward the refrigerator. It contained half of a coconut custard pie that was beckoning to me. I ignored it.

Mrs. Powell, still barely in her towel, was brushing her hair at her dressing table. It lightened as it dried and easily fell into place because of a perfect cut. She had not put on any makeup, but there was a trace of Clive Christian's 1872 *Eau de Parfum*—citrus and cedar filled the air. Maybe it wasn't the best thing I ever smelled; maybe it was.

"All done," I announced. "In the blue hamper."

"Thanks. Sit there." She pointed to a chair in the corner near the door. It rested kitty-corner at the meeting of the hall and closet walls.

I sat. The sandy-colored chair was soft and comfortable.

"Tell me what you've learned," she said as she walked into the closet and dropped her towel. I could tell because, although my angle gave me no direct view into the walk-in, the triptych mirror was positioned perfectly to show me everything.

And everything is what I saw. Her all natural breasts (I still would guess 36C, though now I'd estimate a full C) were topped by poker chip–sized aureoles, and crowned by gumdrop-shaped nipples. They were hard.

Mrs. Powell's trim and athletic build presented toned and defined muscles, which undulated with each graceful motion. Her dark tan made the unexposed areas seem even whiter, and her pubic hair was trimmed only enough to be eclipsed by bikini bottoms. Her ass *was* perfect.

I started talking, cleared my throat, and told all I knew and what I had seen so far (except for my visit to Bindy). She casually pulled on a pair of panties (buff-colored twins to the pair I had already seen), wiggling her hips and then smoothing the sheer fabric over her cheeks with both palms. Her bra was a warm nude-colored lace plunge, again Victoria's Secret. Light blue Old Navy drawstring shorts and a white Calvin Klein cotton tank completed her outfit.

She turned slowly as she finished and looked into the mirror, directly at me. She knew I knew she knew I had been watching. I didn't lower my eyes as I told the last of my scanty bits of information. Neither did she. She didn't even bother to hide the shade of a smile.

I should have been angry at her smugness—that she felt she could use, control me, order me around, expect me to put myself in danger—but I wasn't. I was willing to go along on *this* ride all the way to the last station, wherever that was and whatever *that* meant.

Mrs. Powell stepped over the wet towel, came out of the closet and walked toward me. The scent got stronger. She stopped about a foot in front of me and lifted the bottom of the tank top past the waistband of her shorts. She had an "inny" navel and tiny sunbleached hairs that trailed downward from it in a graceful line to her waistband (and I imagined, beyond).

"Can you tie a pretty bow?"

I didn't think "no" was the right answer here, so I leaned forward, grabbed the drawstrings on the shorts, and started to tie the most perfect bow of my life.

She bent forward and whispered, "I like it tight."

I tied it tight. My pants got tighter, too.

Then she dropped to her knees in front of me, the thick, soft, pale-gold carpet absorbing her. Her hands, pressing on my lower thighs, steadied the descent. Her eyes were almost even with mine as she rested there a moment and stared softly.

"Do you know what I want, Myx?" This whisper was a little louder than before.

I knew what I wanted her to want, and wanted to tell her my wants, but heard myself say, "Justice. Revenge. Your own way."

"You're a smart boy. Maldonato told me so, and that you had methods of cutting through shit and getting results." She began to talk with clenched teeth, her full lips making slightly exaggerated movements. "I need you to find the monster who could do this to my daughter, do this to my baby. Then, you tell me before you tell anyone else. Do you understand? Will you do this for me?"

There are limits. Just because a beautiful woman sends out all the right promising signals, it doesn't mean you in turn agree to become an accessory to murder, no matter how guilty the target. I explained my logic and feelings to Mrs. Powell by feebly saying, "Yes." My voice was white.

"I knew I could count on you." She reached forward and ran a finger across my lips, then relaxed and sat back on her heels.

"Help me up and you can see Shelly's room." I did, and she led me by the hand across the hall. The curtains and spread were different from the last time I had been there, but the stuffed animals and wall hangings were the same. It was darker in here; the windows faced east. I was used to looking around houses during the middle of the night with no lights, so this was fine.

"The police have already been through here and just took her computer, so I don't know what good this will do. Seemed like they just did it all by routine."

Shelly's computer. I should know something about Shelly's computer. Hadn't I checked through it the last time I was here? Didn't I always do that? I couldn't remember, and my stomach suddenly churned and hurt. I remembered looking at the computer in this room, then there was a blur of noises and colors. After that, I could see clearly again as I left.

Why was my mind failing me?

"Myx?" Mrs. Powell was shaking me by the arm. Her hand left warm, snug green rings. I seemed to be sensing things okay now. It was some memories that were jumbled and unavailable.

"Yeah. Thinking for a minute." I smiled; I didn't know if it was to give me or her confidence. I did know I wanted to go through Shelly's room alone. I also needed to find out what Mrs. Powell knew.

I pointed to Shelly's bed with my chin. "Let's sit for a minute and talk before I start looking in here." The bed sagged under her. I pulled Shelly's desk chair out and straddled it backwards, my hands holding the top rail. It was cool and smooth.

Mrs. Powell crossed her shiny, hairless legs and let one set of painted toes lightly brush back and forth on my left leg as she rocked her foot unconsciously.

I thought the best way was to get right to it. "I mentioned a tattoo on the phone. Did you know Shelly had a tattoo? Inside her lower lip?"

Her eyes moved up and to my right. She was remembering. Looking. She shook her head. "I never knew about it if she had one. Last November she said she bit her lip, and it was a little swollen. Could that be it?"

"She could have used that excuse to cover up. We think she got it at Skin Sins, since Dragon was shot too. Was there any design or pattern that she was into—something she would want to make permanent on her body?"

"Other than piercing her ears, Shelly wasn't interested in any of this stuff. This body decorating. I know you're probably right about this, but it's a real surprise to me that she would do it. I have no idea what would make her get a tattoo. And why would she keep it a secret if she did?" She was talking as much to herself as to me now.

"Where was she killed, shot?"

"Some kids found her. Looked in her car at the High School parking lot a little after eleven last night. She was lying in the back seat, face down, blood all over. Alone, all alone. Shelly." Tears welled and rolled; her voice had risen in pitch.

I pulled a tissue from the box on Shelly's desk and handed it. She took it and grasped my fingers for comfort, for touch of a human being, for thanks. The seductress was submerged by the mother. Mrs. Powell dabbed her eyes, blew her nose softly, and continued.

"The boys thought she was a Friday-night drunk sleeping it off. They said they rocked the car a little. That turned her head enough to show them the blood. That's when they called the police."

"When did she leave here?"

"Oh, she was always in and out. I didn't keep track of her like I did when she was younger. But I don't think I saw her after eight o'clock." She looked away and added, "Just this time yesterday, she was still alive. Still alive …"

This was harder than I had thought.

I knew that Kat Andrews and Cyndi Bellacqua were Shelly's best friends. They had always been together in school. I asked Mrs. Powell if this was still true and if there were any other new people that Shelly had been hanging with.

"No. Just Kat and Cyndi. I didn't know about this Ramone. How can a mother not know who her daughter is dating? What kind of person, what kind of mother can I be not to protect my girl?"

I reached out and gave her knee a light rub and then a squeeze. It felt warm and a little slippery from lotion.

"Mrs. Powell, I learned in the last few years that people are really good at keeping secrets they're afraid or ashamed of. They find ways to protect themselves. Sometimes that's good. Sometimes it's a trap that won't let them out. They don't give them up, especially to the ones closest to them because they don't want to let them down—especially them. So don't beat yourself up over that part. Shelly was smart, and she was strong enough to have her way. The rest of us didn't stand a chance." My voice wasn't as dark as I had expected.

Mrs. Powell laughed and cried at the same time while saying "yes" silently with her head.

I heard a key in the back door downstairs. It opened.

"Patty?" It was Mr. Powell. Good. Maybe I could look around here alone for a while.

"Be right down," she said loudly, her voice rattling with tears and congestion.

I got up and tucked the chair back under the desk. When I turned again, Mrs. Powell had stood up, her face an inch above mine—not as much difference now that she was barefoot. She put her arms around me and hugged tightly. I hugged back and she melted there for a moment. She pulled away just enough to look into my eyes, and then leaned close to lightly kiss me on the lips.

"Thank you, Myx. Remember what we said before." She pulled away, walked to the door, and gestured in a wide sweep with her hand. "Now find something useful." She disappeared down the hall for a second, and then stuck her head back in and said, "You little shit!" She laughed and left.

As soon as she was gone, I stuck my head out to see her bounce down the stairs. I headed for Mr. Powell's room. I could always come back to Shelly's. Before I entered the other bedroom, the one opposite the bath, I stood still and listened. They were in the kitchen, and the tone of their voices was uneasy, red and brown with spicy edges. Mr. Powell didn't want me here.

I'd been more unwelcome in better places than this—and worse. I turned and went into his room.

She didn't keep it up for him. It wasn't exactly dirty, but it didn't match the rest of the house in tidiness or cleanliness. It had that real lived-in smell. There was a double bed (pulled up, but unmade), a chest-on-chest dresser opposite the bed and a double dresser with a mirror above just beside it. A matching nightstand was next to the bed. It was all oak, a blue on blonde Euro style. I kind of liked the look; it felt fast and free.

I listened—they hadn't moved. Nightstand first. I felt behind it, running my hand all the way down to the floor. Nothing taped or slid

MIRACLE MYX ■ 133

there. I lifted the drawer a little so it didn't make a sound as I opened it: prescription pills—sleep, depression, and high blood pressure medication—the usual. One lonely condom. A pen and pad. It had some notes about his dreams and some doodles. They sounded harsh. Other pages had phone notes. A black phone was on top of the nightstand. I picked it up and smelled the receiver—sour. An envelope full of photos (processed at CVS) was tucked in a corner of the drawer. They showed a vacation on Cape Cod; Shelly was a few years younger. Most were of Mrs. Powell and Shelly together, some on the beach. Mrs. Powell looked great in her Ralph Lauren pink and green bikini. Shelly looked okay in her one piece. Mr. Powell was in two pictures alone. He wasn't smiling.

I pulled the drawer completely out and looked inside the hole it left. Nothing. Sliding my hand under the drawer and along its back edge didn't produce anything either. This sure was easier when no one was sleeping a foot away from you.

I was constantly listening for any movement in my direction by the Powells. This was a habit I didn't have to think about any more. I'd never been caught yet. With Dr. Zylodic's help, I had come to rely on my synesthesia to keep me safe and invisible. Which was part of the reason I found these memory farts so bothersome. What would happen if I suddenly couldn't trust myself in dangerous situations? Better to just not think about it now.

Under his bed hid shoes, a crumpled pair of boxers whose location he had probably once wondered about, a box of winter clothes, and lots of dust bunnies. This room, unlike the rest of the house, had no carpeting, but a hardwood surface.

Piles of Zaytheon notebooks and memos were on the floor. There were minutes of Selectmen's meetings. He must have used this as his home office too. There wasn't another room for it in the house. Maybe this had been the home office before he made it into his bedroom.

All the piles were even except one. There were a few irregular breaks in the symmetry in that one stack in the corner. The irregularities turned out to be several recent copies of *Uncut Hunks*. These showed guys with very little body fat and very prominent foreskins. They made me think differently about the final destination of that condom.

I restacked the pile perfectly (by perfectly, I mean as it had been before) and moved on to the dressers. The fourth drawer down in the double dresser held a gun. It was under the pair of white athletic socks. Loaded, safety on. I picked it up with a sock and smelled. It hadn't been fired recently, and it was a .28 caliber, just a little thing. Probably made him feel safer at night though.

The rest of my efforts, including the closet overstuffed with clothes, didn't reveal anything out of the ordinary. I came away feeling that Mr. Powell was very alone here in the house.

My search had only taken a few minutes; I had gotten faster this past year.

I gave the bathroom a quick scan before heading back to Shelly's room. It still had a sheen from steam on its tiles. And a scarcely-tainted (yeah, I looked) tampon wrapped in toilet paper rested on top of the wastebasket trash.

The talk downstairs had calmed down, just one-word interchanges now.

I went for Shelly's closet and hamper first. The small gray metal box was still there (the police missed it), under about a foot and a half of dirty clothes. They had been soiled when her body still had soiling power, a quality to be envied once you're dead.

The box was light; even before I opened it with the key from my pocket, I knew the diary wasn't there. The box held some handwritten notes from Kat and Cyndi. They talked about school and how hot they thought Hector was.

So they knew.

There was an open pack of Wrigley's Spearmint gum. It made the whole box smell sweet and tasty.

A key, gleaming and new and sharp-toothed, lay at the bottom. It had a few file marks on it. This was Benny's handiwork. I should know what this key is. That feeling came again. I didn't want to get used to it, so I let it hurt.

I pocketed the key.

There were some photos. Shelly was pulling up her shirt and showing her boobs in one, and on all fours, sideways in the other. She was completely naked in the sideways one. She was smiling in both of them. They were printed on regular computer paper and cut out with scissors. Digital. Most cameras had a timer or a remote control, so she might have taken these by herself. Or someone she trusted had been there.

I hadn't seen a digital camera in the house. Maybe the police took it. What they didn't take was the Kingston 512 megabyte CompactFlash card here in the box. I put it safely away with the key in my pocket.

I wondered what was on it and why it was hidden.

"What have you got there?" Mr. Powell was looking for a reason to be angry with me. The naked pictures should easily provide that.

I had heard him coming, of course, but made no effort to hide my actions. I had permission, after all, from Mrs. Powell.

I put the box on the bed. "Found that in the closet." I had put the photos face down under the notes. It took him a moment to fish them from the box.

He exploded.

"My daughter's dead and you're here staring at these?"

Had I been staring?

His shouting brought Mrs. Powell running to the room. As soon as she came in, he threw the pictures at her with a backhand toss. They fluttered to the floor. She squatted, turned them right side up, and left them there as she looked.

Never tilting her head upward, she said, "Amens, where did you get these?"

Was it the subject matter or Mr. Powell's presence that added the layer of formality? I had no reason not to tell her. "Hamper."

"They were in here." Mr. Powell shook the box. The gum and notes made soft slithering papery sounds.

She stood and scrutinized the contents for a second. "Is this all that was in here?"

"Yes." I bleached my voice as much as I could, which was saying it was pretty pale.

"You wouldn't lie to me now, would you? The Chief didn't trust you. Why should I?" She stared unblinking into my eyes.

I simply raised my eyebrows in a momentary conspiratorial arc. I wanted her to believe what she already wanted to believe: that she had control of me and I'd be afraid of losing her favor. I had to admit though, that *would* kind of suck.

"Just don't let him be here when I get back," he said, handing the box to Mrs. Powell. He stopped at the door on his way out and waved his finger at me a few, wordless times in anger. I could hear him leave the house.

I mouthed wordlessly, "Or else what?" as he left. Mrs. Powell laughed silently, letting her shoulders shake.

"Maybe you *should* go. This is a very hard thing to go through." She put the photos back in the box and closed it. "I don't know why Shelly took these and saved them here. Who knows what goes on in a young girl's mind? Looks almost like she's playing. It's just that she's playing a dangerous game, one that can get out of control. She was a beautiful girl."

The word "was" hit her after she said it, and the tears started again.

This probably was a good time to leave. I took the box from her and put it on Shelly's desk.

Mrs. Powell grabbed my hand and led me downstairs to the front door. "Hold me for a minute," she sighed.

I did. She was hot from holding in her breath and sorrow.

"It's okay to let it out," I said while rubbing her back slowly with my left hand.

She put her eyes on my shoulder and said, "I can't believe it, I can't believe it."

Finally, she pulled away and asked, "Do you think we'll find out who did this?"

"Some things aren't meant to be found out," I said while going through the front door she had opened. At the bottom of the steps, I turned and added, "This isn't one of them."

Chapter Fifteen

The sun was low, buzzing with small variations there on the horizon. A southern wind carried warmer air. It was a pleasant walk to Beverley Street. Every walk for me was pleasant.

What wasn't pleasant was this day's events so far. Yesterday at this time, I was only thinking about getting that key back from Mrs. Walker.

Now I had two problems: the murders (which was at least interesting), and "my" Louis Vuitton suitcase.

I felt like I ultimately got a gold star on my paper today from Mr. Damianzo, Mama, and friends. But that was polluted by the 4.8 million demerits I had cached. Not that it was 4.8 any more, either. I had spent a little and given away some—anonymously, I hoped. Almost a quarter of a million dollars was gone. Handing back a less-than-full load would bring unwholesome results. These guys didn't give up.

They were like me.

Sarge Halpern's house was a huge Victorian Queen Anne. It had beautiful porch posts and ornamental spindles. Nothing was in disrepair, nothing wasn't perfectly painted. Every bit of it sang in one harmonious chorus and looked ready for a magazine cover.

I saw all this from four houses away and across the street. This was as far as I was going; his truck was still in the driveway.

Good. This gave me time to have something to eat and check my email. Darkness was better for my kind of visiting anyway.

Miracle Meals, my favorite diner, welcomed me from Main Street. It looked like a classic but banged-up railroad car. They closed at 5 P.M. every day but Saturday, when they stayed open until eight (they were closed Sundays). They gave you a huge portion of meatloaf, their Saturday special. It came with corn and piping-hot mashed potatoes and brown gravy. The meatloaf had onions and little red peppers flecked through it.

I pulled open the sliding door. "Here comes trouble," sang Birch Paget, waitress and wife of Petey, the owner and cook.

The four customers at the counter turned and played along by muttering a variety of good-natured insults. They were all regulars, just like me. I took my usual stool (it had a red plastic cover with a piece of silver duct tape sealing a rip) at the counter, the third one from the left.

"What's good tonight, Birch?"

"Meatloaf, extra gravy," she called towards a small window to the back kitchen. Petey was back there as always, doing some magic—his food was the best.

It was always kind of steamy in here, and full of coffee and cooking smells. The sight glass on the old coffee urn showed there was plenty still. Birch was already pouring me a mouthful or two into an overly thick blue-rimmed white mug. Why did it taste better in that?

"I like it light, Birch," I said.

"What, I don't know you?" She pulled a thin paper napkin from the stainless dispenser and put it down in front of me, then settled the cup on it. She gave my face a squeeze and a shake.

Birch and Petey worked about a thousand hours a week. Their son was studying at UMASS Memorial Medical Center to be a renal specialist. About two months ago they had received a package and letter from an elderly woman stating that they must be proud of their son and she hoped the contents of the package would help with his expenses. The letter had 250 one-hundred-dollar bills in it.

I had used Eleanor Roosevelt's handwriting.

They had kept quiet about it. Good.

Steam from the plate was swirling as she put it in front of me. Birch leaned close and said, "You hear about what happened? You know anything?"

"Police have been busy. What's going on?" I always learned more by asking than talking.

Birch told one series of events with lots of misinformation. The other regulars added particulars, but contradicted each other, and all together made a jumble of half-truths out of the murders. I didn't learn anything valuable, but shook my head in awe as though it was all trustworthy.

I finished the meal by mopping the plate with the last piece of bread from the "setup" she had given me, the two slices of Italian bread with a pat of butter on a little plate.

It cost $4.50. I tucked a five and a one under my plate, wiped my mouth, and said, "See you tomorrow."

From the back, Petey hollered, "Closed tomorrow, wise guy!"

We all laughed.

Martin Aubrey lived in apartment 214 at the Blended Willows complex. He had a big territory, most of New England, and was gone a lot. Medical supplies. He gave me five dollars a week to take in his mail, water his plants and feed his fish.

He had a powerful computer with a huge hard drive hooked up to Comcast broadband. This was perfect for me. I considered it my computer since I used it much more than he did. Email, Word,

Excel, and PowerPoint—that was all he did on it. I don't even think he surfed. At least his history didn't show anything.

I did more intricate things.

Of all the places I'd been through, his was the least interesting. At first, I'd wondered if he ever kissed a girl. Now I wondered if he even *knew* a girl.

He was due back for Founder's Day, and then off for a swing through Maine for ten days starting Thursday.

His "secret" password was *Albert*. It was the name of one of his fish, one of the Red Top Zebras. Pseudotropheus Sandraracinos, he had told me while watching it closely at the tank.

That got me into his computer. I checked email first. I had two types of account: spamalicious and spam-free. I used the spam-free accounts to receive mail. I used the others to be visible on the web; these addresses got harvested and spammed, leaving me with loads of useless hype filling the inbox. I deleted them all without looking.

There wasn't anything urgent in my other email except Dr. Zylodic's request that I participate in yet another study of his. These studies, which he then wrote up for medical journals, consisted of my memorizing long random numbers or nonsense syllables to test the limits of my synesthesia-powered recall. Talk about boring.

I was anonymous in his writings. He identified me as MA, which I thought was funny. Could be my initials, could be Massachusetts. Funny. I hated doing the tests now because they had become so long. Still, I figured I owed him because of all he did to help me when my synesthesia had overwhelmed me early on. And later, he gave me the encouragement and tools to cope with my sleeplessness.

I didn't write him back even though I should have.

Out of habit, I was quiet for a moment and listened. Just

apartment noises from other tenants. I had been through lots of these apartments since I had made myself a master key. They were generally nice people; I knew lots about them.

Amber lights on the front of the computer blinked when I inserted the CompactFlash into the built-in card reader. This was the one I found in Shelly's room.

A dialog box asking if I wanted to open the folder appeared on the screen. I hit okay, and a text file plus a series of small photos, thumbnails, showed up. There were twenty-three of them. Two were the ones that had been printed and kept in the box. Eighteen of the rest were far more revealing. They showed Shelly naked on her bed in many different poses.

The remaining three photos showed tattoos.

One was a close-up of the inside of a lower lip; one was of the shaft of a skinny penis. The last was taken about fifteen feet away from two naked asses. The owners of the asses were bent over, their heads not visible. They wore thongs, and their jeans were pulled down to their thighs. I assumed the little dark shapes on their left cheeks—one each—were tattoos.

If the camera used had a macro setting for taking photos at close range, they ignored it. The close-ups were blurred and overexposed.

I double clicked the lip thumbnail and it opened up in Photoshop. I was pretty good with this program, but couldn't do much with any of the tattoo pictures: the close-ups were too blurred and bright; the asses were just too far away. I wasn't able to tell what the tattoos really looked like.

One thing the program did tell me was when they were taken. Lots of digital cameras create a file (Exchangeable Image File, or EXIF for short) that travels with the image. This identifies the camera and its settings along with the time and date the photo was snapped. It was an Olympus camera, and these were all taken on 11/11/04. The dual asses was taken four hours before the others.

Since only a zit was on Shelly's ass, I ruled her out. So, who could the mystery butts belong to? Safe to guess Kat and Cyndi, her best friends. Could they be dead too, or next on the list?

I'd look at the text file later. This seemed like a good time to visit the girls.

Chapter Sixteen

Hard or easy? I decided hard first. I always did the hardest thing first.

Kathleen "Kat" Andrews was a junior at Miracle High and bitch-in-training heir apparent to Shelly's territory. She'd be hard. Cyndi Bellacqua was a senior and just seemed happy to hang with popular friends. She'd be easy.

I had looked at all Miracle High's student records at the beginning of the year. I visualized Kat's entry and saw she lived about four miles away. I could walk or run there, but didn't want to take the time.

Not having a driver's license sucked. I pulled my cell out and called Red Top Cabs, Miracle's only taxi service.

"Red Top!" an overenthusiastic singsong voice chanted.

"Blended Willows. I need to get to Farmer Street now."

"Awwww, Myx. I can't drop everything every time you need a ride."

"What are you dropping, Cabbage?" I had guessed that Leo picked up the nickname "Cabbage" from some playful erosion of the word "cabbie," but never asked.

"That's not what I'm talking about. I don't want you to think I'm your personal transportation all the time."

"I don't think that *all* the time," I said.

"What if I say no?"

"That's your right. I just move you from one list to another list," I said.

"You got lists?"

Silence.

"Blended Willows? Five minutes," he said.

"Bring donuts."

He sighed and hung up.

I ate a glazed and a cinnamon by the time we got to Farmer Street.

Cabbage had some variations of the same misinformation I had heard at the diner. Nothing new was coming from outside the investigation. Leo was usually a good source of street talk.

But his cab really stank. "You should clean this up once in a while," I said as I got out at the intersection of Farmer and Castle. I wanted to walk the rest of the way and look at Kat's house before I talked with her. I always liked to see where the doors, windows, and fences offered themselves to me.

As Cabbage drove away, he called back through his open window, "Nobody else complains … hardly."

It was dark enough now that lights were on in most of the homes. In the dusk, they tasted yellow through their curtains.

I went into the backyard of a home two houses up from Kat's. I kept close to the foundation and took a glance. There was a deck with a covered grill on it. Two downstairs windows and three upstairs. It was a colonial. The back door opened onto the deck. A side door on the ground floor led into the garage. Lots of ways in and out.

The front of the house had a porch with a low overhanging roof. A big man, dyed black hair, striped Lisle gold Polo shirt, answered the door when I rang the bell. He had the *Boston Globe* newspaper and glasses in his left hand.

"Mr. Andrews? I'm Myx Amens. Could I talk to Kathleen?"

"She's not having any visitors today." He sounded sure of himself. "Or going out. She's in her room resting and staying there." Even more positive.

"Oh, this will only take a few seconds. I ..."

He cut me off. "Don't you know what's going on? You look like you're smart enough to see when to back off. Call her next week." He shut the door before I could prove I wasn't that smart.

Why did I even try Plan A any more?

Plan B was to stand on the porch railing, pull myself up to the roof and find Kat's room. I did this within seconds of the door's closing.

Her screened window was open. No light on, but I could see her lying face down on her bed. I breathed in a faint makeup scent.

"Kat." She stirred. "Kat," I said again.

"Dad!" she called out in a high and surprised voice. I heard footsteps on the stairs.

This was a perfect time to get away either by dropping off the side of the roof, or jumping from where I was to the main roof and climbing over it to the back, and then down to the deck.

Instead, I said, keeping my tone calm, "I know why Shelly was killed and why you, without my help, could be next." I had barely flattened my chest against the house to the right of the window, keeping just the corner of my eye peeking into the room, when Kat's father flung the door open. I wondered what she would say.

He flicked on the light switch next to the door and two matching lamps on the dresser threw their 60 watts each onto them both.

She hesitated and said, "Who was at the door?"

There was rustling. He still carried that newspaper. "Kathleen! You make me run up here for that? Why don't you come down for a while? You've been here all day."

"Maybe later. Who was it?"

"Some kid. He had a funny name. I think he said Mix."

"Thank you, Daddy. You know this is hard for me. I'll be down later."

Mr. Andrews sat on the bed next to Kat. She had raised herself to a crooked elbow. He stroked her brown hair backwards, bent, and kissed her forehead. "We'll make it, Kitty."

He left after she said an unsure, "I know."

"Kitty?" I asked.

"Shut up and get in here," she said, raising the screen. I climbed without touching the casing. Kat walked over and locked her door. She put a finger perpendicular to her lips in the silence signal.

She whispered, "Shelly hated you."

"That's not a small club," I said, matching her volume.

I left it there for her to wonder if I meant the people who hated me, or the people that Shelly hated.

"Why are you here? Why are you scaring me? Tell me now or my Dad will hurt you bad."

I give her credit. She recovered quickly and was trying to get control.

"I'm here to look at your ass."

She breathed in a chestful of air and opened her mouth to signal for Daddy again when I used her silence signal.

"Tattoos. They were killed because of their tattoos. You and Cyndi got tattoos on your butts that can get you shot and cut the same way."

"Cut?" All that air, and the sound was only a muted rush.

"After they were shot, the tattoos were cut off. Taken away."

Kathleen staggered in small shuffling steps until the backs of her knees touched the bed. Then she dropped down, sitting heavily there with her shoulders slumped, head almost to her thighs. She started crying.

I let her.

Finally she straightened, wiped her face with a palm, and asked, "Why did I get that damned tattoo? This can't be happening! It can't! She can't be dead because of some friggin' mark on her skin." Her voice was growing and becoming laced with jagged red lines. I made a lowering gesture with my right hand. We didn't need her dad up here anytime soon.

She went on in more or less a whisper, "It doesn't make sense. And now you say that same bastard's after me? After Cyndi? How can I stop this?

"Help me figure this out."

"Why are you doing this?"

"Mrs. Powell."

"She always gets what she wants, doesn't she? Shelly always said that."

I tilted my head, hoping she got whatever meaning she most wanted from the gesture.

I'd found lots of emotions can be turned into anger. Kathleen transmuted some of her fear and grief now.

"I used to tell Shelly not to care what her mother said. That she was jealous and had to be in control all the time. And her father—I don't even want to think about him." She shook her shoulders in exaggerated revulsion while scrunching her pretty face into a fierce and hard mask.

She looked at me. "And now she's got you trained."

"I'm easily led," I said. I thought resistance would be unproductive. "But," I added, "I might be the only one who can get you out of this alive." My voice was cloudy. I didn't really know if Kathleen would be a target or not.

"What can I do?"

"First of all, show me the tattoo," I said.

"How do I know you don't just want a look at my ass?"

"You don't. Come to think of it … I don't." I pushed playfully at her shoulder and smiled.

She looked down a moment and then made up her mind.

"Okay, but no touching," she said, offering me her hand. I pulled her up.

She was wearing Patagonia's Baggies shorts, Iceland blue. Kathleen turned her back to me and tugged them down to her thighs. White Hanes Pure Bliss bikinis clung tightly underneath. Her thumbs hooked the elastic waistband and pulled until the tattoo and an extra few inches of skin were exposed.

I dragged my eyes away from her ass crack, and stared at the blue symbol.

It was just a one-inch swirl, a gentle arc that flowed on the diagonal. The ends were tapered to points. The only remarkable thing about it was that I had seen it before—but couldn't remember where or when.

I tried to access my other senses, to match its taste or feel or sound or smell, but got only weak reactions, as if the volume or current had been turned way down in each of them.

Why?

"Okay," I said.

"That all you want to see?" She couldn't resist teasing me, even now, even in this situation.

That same music. Girls know they play it. They want *you* to know they play it, and let them know you listened.

"I want to see it all, but saving that pretty butt of yours is the first thing we should do," I said.

"You think my butt's pretty?"

"Prettiest one I've seen today." My voice was dark.

"My boyfriend would kill you if he found out."

"That's been tried before." Then, for the record, I added, "He won't find out from me."

She released the waistband and it snapped back into the red-tinged groove that tight things leave on your skin. She turned toward me before pulling up her shorts. She wanted me to see all of her sparkling white panties, I guess.

I did. It was a nice sight.

"Who took the picture of you and Cyndi?" I thought it best to get on with this before she entertained herself with more of the popular "let's beguile Myx" game.

"That was Shelly. This was all Shelly's idea."

"Is Hector Ramone circumcised?" The photo hadn't shown the blurry business end of his penis.

"How would I know?" Kat said this a bit too loudly, and I made a "lower it" sign with both my hands. Let Dad finish his paper.

"Were you there when Shelly and Hector took pictures of their tattoos?"

Kat squinted at me and said, "I didn't even know he had a tattoo. I thought it was only the three of us until you told me he died because of one he had."

"Did you get the tattoos together from Dragon?"

She sat back down on her bed, as if that were a comforting and safe spot to recollect from and then repeatedly smoothed the edge of the flower-patterned bedspread with her right hand. "Shelly came to us all excited last November about how she was going to rock the whole town. But how she needed our help. Turns out she wanted us to get these tattoos. She had them on three pieces of paper."

"Drawings or a photo?" I asked.

"Definitely a photo. I could tell it was from a printer. There were little dots if you looked close. It looked like blue lines painted on wood."

"Are you sure there were only three and not four?"

She nodded, "Only three, one for each of us."

"Do you remember the other two? Could you draw them?"

"No. They were like mine, but different. You know, different squiggles. You want to see mine again?" She started to get up.

I put my hand on her shoulder. "Nope. I got it." I didn't bother to show off and draw it exactly for her.

"Whose camera did she use?"

"That was Shelly's."

"What was Shelly's big plan about?"

"She said it was going to make us famous, and be the coolest thing that ever happened here. It was going to be on Founder's Day."

Kat's head angled toward the floor while she talked. Now she looked up at me with a realization. "That's not going to happen now." And the tears came.

Big recent hurts slip from your mind again and again until the shock of remembering finally makes them a sad part of you. The busted plan had reminded Kat that Shelly was gone.

I gave her time before I asked, "Did you ever see the fourth tattoo,

Hector's?"

"No. The three of us got drunk after the home game against Eastboro. The one we won on the fumble. Cyndi and me, we didn't want to get them, but Shelly, along with the beers, pulled us into Skin Sins. We all did it. Shelly wouldn't tell us why she got hers on her lip. That grossed me out. She got hers last."

She thought for a while and said, "This is all about her father. About her father and Founder's Day. She was going to tell us on Monday, the day before."

"You got a camera?"

"My father does."

"Digital?"

"Yeah, he's a gadget lover."

I bent down, my hands braced against my thighs, and explained, "I think that the murders happened to keep these tattoos a secret. If your tattoo is made public, if the police know about it, then there's no reason for you to be in danger. Cyndi too. I want to take a picture of it, so close it's just the tattoo, so don't worry about anyone recognizing you. Then I want you to call Cyndi and tell her I'm coming over."

She stood up. "Better still, I'm coming with you." There was no doubt, no hesitation. She was used to getting her way.

I would reason with her. "That's not a good idea because …"

"Look," she interrupted, "I have the tattoo, I have the camera, I have a car." As she slipped into a pair of Blue Label Marianna Suede Sandals (lime green), she looked my way and said, "And I may let you touch my ass."

I protested with, "Meet you at the corner."

Chapter Seventeen

Kat drove too fast and didn't stop much at intersections. It didn't help that she was on the phone too.

We were in her blue 2001 Dodge Neon.

"Yeah, we'll be there in five minutes," she said into the phone while turning with one hand. "'We' is me and Myx Amens." She listened for a few seconds, looked at me and said, "Yeah, the weird one. That's him. He's going to help us. Help us not end up like Shelly." She got frustrated and said, "Just stay there and wait for us. I'll explain then."

She hung up and threw the phone in her bag.

"Cyndi's nice but kind of flaky. She's scared, too."

"You think she'll show me the tattoo?" I asked.

"She'll give you a blowjob if I tell her to."

"And … ?"

"Tattoo only," she laughed.

Then her face lost the laugh and she said, "You know how I said you were weird?" She didn't wait for a reply. "Well, I didn't mean anything bad by it, but you are real different from anybody else. They say you talk with the dead. Is that true?"

"I may talk to them, but they don't talk back. Like Shelly and Dragon today. I saw two dead people. But I saw them just like you would. The difference is … I ask them a question. A question because of dreams I had once—or twice. I don't really expect an answer from them. I guess I want to suddenly realize something even though I don't know what that is. It's just kind of a feeling. Like I'm on the verge of finding out something I already know."

Kat didn't ask what I asked dead people. Good. I didn't know why I was telling this to her. I usually didn't talk about it. Maybe showing me your panties made me think you're my friend.

"You're weirder than I thought. Than any of us thought." She laughed nervously.

"Luckily *weird* is going to help you more than *normal* today."

She relaxed and almost stopped at the next intersection. I pulled the camera from her bag and looked at it. A Sony P150. It was smaller than my hand. Without turning it on, I held it up and pointed it toward Kat. She shook her hair back from her face, expecting me to click a picture.

"Do you think I'm pretty?" Maybe the distress of the day had opened her. Her voice was white.

"Remind your boyfriend for me that he's a lucky guy." She *was* pretty, and she knew it. But it's always nice to hear someone else knows too.

She smiled. "Myx, you're kinda sweet—in a spooky sort of way."

This was probably as nice as she got. I didn't say anything, determined to save my thanks for after she let me touch her ass (if, that is, she was going to let me touch her ass).

Her headlights gleamed minty blue and felt heavy on everything they touched. They finally touched Cyndi's house on Gillian Circle when she turned up the driveway.

Through the windshield, Kat pointed to the left window on the second floor. It was darkened. "That's Cyndi's room. See you up there." She turned to open her door.

"Don't I get to come in with you?" I asked.

"Easier this way. Don't you think?"

Before I answered, she was out and up the one step to the front door. I got out and shut my door just before she locked it with the remote on the keychain I had looked at and admired in the car.

I usually like to circle a building before I climb all over it. I didn't this time. Kat had walked into the Bellacquas' home as if it were her own, and a moment later, Cyndi's light went on.

There was no convenient lower roof for me here. It was a brick-face resurfaced exterior—not the strongest climbing medium—but there were a lot of little projections that made it easy to scramble up if you didn't stop.

I started only when I saw the window open and Kat stick her head out. I completed the twelve or fifteen feet in just a few seconds. Kat grabbed my belt so I wouldn't fall back as I crawled in. I was beginning to like her.

She closed the window while I looked at Cyndi, who shrank away from me toward the closed door. Only her desk lamp was on, a glaring bulb with yellowish light. Bitter.

"Hi. I'm Myx Amens." I tried to sound helpful and cheery. Cyndi had a little extra weight on her, but it was so proportional that it fit perfectly; any reduction would have made her less perfect. Dark eyes, dark hair, and the sharp shadows painted by that one light made me want to look at her longer than necessary.

"I know who you are. My father would kill you if he knew you were up here. My boyfriend would too." Her words sounded nervous with little gusts of hysterical.

"Then let's not tell them," I said calmly.

"Kat, this isn't a good idea. I—"

"Shut up," Kat said. She had put her bag on the bed, walked over to Cyndi and physically turned her around so her back was to me. Kat dropped to one knee, and roughly dragged the stretchable waistbands of Cyndi's shorts and panties to just below her ass cheeks.

Cyndi yelped.

"Quiet. You want your father up here seeing you with your pants down?"

Obviously Cyndi didn't want that, and saved her breath for a series of nasal exhalations that were noisier and quicker than normal.

Of all the tushes I had seen today, Cyndi's was the worst. That wasn't a criticism, just a fleeting comparison. On any other day, it might have been the best. It was just a little rounder and plumper than the others.

I got closer and looked at the blue swirl ingrained there. I had also seen this one before. It didn't cascade any other valuable information like where or when, though. I was getting more comfortable with my mental inadequacies. Not a good thing.

"Hold still," I said as I walked to the bed and grabbed the camera from Kat's bag. She had a box of Tic Tacs, half full. I took two and sucked on them. Original mint. I rattled them towards Kat, but she shook her head.

"What's he going to do with the camera?" Cyndi asked. She sounded frantic again.

Kat walked halfway around Cyndi and pointed at me with her chin. "He thinks Shelly was killed because of the tattoo she had. We need pictures so our butts aren't the only place they show up. Shelly had hers cut off and taken."

Cyndi shot her left hand to her mouth and stifled some sort of cry. Her right hand went to her shorts and tried to pull them up. Kat slapped that hand. Slapped it hard, and away from the material.

"Take the picture," she ordered.

"Nooo!" Cyndi was whining now.

"Look. Take mine first," Kat said as she turned and tugged her own clothes down, just as low as Cyndi's.

It was a strange sight, these two like this.

"I'm taking a real close shot so nobody can tell who it is. It'll just be a little skin and the tattoo. That's all. It's called a macro shot," I explained, hoping that would make the process more antiseptic for Cyndi.

I turned the camera on and fiddled with it for a moment to find the right setting. There's a little black flower that shows up on digital camera LCD screens when you set the camera to macro. I reached around and showed Kat, for her information. Who knew if I was going to need her to record something for me in the future?

I crouched and positioned the lens about five inches away from Kat's tattoo. I pressed the shutter button halfway down, heard it focus and set, then pushed the rest of the way. It flashed with a sweet click and an orange tinge.

"One more to be sure," I said. Kat never moved. Neither did Cyndi.

The two of them, standing with pants at half mast, incensed the room with their girl spice. It flushed the space with soft waves and curls of magenta.

"Okay," I said to Kat as I positioned myself behind Cyndi. I watched Kat though, as she wiggled her panties then her shorts up.

I told myself to concentrate and took two quick pictures of the second tattoo. "Okay," I said again. I didn't watch Cyndi rearrange.

"Cyndi? Everything all right? I made some popcorn," called a female from downstairs.

Popcorn?

"My mother. I'll be right back." Cyndi closed the door after she slipped through it. I heard her talking downstairs. I hoped she had the good sense to bring back the popcorn.

Kat was looking at me. I felt it before I glanced up from the camera's monitor.

"Well?" Kat looked expectant.

I knew what she wanted. "Your ass is way better than hers. You're amazing." I looked back down at the monitor and started checking the photos to make sure they came out.

Kat stepped behind me. She draped her chin over my shoulder and viewed them with me. "You may get that blowjob after all—and not from her." Her voice was cloudy, but it was nice to hear anyway.

The four shots of the tattoos were perfectly focused and exposed. There were six other photos there: all of a good-looking woman in her late twenties. She had long dark hair and wore a short khaki Izod Scooter skirt with a pleated front. A slate sleeveless tank by Nicole Miller finished her outfit.

The images were taken in an office. One had her sitting on a desk with her legs crossed. She had killer legs, long and muscular. She was smiling in all of them.

"Your mother's pretty," I said jokingly.

Kat seemed disgusted. "That slut is my father's secretary. And look at those 'fuck-me' shoes. What do they say to you?"

"I can type fast?" She was referring to a pair of rsvp Venice camel leather sandals with open toes, ankle straps, and 3 ½ inch heels. They went perfectly with those legs, that's for sure.

"Where did you *get* this camera?"

"Out of his briefcase." She laughed.

"That's where it should go back to when you get home. So he

doesn't know you saw these. A little advice: don't let people know what you know until it does you some good." Why did she make me want to tell her things? Very unlike me.

I shut off the camera and sat at Cyndi's desk. I woke up her computer there; it wasn't password protected.

"What are you doing now?" asked Kat.

"I'm going to email the pics to myself and then delete them from the camera so your dad won't see your ass, or Cyndi's."

"Email them to me too—all of them."

This probably wasn't going to be good for daddy, but I kind of admired that she was thinking ahead.

"Is that an order?"

From behind, she gently combed my hair for a second with her long-nailed fingers. "Request sounds better, doesn't it?"

"What's your email address?" She stopped combing and told me.

This was a Sony Vaio computer, and I knew it could read the 128 megabyte Memory Stick I pulled from the camera. I pushed it into the slot on the front of the computer and used one of my Yahoo! email accounts to send the emails. I didn't send Kat the tattoo photos; I wanted to control those. She was still standing over me, but didn't notice. She did notice I sent all the pictures (including the secretary) to myself.

"What are you going to do, masturbate to those?" she asked, a little red tinge around her words.

"Are you kidding? The next time I jerk off, I'm going to be thinking of you!" I said it with just the right amount of enthusiasm.

"Awwww! That's sweet. Disturbing, but sweet."

We both laughed.

I deleted the photos I had just taken then returned the Memory

Stick to the camera and handed it back to Kat.

"Maybe I'll let you take some other pictures of me someday."

Her empty promise sounded much better than it should have, and I gave her a big smile.

The door handle rattled, and I stepped into the closet. I peeked back out after someone entered and I smelled popcorn. It gave my tongue little twitches before I salivated.

We all sat on the bed, Cyndi in the middle with a big bowl in her lap. We picked at the popcorn and talked. She had brought some napkins and a big glass of Diet Pepsi, too. I took the bowl and finished it when everyone else had their fill.

"What are you going to do with the pictures?" Cyndi was visibly uncomfortable, I think as much about having a naked photo of herself floating about in cyberspace as about the danger she really didn't have a grasp on yet.

"You can't tell it's you—or me," Kat said, intuitively interpreting her friend.

"I'm going to get them to the police. Once it's public that they've seen them, you shouldn't be in any danger. There'll be no reason for someone to hurt you to keep them secret." I didn't mention the other plan that occurred to me: to leak that Cyndi had the tattoo and wait to see who showed up. This would be making Cyndi the bait. I seemed to want to protect Kat more.

I decided to go with the police plan. "Would you two feel safer if the police knew who you were and maybe watched you until this was over?"

Cyndi jumped at that, "I want the police to be here now so nothing can happen." Her hands were clenched and punctuated the last three words with soft pounding of her thighs. She was going to cry.

Kat was quiet for a moment, and then asked, "What do you think, Myx?"

"Why should we trust him, what he thinks?" Cyndi waved a hand at me.

I put the empty bowl on the floor, wiped the fingers of my left hand with a napkin, and then took a sip of soda, drinking from where Kat's lips had been.

"Look around, Cyndi. Who else is helping us?" Then to me, "You're good at this stuff, aren't you?"

"Real good." My voice was white.

I was willing to gamble even though I realized I was gambling with their lives. But I thought my reasoning was pretty sound. I wanted them to feel safe enough so they wouldn't do anything stupid on their own.

"I think whoever killed Shelly and Ramone and Dragon didn't know about you two. I think if he did, you'd both be dead now."

I waited. I wanted that to sink in.

They sat with their mouths open while it sank.

It hit bottom with Kat first, and she asked, "What should we do?"

"Let's not tell the police who you are. I'll take care of that. I'll send them the pictures and not tell them anything about you." The Chief would get an anonymous email later. I'd hook up to a proxy server so that whatever computer I was using couldn't be traced.

"You hear that, Cyndi?"

"I have to tell my parents, they have to know. And Artie, too."

Kat pinched the back of Cyndi's arm, near the triceps, very hard. Cyndi screamed. "Shhhh!" hissed Kat, and then pinched again, adding a twist. Cyndi muffled her response.

"You're not telling your parents and you're definitely not telling that asshole boyfriend of yours."

I didn't resist, "And *your* asshole boyfriend?"

Kat squinted at me, "Good point. Him neither."

I turned to Cyndi and asked, "Was Hector circumcised?"

Kat sighed and said, "Will you stop with whether he was—"

"No," Cyndi quietly interrupted.

Kat looked at her and shook her head as if waking up. "How would *you* know?" she finally asked.

"Well ... one time Hector had to give me a ride home ... and something happened. It was just that once. Really." Cyndi was almost pleading.

Kat's jaw tightened and she spoke with lips drawn back over her clenched teeth, "Billy gave you plenty of rides home. Did anything just happen then too?"

Billy Westlake was Kat's boyfriend.

"Nooo! Kat, I made a mistake once. Just that once."

Them fighting didn't do me any good right now. "Did he have a tattoo on his penis?" I thought I sounded very professional.

"Yeah, I saw it."

"I bet she got a real close look at it, too." Kat wouldn't let up on being pissed. Her face was red.

"Can you draw it?" I wanted to keep this rolling.

"His cock?"

Cyndi was a real project. I hadn't known her well enough in school to guess that.

"Just the tattoo would be enough," I said, hoping I hid all snide thoughts I had just found funny to myself.

"Let me try," she said and then went to her desk. She sat and opened a blue spiral notebook holding lined paper. She let a pencil tip hover over the page before making little flight patterns without touching.

She did this several times before turning to me and saying, "You know it was shaped different when it was ... you know."

"Hard. Erect. Stiff. Wood. We get it." Kat stood with her arms folded behind Cyndi and gave no sign of giving up her self-assumed position of moral superiority.

I put my left hand on Kat's back. I rubbed twice and patted twice. Kat relaxed and dropped her arms to her sides. I hoped this meant she was going to keep her judgments internal at least until Cyndi finished.

Cyndi had finally drawn something—but then scribbled it out. Just below that, she tried again. She repeated this four times.

The fifth try pleased her. "I think this is it."

"Why don't you put your mouth on it to make sure?" Sarcasm always looks pus yellow and tastes sour to me. Kat had a practiced flair to hers.

Cyndi was hurt and started to scratch out her latest effort when I put my hand on hers. "Thanks, Cyndi. This is really going to help." I took my hand away, and she put down the pencil.

"Were the ends thinner than the middle? Tapered?" I asked because this was looking familiar, just like the others. I thought Cyndi might have done a good job here.

"Oh yeah. Right." She took the pencil again and thickened a portion of the curve. Somehow, I felt that was it.

I now knew what three out of the four looked like.

"How about Shelly's? Can you draw hers?"

"She would never show me the whole thing. She would pull her lip a little bit and I could see a piece of blue. That's all. I knew she had it for sure, but not what it looked like."

I turned to Kat. "You saw the papers, what they looked like. Could you draw Shelly's?"

"I couldn't draw the one on my *own* ass. Obviously I don't have the talents *she* has." Kat was revving up again.

Cyndi apparently was ready for it this time. "Oh, and do you want me to tell him what talents you do have? What *you* like?"

"Shut up!"

I usually like watching girls settle their differences in both verbal and physical ways, but not when it's going to get in my way.

"Listen," I started. "You both lost Shelly today. You still have each other, and you both need each other. Some things happen and we can regret them. What we do at our worst or weakest isn't who we really are."

They looked at each other and through tears said they were sorry. They hugged. I was hoping they would kiss each other on the lips.

They didn't.

When I thought enough time had passed, I asked Cyndi, "Did you know what Shelly had planned for Founder's Day?"

She shook her head and then hugged herself and rocked slightly back and forth. "She was going to tell us on Monday. She said it was going to be crazy and we should be ready for something big. She got excited every time we asked her. At first I thought the tattoos were just something that we did because we got drunk. But Shelly had this planned out. I was really surprised when …" Cyndi turned to Kat, paused and then went on, "… when I saw that Hector had a tattoo with the same kind of pattern. That's when I thought this might be for real, that Shelly was going to do something freaky. It kind of scared me."

I tore up the paper Cyndi had worked on and threw the small pieces in her basket under the desk.

"Won't you need that?" Kat asked.

"I got it if I need it." Should I try to impress her by reproducing it or her own handwriting? No.

Before we left, I emailed the photos to the Chief. While the girls were chatting, I also copied everything that looked interesting from the computer onto my flash drive. They never noticed.

When it was time, I dropped from the window to the soft lawn. I met Kat down the street.

"I'll drive you home," she said.

"Not going home."

"Won't your parents worry?" She sounded truly concerned.

I never looked at Benny and Bunny in a real and responsible parental light, so it struck me from a different angle this time.

"Oh, they don't care. I'm always in and out."

"That's kind of sad, Myx. I wish all the time that my parents would leave me alone. But I don't know what I would do if I thought it didn't matter to them where I was or what I was doing. I feel safe because they are somewhere hoping for the best for me."

"I don't think anybody hopes the best for me." My voice was white.

She was quiet and finally said, "Then I guess that'll be my job."

I had Kat drive past Sarge Halpern's house on Beverley. His truck wasn't there, but most windows glowed from dim lighting within (shades were pulled down on most of them). She dropped me off up the street and I watched her tail lights until they disappeared around a corner.

166 ■ DAVE DIOTALEVI

It was nearly midnight and clouds hid the moon. Good. I liked the darkness when I was studying a house I had never visited before. I wanted to find out why, if I could, ol' Sarge had been following me, and what he expected our meeting tomorrow to bring.

I felt in my pocket for the key I had made that afternoon. I had seen Sarge's house key when we met on the street; the copy slipped neatly into the back door. I smiled.

This was going to be quick and easy.

Chapter Eighteen

It had the clean smell of polish and mineral oil. The whole house.

I listened. Nothing. Nothing but a clock's ticking in a room somewhere behind the swinging door that led from this kitchen.

I closed the Dutch door behind me. The top and bottom were held together by a shiny brass pin.

Shiny. Polish.

This meant surfaces that could show fingerprints easily. I pulled my latex gloves from my back pocket and stretched them on with a soft snap that tasted a bit bitter. I paused again to listen. The snap had sounded louder than it should to me.

A blue plastic seashell nightlight radiated from an outlet next to the refrigerator. It barely hummed to my sight. I tore a paper towel from a roll on the wall. The rack was made of a dark wood, its two end pieces perfectly symmetrical and intricately lathed.

I wiped the door handle inside and out, then decided to keep the towel when I found the wastepaper basket had nothing in it. Why call attention to yourself?

The counters and cabinets were red beech, finger-jointed. Beautiful work.

All the cabinets were fully stocked. There was no other car in the driveway. I assumed he lived here alone. This meant he cooked.

I dined on some roasted chicken from the refrigerator. I cut away a piece of apple pie and ate it right from the pie plate before I washed the knife and fork, dried them with my paper towel, and replaced them exactly where they came from in the smoothly opening silverware drawer.

I felt better. My stomach gurgled. Maybe I should use the bathroom; maybe I should wait. I decided to wait.

The swinging door opened to an oak-paneled hallway leading to the main entrance and the stairs on the right. Surprisingly, there were no openings on the left, just a blank wall with lots of ornamental molding. On the right, under the stairway, was an office.

A big oak desk rested in the center of it, taking up most of the space in the small room. I hooked my fingers under its top and hefted; it didn't budge—real heavy. A swiveling Captain's chair sat behind it.

I listened before I turned the small desk lamp on. There was no sound of approach or attack, so I continued. The hardwood floor gleamed.

In addition to a handcrafted pendulum clock (there's the tick), there were seven framed photos on the walls. He was a hunter, and proud of it. They showed him with deer, geese, pheasant, wild turkeys, a black bear (a big one), a moose, and a mountain lion. Sarge was the live one in the pictures. The live one with the rifle or the bow. He had a Ka-Bar USMC combat knife on his belt in each shot.

I listened again. I didn't want to be in photo #8.

His desk was ultra neat. This wasn't coming as a surprise any more. He seemed very meticulous. There was an in/out basket, a small holder for paperclips, a cup with pens and pencils, a phone (white), and a large black blotter. Not one paper littered the desktop.

I sat in the chair and swiveled a little to get the feel of it. Not a creak or rough spot. The left drawer was deep and had a series of green hanging files on rails. They were all hand-labeled. Business-related. The other side drawers held the usual supplies.

The center drawer was broad and glided open with a nearly-hidden hiss. It held very little: scissors, a paper punch, rechargeable AA batteries, some stamps, a St. Christopher medal, an invoice pad with his company name, and a wallet-sized photo which was creased once and dog-eared on the upper left corner.

It was a young girl, maybe about seven years old. She had dark hair and eyes and two oversized upper front teeth with a gap between them. She wore a white v-neck sweater with thin red and blue stripes lining the neck. On the back in precise printing with a blue ballpoint: Lisa 28 Feb 91.

I pushed the drawer back in, pulled it out again, and then pushed it back in. I did this five times. Something didn't feel right. I bent even with the face of the drawer. A thin line, hardly noticeable, about ninety percent of the way down, ran straight across. I wiggled my thumb on it. There was no feel to the edge, but I heard a small "blip" sound. It was a seam.

I raised my eyebrows like I was sly and grinned.

My grin disappeared when I couldn't figure out what the seam was for. I pulled and turned and fretted at it a while. Nothing.

I wanted it to come out. All my effort pointed at getting it to pull toward me. What if it was meant to go the opposite way?

I pushed. Nothing.

I smelled along the edge. Like polish mostly, but on either end, down at the bottom, there was a smell of soap. Zest. I hooked my fingers over the top edge of the drawer and pushed the bottom corners with my thumbs. Nothing. Then I tried my right thumb first, and then my left—there was a click. The bottom of the drawer slid forward an inch; it was free.

I pulled the drawer completely out and then dragged the hidden compartment tray from the inner end. It held a few envelopes, some documents, cash and a photo.

Sarge Halpern wasn't Sarge Halpern. Or at least he was also Brian Halders of Wolf Point, Montana. There was a valid Montana driver's license, a passport, and a Social Security card among other things. The picture on the license showed him with his head shaven and no facial hair. He looked totally different from the man I saw today. But it was him. A map of Mexico showed a small red pen mark on Durango. One of the letters (on Halpern Funeral Home stationery) was from his father and postmarked Great Falls. Sarge was also keeping an apartment in Wolf Point. There was $8400 in cash too. A storage receipt for a garage made me think he had another vehicle ready.

Looked like Sarge had an alias set up for himself. My experience told me people did this for two reasons: they had run away, or they were going to run away.

A thin metallic tube, almost needle-like, had punctured the side of an unsealed envelope. It had a sharp three-sided tip. The word "trocar" came into my mind. I had seen it once in a book. This was used in funeral homes. A memento from daddy?

The photo showed a younger Sarge in fatigues and dark glasses. He was standing next to a half-buried, shattered Iraqi tank. On the back was written, 22 January 1991.

I slipped the drawer together and replaced it in the smooth grooves. While crouched there, I noticed a glint at the top of the modesty panel under the desk. I listened before I crawled into the dark shadow of the recess and retrieved a key ring from its brass hook home. Four keys, different types. I looked at and then pocketed them. They'd go back after I was finished.

Although fascinating (I really wasn't surprised by much any more), this still didn't give me any ideas about why he was interested in me. Maybe he just wanted a buddy to share a road trip to Montana with, and I looked like a great conversationalist for those long stretches of flat highway.

I shut off the desk lamp and walked down the hall to the front door. I braced my hands against it and stretched upwards to look out of one of the two small glass panes about six feet from the floor. All dark and quiet, just how I liked it.

I concentrated my search on the only other room downstairs. The brass lever handle wouldn't move. Locked. It belonged to the interior door at the bottom of the stairs. I knew which key would fit; it did, and opened a room which I had seen many times before—just not here.

One Paul Revere punched-tin nightlight on the far wall sprinkled tiny diffuse shadows across the ceiling and walls. Patches of light and dark with no hard edges. A cello sound in one long soft pull of a bow.

This was an exact replica of the West Room at the Sonnet House. The woodworking was flawless (I wondered how the joints were); the details of the map were exact. It all sang together with only a slightly different tune than the original. It was really remarkable work. I had increased respect for Sarge's mastery.

At the far end, in a wood and glass case, sat Sonnet's box and key.

I pulled my cell phone out and dialed. It rang three times before a sleep-gurgled voice said, "Sonnet House."

"Hi Brass. Myx."

He cleared his throat a few times. Once so hard I thought he would hurt himself.

I went to the front door and looked out while talking. I didn't want an unexpected visitor while I was talking (I had learned not to get distracted the time I finally had found Thomas Alva Sykes, the serial rapist). No traffic. I was safe.

"Coming over tonight, keep an old man company? I'll tell you the time we went on tour to every bar on the Mississippi for a hundred miles." He chuckled to himself, enjoying the memories. I had heard about this tour so many times, I could smell the sweat and smoke.

"Maybe if I finish my errands," I said quietly. It echoed, bare wood reflecting it.

"Bring me one of those spicy sandwiches and I'll owe you."

"Brass, the big day is coming up. Sonnet's box all ready?"

"Sitting here quiet as a nappin' cat," he said.

"No extra excitement then?" I now felt a little silly that I had checked. Anyone who could copy the West Room could copy the box.

Brass went on to tell me about the murders. I let him to see what he knew. Just rumor and hearsay.

Then he added, "You know Ramone's car was parked near here last night for a while? I saw it."

"Sure it was his car?" I laughed. Hector Ramone had the Puerto Rican flag painted across his hood.

"Now you're playing with me, boy."

"See you, Brass." I hung up.

I made my footsteps quieter as I approached the box. The case was identical, too. I fitted another key from the ring into the lock and opened it.

Last May was the only time I had ever held Sonnet's Box. Sarge had outdone himself here. It felt exactly the same. Same weight, same texture, same sound, same taste. How could he do this? Was he that good a craftsman?

The parquet symbols covered the box darkly in the dim light. One—I turned the box—two, another turn—three. All three. Tonight I had seen two of these on Kat and Cyndi. Cyndi had drawn the third. None of them were perfect representations, but certainly close enough to be distinct and identifiable.

What was the fourth?

The key. Maybe the wooden key would make this easy for me. I liked easy.

I replaced the box and picked up the two slabs beside it. It was a wood sandwich four inches square and two inches high. A purple wax covered the seam between the pieces. A signet imprint showed on one edge.

Do I or don't I? It didn't take me long to run the sharp point of my knife all around the edge and break apart the duo. One in each hand, I turned the inside faces toward my own.

Bare, recently sanded, unfinished wood. Not a mark on it.

So much for easy.

I looked and shook, smelled, and even tasted those short blocks, but I found out nothing further. I clunked them together. The sound told me they were solid. I surmised Halpern couldn't duplicate the key; he never knew what was in the original since it was still safely waxed together at the Sonnet House.

I nodded to myself in the murk. Seemed reasonable.

So the murders are connected to the tattoos and the tattoos are connected to the box. Could Sarge be another connection, maybe the final connection to the shootings? I wouldn't be surprised. After seeing this room, I was incapable of further surprise in this house.

The other thing I learned here was the purpose of the key I had found in Shelly's room. It wasn't an exact match for the key that had opened this case, but it was close enough to tell me they belonged in the same family. I bet her key opened the case at the Sonnet House. Through ceremonial tradition, only the town leader had control of the Sonnet Box. Being Chairman of the Miracle Board of Selectmen gave Shelly's father that right and responsibility.

Shelly had "borrowed" the key and brought it to Benny, who shoddily made the copy in my pocket.

These things coming together almost made me feel better about my recent memory farts, the lapses and the blurs. Seeing the symbols on the box made me realize I had thought this through before, but now couldn't remember the outcome.

I locked the case and then the door behind me.

Upstairs or downstairs first? Cellars were always more fun and interesting in a guy's place, bedrooms in a girl's.

I had seen the cellar door in the kitchen. On my way back, I trailed my right hand along the hall's wall and moldings as I walked. It made that "blip" sound to me again, the one I had felt on the drawer.

Another seam? It was too dark in the hall to see. Especially when it could be still another example of Halpern's abilities. I was beyond just respecting the precision of his craftsmanship. It tested me. So far I had a passing grade.

A car was coming. I ran to the front door and looked—it drove by.

The light from the desk lamp spilled enough into the hall once I turned it. There, right where I had felt, was a barely-noticeable edge joining of two separate pieces of wood. I traced around it with my left index finger, a rectangle a foot wide and three feet high. I pushed on the corners, one at a time. Nothing. Then I pushed the center of the left edge. It receded a little and sprang towards me when I released it, revealing its function as a door to a shallow recess. Clever internal hinges were invisible from the outside.

It contained a lead-gray cylinder about a foot in diameter with the letters "CO" stenciled near the top on the side facing me. I tested the valve; it was shut. A one inch hose trailed from the nozzle up through the wall and out of sight.

Why would anyone want air from Colorado?

I laughed at my joke. This was carbon monoxide, and its fun uses were few as far as I could remember.

What are you up to, Sarge?

A button and a switch offered themselves to me from the back wall of this chamber. The round white button looked like a doorbell. The switch was a simple silver toggle set to the down position.

Hesitating and thinking take too much time when in someone else's house. I pushed the button. I had learned that if nothing happens, it's probably an alarm, so get out.

Something did happen though. I heard the hum of a motor, and one of the panels in the hall slid to the left into the wall. Springs were stretching, their pitch rising as the distance from their resting length increased. A secret sliding door. It extended all the way to the floor; the opening measured six feet high by two and a half feet wide.

The interior was black from my angle while I stood several feet away. That darkness disappeared when I flipped the silver switch up. The interior spilled over with bright light. It was faintly pink and tasted malty.

I ran to the kitchen and brought back one of the heavy oak chairs that sat around the kitchen table. Its seat was two inches thick. I had learned my lesson about spring-loaded doors when I tried to retrieve Alice Samuelson's engagement ring from her ex's body shop.

I propped the chair in the door opening. Then I looked up into the room.

Sometimes I lie to myself to gain confidence, sometimes to get myself to do the right thing (or the difficult thing). Other times I lie to myself unintentionally out of undiluted ignorance.

This was one of those times.

I had thought I had already uncovered the biggest surprise in this house. What faced me in this hidden room didn't just surprise—it shocked.

Unconsciously my lips moved, but no sound came as I asked the question.

The glow room?

Chapter Nineteen

They looked at me. They never blinked, their blue eyes shining and staring.

I knew them. At least I recognized them. They were the five sisters. That's what the newspapers finally labeled them.

All five were blonde, blue-eyed, fourteen-year-old girls. The first one had disappeared from New York in December. Then New Hampshire, Connecticut, Rhode Island, and finally Vermont— one each month. A writer for the *Hartford Courant* had made the connection at the end of February, calling them the three sisters at the time. Two more had been added since, the last in April.

I stepped over the chair and into the room. I measured with my eye. It was twenty by fifteen with a ten foot ceiling. Unlike the rest of the house, there was no wood here. It offered unrelenting white instead. White plaster for the walls and ceiling, white ceramic tile for the floor. A white metal bench hugged the right wall. Above it on the wall, just waist high, six thick flat head screws held a circular chrome plate with an eyebolt in the middle. Handcuffs hung from the eyebolt, one end waiting for a wrist.

Each girl sat in a separate glass case, all arranged in a semicircle facing the front. A sixth case, facing the others, waited at the center of the circle. This sixth was empty.

I looked at the ceiling behind me. Seven track lights. A not-too-bright pale pink spotlight shone on each case. Their reflections off the immaculately clean glass followed me as I moved.

The trocar, the needle-like instrument from the desk, I had thought was some keepsake from his father's funeral business. Now I knew Halpern had more talents than just woodworking. These girls were expertly embalmed, preserved for display. I also knew what I would find in the cellar—an embalming studio.

All their eyes were open and made of glass. That didn't stop me from looking into them one at a time and asking, asking my question. I got the same answer.

Each case rested on a white plastic pedestal about a foot high. The same plastic covered the edges.

They sat there, hands folded in their laps, feet flat, as if waiting. They wore plain full-length cotton dresses with long sleeves. A different soft pastel shade for each. White opaque stockings showed above their shiny patent leather dress shoes. I could see the lights in them.

Pale dried-flower garlands circled their heads, resting about an inch above their brows.

"You're all pretty." I don't know why I said it aloud.

My voice disturbed the quiet.

The next sound was more disturbing. A faint buzz in the wall preceded the sliding door slamming against the chair, easily splitting the thick seat and sending broken pieces across the floor. The other half of it was outside. Outside—where I instantly wanted to be.

I didn't have to look around again to see there was no other exit, but I did anyway.

I pulled out my cell phone. No signal. Was he jamming or blocking? Didn't make much difference; I was on my own.

The door had a coat of white enamel. I tapped on it. Metal. No wonder it sliced through the chair.

"Glad my fingers and toes weren't in there," I said to give myself something to be thankful about. That was all I was thankful about.

On the door, an eight-inch square panel centered itself at eye level. I surmised this could be opened to view the room from the outside. More of Sarge's hidden ingenuity.

I ran my hands over the door and walls and even the floor, looking for a release mechanism. Nothing. The only breaks in the interior were two small vents in the ceiling, right near the track lights. The door probably could be worked by remote control.

I didn't have one, so I decided to wait. I liked deciding things that were forced on me anyway. It made me feel like I was still in control.

I wasn't in control though, and this was a very bad spot to be in—even for me.

I sat on the bench, resting my back against the wall. It was cool. I laced my fingers together and held my right knee after I had crossed my legs. I looked down and debated whether to take my gloves off. I looked silly with them on here. After all, fingerprints weren't going to be my main concern when Sarge found me.

I won the debate and kept them on.

During the next forty-five minutes, I kept busy by playing with the handcuffs and inspecting the cases again and again.

When I heard the muffled sound of the back door, I sat on the bench and waited. I heard Sarge's voice swearing. The desk lamp and the broken chair must have given me away. I smiled at the thought of him coming home to see the mess.

Myx, get serious.

This hadn't been as quick and easy as I had planned.

There was fumbling at the sliding window before it opened with an easy, almost noiseless pull. It felt round and green.

Sarge was the nervous type. He had quick, jerky movements. A glance to the girls, and then a startled look at me sitting there—sitting there with my gloves on.

A thick wire mesh interfered a bit with our stares.

Sarge wore a dark blue baseball cap. The red "B" stroked in white signified the Boston Red Sox. I could see he still had on the same shirt from earlier.

"How 'bout them Sox?" I offered before he could say anything. Maybe I'd get on his good side.

Sarge started laughing and continued for a long, long time with increasing volume and animation.

I usually enjoy when people appreciate my attempts at humor. I *wasn't* enjoying Sarge's display.

He added some hand clapping while throwing his head back with a last, almost hysterical howl.

Not many people are happy about my visits to their homes, but their usual reactions were less distressing than this one Sarge was joyously demonstrating. I didn't have to be clairvoyant to foresee he had plans that required my unwilling participation.

"This couldn't have worked out better!" He spoke with almost a shrill tone.

"For you or for me?" I didn't expect an answer to that.

"You act so smart, but look at you there ... right where I need you to be."

"Speaking of smart, did I trip something in here to shut the door?" This is an answer I'd appreciate—in case there was a next time (which didn't look all that guaranteed right now).

He shook his head, waited, savoring his apparent good fortune, and said, "Simple timer. Three and a half minutes."

I nodded. It had to be digital. I hadn't heard anything ticking or turning.

"Well, you got me. Now, let me out and we'll keep this," I pointed with the top of my head towards the glass cases, "just between us guys." My voice was very cloudy.

He ignored me. "You know who they are?"

"They're the five sisters. You know, you still haven't touched Maine or Massachusetts. That's two whole months yet. You don't need me. Girls seem to be your thing." I tried to appear logical with my inane reasoning.

"You don't understand, Myx." He was getting personal, friendly. How many friends like him do you need?

"These are the five princesses of light from encompassing lands," he continued. "That final case is for the thrice-born dark prince. That display is yours."

Usually, I welcome gifts and honors. Well ... if I ever received any gifts or honors, I would welcome them. But picturing myself inside that transparent vault staring glassy-eyed at my tragic bevy evaporated any joy, leaving the realization that this could be my one and final end.

"Thrice-born?" I knew where he was going with this, but the more he talked the less he turned on the carbon monoxide. If he did that, I wouldn't be waking up to Dr. Fabrizio's face again. I would meet Sarge's embalming needles pumping formaldehyde, methanol, ethanol, and other solvents to the farthest retreats of my body. I wanted to keep coursing blood in those retreats for as long as possible.

"You know it was in the papers. How you cheated death. How you did it not just once, but twice. Along with your original birth, you are now thrice-born. Just like it was written in his words." He sounded sure and satisfied; I preferred when I sounded like that better.

"His words?" He sounded like a Bible thumper, but this wasn't matching any Biblical text that I had just visualized.

"Sonnet. Elbridge Sonnet. He was a modern prophet. I came to Miracle because of his craftsmanship, but that was just the nectar that drew me close to the message, the beauty of the light. I knew he had chosen me to carry out his plan to bring about the miracle this week with the opening of his box."

He wasn't looking at me. Halpern, or Halders, examined the five, his eyes moving constantly from one to another.

Finally, he returned to me and said, "It's all in his words, his library. His greatest work was in his revelations, not in wood."

I had looked through all his writings, but couldn't remember them. I couldn't recall them to my inner sight.

That feeling again. This time on top of a trapped feeling.

"I looked at those, but ..."

"Your mind is confused now, confounded. Sonnet said the dark prince's powers shall be clouded by the light." He tapped the wire with his finger, pointing at me with a snarling, vicious emphasis. He said the last words through clenched teeth.

That clouded part affected me more than it might otherwise. It was easy for me to grasp at the first solution to my recent memory hitches, and forced me to question if there were unnatural or supernatural forces working against me. It wasn't a comforting question, and I had no soothing answers.

"Nice copy of Sonnet's box you made." Sarge seemed like a guy who would soak up some naked flattery.

"Copy?" He smiled tight-lipped and waited.

I looked and read him: so sure, so pleased. It was then I knew. "The box, the one in the other room. It's the original, isn't it?"

He closed his eyes and tilted his head slowly to the right. That smile remained. This had become a slow orgasm of self-congratulation for him.

"They hired me to clean and restore Sonnet's woodworking. My humble talents made it easy to put a replica in place."

"Why did you open and ruin the key?"

Keep him talking, Myx.

"That *is* unfortunate. The key is lost. But I'm confident I can open the box with minimal damage. I just have to break the first joint, which only I could have found. Found only after studying his methods and interpreting his visions for so long."

"Maybe I can help. I'm good at looking at stuff and figuring it out." This was my let-me-out-and-we'll-be-on-the-same-team approach.

"The way of the wicked is lacquered in blood. The just shall find rest on a bed of tears." He was spouting again. More Sonnet, no doubt.

I didn't think he was going to let me help.

"What does the map mean?" Just because you're scared of being gassed to death at any second doesn't mean you can't be curious. He was obviously an expert on all things Elbridge. I might as well take advantage of our time together.

"The map of the West Room concerns itself with the inferior path: the ways of the world, the hungers of man. I won't bother with its interpretation. I only care about bringing the secret of the miracle to fulfillment."

"Why do some of the tiles look different?" I asked, but was beginning to expect less than informative answers.

This got his attention, though. "You have the sight? You can see them, the cursed? This proves you're the right one. I'm saving you while perfecting the miraculous."

"Thanks," I said. My voice was dark.

"Look at them." He gestured to the girls with his eyes. "All immaculate. You'll be the same."

"What will I be wearing? Blue is my best color."

He ignored me.

"Myx." There was a gentleness to his tone that made me shiver. "It's time. Time for you to take your place. You were meant to be here. You were given to me for this purpose."

Sarge disappeared from the screened window and I heard a screech of metal on metal. He was opening the valve of the gas canister. The two vents above the track lights hissed. There was no use looking there; carbon monoxide was colorless.

I looked anyway.

Sarge was back. He looked ready to shut the window and seal the room.

But I wasn't ready for the dizziness, headache, confusion, collapse, coma, and death that was minutes away. I had wanted sleep for over three years, but I was determined it wasn't going to be this way, and it wasn't going to be tonight.

I hadn't moved in more than an hour. I moved quickly now. To my left, near the door, lay the pieces of the broken chair. I freed the two thick oaken legs from the splintered seat, and ran to the nearest sister/princess. She didn't acknowledge my approach.

I swung hard in a diagonal arc. It wasn't safety glass and shattered easily with discordant red and orange sounds.

The case had been evacuated of air. It rushed in now and caused her to jump a bit, as if startled—her eyes a little wider, her clothes and posture jerking.

It smelled of chemicals. I read they had dipped the corpse of Lenin in glycerol and potassium acetate periodically to preserve it. I didn't know my preservatives like I knew perfumes, so I only wondered what these odors were.

Behind me, Halpern screamed, "Nooooo!"

They were immaculate. That's what he had said. I was going to change that. Change it before the gas got too thick or he could react.

In one motion, I dropped one of the legs and replaced it with the lighter from my pocket.

Without hesitating, I said, "Sorry," then lit her hair on fire. That kindling ignited the rest of her in a whoosh that threw me back a step and made me glad I had reached in from an angle. The mystery chemical was flammable.

I heard the door open before I could break the second case. I had retrieved the chair leg, and again had one in each hand.

Sarge carried a small red fire extinguisher. He wasn't so intent on putting out the fire that he didn't easily and expertly parry the backhanded slash of the wooden club in my right hand with the extinguisher. It rang. All that military training, I supposed. What he didn't expect was the follow-through of the other leg in my left hand; it was an overhand chop too quick to see that caught him on the right ear. The leg's slivered end lacerated the flesh after its blunt force pulped it. This only partially jarred his cap loose. He went down, rolled (that's when his cap flew off), and groggily went for the knife (the one in the pictures) on his belt.

I hit that wrist hard and heard it crack. Wood on bone—wood

won. I hit it again. There was a softer sound. He yelled in pain. Not out of control though. Maybe he was used to pain.

He'd better be.

I knelt, took his knife, and held it to his neck. It shone in the spotlights and my hand told me it liked me. "You move, I cut your throat." My voice was white. I had been impressed by the Indian's economy of words three years before. Threats seemed more powerful when compact.

I dug into his pockets and threw the contents to the doorway.

The carbon monoxide spewed still and the fire glittered with small strips of black ash that glowed orange when touched by one of the feeding flames. She wasn't immaculate any more. I needed to take care of this fast.

I dragged Sarge across the floor to the handcuffs by the bad wrist. But only after I had laced him hard across the left quadriceps with one of the oaken legs. That was to lessen his mobility and maybe discourage his resourcefulness.

More time would have made me more gentle. Right now, I had to get that fire out and the carbon monoxide throttled off.

I did both of those things after hanging Sarge from the handcuff. I took the bench away so he was suspended there, quite painfully from the look of it.

I found another hidden compartment near the gas cylinder. It held the door timer and a vent switch. I couldn't figure out how to shut off the timer, so I set it for six hours instead of its 3.5 minutes. Sarge probably had a remote control somewhere, but who wants to try and reason with someone you just physically abused?

I flipped the vent switch and heard air rushing into the room. Maybe there would be a slight headache from the residual poison; I would gamble with Halpern's life and welfare.

The carbon dioxide stream from the red fire extinguisher blew out the fire. Its white flow highlighted her blackened face and took paper-thin pieces of ash to the back of the case in its rush.

Her blue glass eyes showed wider now that the lids were partially burned away. We stared at each other. Mine were the eyes that watered in the stinging atmosphere of smoke and chemical haze. I stood there a moment, motionless except for my finger, which wagged down into the dent I had made in the extinguisher with my first swing.

Sarge coughed and hung limp. The bashes to his head, wrist, and thigh would make him behave while I checked the rest of the house.

The third key from my found set opened his gunroom upstairs. Several hunting rifles hung on the walls. A loaded Beretta 92FS, which uses a 9 mm cartridge, was the only handgun. It felt cold in my palm. I took it with me.

I was right about the cellar. The final key on the ring opened his laboratory, spotlessly clean but stinking of those same chemicals. He had a large wooden toolbox with a false bottom. It was big enough for any of the sisters. Probably how he transported them. I looked at a drug encyclopedia once. Midazolam causes unconsciousness. He had syringes and a supply of this. The girls didn't have much of a chance, did they?

Sarge was trying to stand by the time I got back to him. I let him struggle while I chose a place on the floor about six feet away. I sat cross-legged, facing him.

"You killed the five girls."

He looked at me, his glance filled with the weariness pain brings.

He didn't say anything.

"They were a part of your plan. So was I. The Sonnet thing. But why did you shoot the other three last night?"

He shook his head. "Not me. Not me." The words were slurred and thick and not very loud. His voice was white.

The girls were just victims of a fanatic, a zealot. He perverted something he found in Sonnet's writings; this was the outcome. I looked at the cases even though I didn't need to. I would be able to see them forever.

His wrist hung limp in the handcuff. That must hurt. I wondered if the sisters breathed their last moments here, here in this white room. I suspected so, but hoped they had been drugged to death without having to realize they were going to die. I didn't have much hope for that hope.

A court would find him insane. I didn't doubt that. Sarge would live a long life in prison while these girls would be dead even longer.

I decided that wasn't going to happen. I knew what I was going to do.

"Four thousand dollars," he said. "I'll give you four thousand dollars to let me go. I'll leave and you can have all that money." He was offering me roughly half of what I had found.

Before she died, I used to give Mrs. Mangasto her insulin shots when her daughter had to be away. Mrs. Mangasto couldn't bear to give them to herself. I was good at it, and she said I didn't hurt her.

I got up and swept Sarge's good leg out from beneath him as he tried to steady himself upright against the wall. The fall hurt; the shot of midazolam didn't.

Before he passed out, he probably heard me say, "I'll think about it."

I wasn't a cold-blooded killer. He needed to die. What's a boy to do?

This is where I should call the police, get Chief Maldonato over here, and clear up the most terrifying mystery New England had seen since the Boston strangler.

I called Mrs. Powell instead.

Chapter Twenty

Being polite shouldn't be required of you at 3 A.M. the day after your daughter's death.

Mr. Powell wasn't and would have hung up if his wife hadn't grabbed the phone.

"Amens?" Her voice sounded rough with sleep. It had green and blue streaks through it and gave my stomach squishy and heavy feelings.

"What we talked about. Meet me at Dunkin' Donuts on Main Street." I didn't want to give long explanations over the phone. She was either in or out.

"An hour." She hung up.

She was in.

Sarge was still breathing. Good. I'd used the right dosage. I took his work boots off and put them out of reach. I didn't want a cleverly hidden handcuff key to ruin my plans if he woke before I returned. I searched him again. Nothing. Maybe I judged him by too high a standard—my own.

I found a Stop & Shop paper bag in the kitchen. It had handles. A perfect tote.

Back in the office, I again opened his secret drawer and took an envelope from it. On a blank sheet from a yellow legal pad, I wrote a letter to Sarge in a shaky hand, folded it using an accordion fold, and slipped it into the envelope. This went into the bag.

After I tore a blank invoice from his pad, I made up a series of repairs, estimated a price, and added a date and address, all in Sarge's handwriting. I found a "Paid" stamp and an inkpad. I stamped the invoice and threw it in the bag, then replaced the drawer.

I couldn't help looking at the sisters again when I checked on Halpern (who slept on—I wondered if he dreamt). I stayed still, gazing more than I should.

Then I was back in the fake West Room. I transferred Sonnet's box and sanded key to my bag. I now had to support the bag by its bottom due to the weight of the box (which I estimated to be almost forty pounds).

I locked the back door when I left, and had fifty minutes to store my "groceries."

After about ten minutes walking, I heard the van. Every vehicle has its own signature: engine sound, lights, suspension, tires. I didn't have to turn around to identify it.

Usually, I drifted into the cover off the streets when someone approached at night. I kept walking, not seeming to care until the van stopped beside me.

"Need a ride?" The sliding door was open.

"You know me, Bindy." I sounded thankful for the offer. I was, among other things. "Going to Miracle Self-Storage."

"I'll take you." Bindy tried not to look at me too long. Instead, it was too short. "I was surprised to see you today, at my house."

"Surprises happen. Like this. *Miracle Daily News* doesn't have a Sunday paper. And here you are. Surprise! That's just my good luck because now I have a ride." I thought I sounded very natural.

"Yeah, couldn't sleep. Thought I'd take a ride. I like to think while I ride."

It was strange to see the back of the van empty of papers. It looked much bigger than usual. Bindy's dirty nylon mini-duffel was the only thing back there. I thought I caught a peppery whiff from it before we started and the wind swept in through the open door.

I was careful to keep my own bag away from Bindy. Its stiff sides made it stand open to anyone who wanted to look down into it. Bindy didn't want to.

He tapped the steering wheel with his left palm the whole three minutes it took to get to my storage unit. He was struggling. I could smell his sweat even though it was comfortable again tonight.

"Thanks," I said while jumping out when he slowed.

"I can wait. Where you going next?" He didn't shut off the van.

"Police station," I lied over my shoulder as I worked the combination lock then raised the overhead door. The indirect glow of the headlights made it much brighter than my usual visits. I didn't need much light anyway; I knew where every item was and how to maneuver around the chaos.

The paper bag went in the back corner. It looked like clutter to the casual eye. (Would a casual eye ever see it?) I opened the green metal box beside it with a half turn of the key I had left inserted there. The letter and invoice went into it. I transferred $75,000 to the box from "my" suitcase. Before closing the luggage, I duct-taped another key to its inside lip. I slipped its twin into my pocket.

The thin metal handle of the box felt sharp on the crease of my fingers. I swung it slowly in a little arc and tested its weight while looking back into the unit before leaving, making sure everything felt right. That's when he spoke. Of course, I had heard him and been waiting for this.

"Why'd you make me do it, Myx?"

Bindy stood silhouetted there at the entrance, the headlights still

MIRACLE MYX ■ 193

angled behind him. Gentle air currents brought in the peppery smell from the Smith & Wesson Model 10 revolver in his hand. This was a .38 caliber. The peppery smell? It had been fired recently. All four inches of its black barrel were aimed at my chest. I took one slow sidestep to my right. It followed.

"Only you knew, and you told somebody who wanted to hurt me and Miriam. He would have killed Miriam. Hector would have killed her like he killed Shelly and Dragon if I didn't do what he said."

Only I knew? Knew what?

I felt like I should know, but that ache of my recent forgetfullnesses returned and made me sick in a whole new way—a pressure in my throat that made me want to gag. With a gun pointing at me, I decided I would save that for later and just concentrate now on surviving.

His hand kept flexing on the gun handle. It shook each time. I hoped he didn't flex his index finger, his trigger finger.

During one of my sleepless and more leisurely nights, I had estimated eight feet to be the maximum distance from which I could rush a gun aimed at me and have a reasonable chance of not getting shot. I was quick and able to read somebody's reactions well.

I was eleven feet from Bindy.

"I knew I'd find you. I knew you'd be out tonight."

I'm out every night.

"When you showed up this afternoon, I figured it was all over. If Miriam hadn't been there, I would have got this done right then. I would have ..."

Bindy brought his left hand to his face, and it was lost in his darkness. But the motions suggested to me that he was wiping tears.

"I had to kill him. Hector. I had to."

"We can fix this, Bindy. You're no killer. You did what you had to do." My voice was white.

I wasn't just playing along, even though that would have been a good idea in this situation. Reflecting back, his own words seemed a good plan.

"That hard-headed little bitch—he cut her. She wouldn't give him what he wanted. He had to go to Dragon. He would do the same thing to Miriam. He said that. That wasn't gonna happen. All I had to do was get the box. That's all. I couldn't, at least not last night, I couldn't."

Tough to read when you can't see someone's face, but his tone was escalating towards some climax. That climax would probably be a burning pain in my chest. Maybe I could change or delay that.

"Think of Miriam at home, Bindy. She wouldn't want this."

"I *was* thinking of her. Thinking when he pushed this gun in my face. That animal looked so surprised when I hit him and grabbed it, and more surprised when it went off." He laughed with no joy.

"You cut off his prick too?" I asked this out of curiosity before considering it might add weight to the wrong side of an already unbalanced mind.

"Yeah—I did it just like he did to Sam Powell's little slut, just like he told me he was going to do to Miriam. I wanted to send his cock to Powell so he could shove it up his ass one more time."

Now that seemed familiar—Powell, Bindy, Ramone ... they were all connected ... up the ass—but I couldn't remember. The bad feeling of not remembering was nicely dulled by the fact I was still in line with the open end of the gun. "You didn't do anything wrong;

it was an accident." I didn't add that the mayhem of emasculation could have been considered going over the line, no matter what the provocation.

"It's all wrong, Myx. All because of you. Too smart. You know so much about so much and you let us all sweat. Why'd you tell? Everybody would be happy if I put a bullet in a snitch like you."

"Everybody" was an exaggeration because that wouldn't have pleased me at all.

"But now I know I can't do that." The words were slow and tired. "I just know I can do this." Bindy bent his elbow and pressed the gun to his head. I wondered if he closed his eyes like I had with Rico's gun. I couldn't see.

The hammer started to go back as his finger tightened. That's when the metal box arrived. It sent the gun skidding on the pavement outside, finally stopping on the poorly landscaped grass in the dark.

I had lobbed it while taking one step forward, hoping to hit him just hard enough to knock it away.

Bindy squawked and held his wrist. He looked down near his feet for the gun, but it was out there lost for now. Without another look or word to me, he turned, ran to the van, and drove away.

There goes my ride.

Without the headlights, it was dark while my eyes adjusted. My metal box was easy to find; it was there beside the entrance. The gun took a few minutes. After putting on another pair of gloves, I wiped it clean of prints (including the bullets) with a paper towel from a roll I kept there. I opened the box, threw the gun on top of the money and locked it. This went into a small blue backpack. It also held some graphic porn magazines that I could act embarrassed about if searched—a diversion that had worked once.

I threw some extra pairs of latex gloves in before walking to Dunkin' Donuts.

It was a nice night for a walk.

It was pleasant to be outside.

It was good to still be alive.

I had finished my coffee and bagel when Mrs. Powell pulled up in her silver RX300 Lexus. When I heard the locks click open, I got in and handed her a bag.

"Medium coffee, light and extra sugar, and a corn muffin," I said.

"How did you know? That's my favorite." She hadn't spoken much yet since she awoke, and her voice was still warming up.

"I'm good at guessing." Real good after I read someone's preferences in a diary.

"Let's get this done."

"You don't want to waste that after I spent my allowance on it." My allowance was still coming from the suitcase. I wouldn't mention that part.

"Can you drive?" She tipped her head downward. I was almost looking through her eyebrows into those blue eyes, a little red still from the lack of sleep.

"Legally, no. Safely, yes."

"Let's switch." She started over the console and I threw my stuff in the back barely before she rested her butt on my lap. I turned my hips and slid her into my seat just as my crotch was awakening. I made what I would call a graceful climb into her driver's seat. It was very warm.

I put the car in drive and got off Main Street. We didn't need any attention—back roads in the darkness suited us best.

Mrs. Powell ate and drank as we went. The coffee mixed with her smelled good in the small volume of the car.

Between sips she asked, "You know who did it?"

"Yeah." That's all the talk we needed. I parked one street over. We got to Halpern's back door through the wooded lot behind his house. I held Mrs. Powell's hand so she wouldn't stumble on the thin vines and fallen branches. The moon gave enough light.

Before leaving the woods, I opened the backpack and pulled out two pairs of gloves. I made sure she didn't see the porn magazines. No sense this thing backfiring on me.

"Put these on." I led by example and then helped her.

Once inside, I put my finger to my lips and listened. No sound, and everything was just as I had left it.

I pulled out one of the three remaining kitchen chairs. "Sit here while I check."

Sarge was still resting. He didn't seem to mind handling the Smith & Wesson (including the bullets). I "hid" it upstairs in the gun room.

Although this only took a few minutes, Mrs. Powell was noticeably nervous and fidgeting when I got back to the kitchen. I guess she wasn't used to breaking and entering, then making herself at home in a strange house while contemplating an execution for revenge.

She whispered, barely audible, "Whose house is this?"

"Brian 'Sarge' Halpern." I spoke in a normal tone.

"The carpenter?" Her voice was louder, but still not normal. "He killed Shelly?"

I wanted to say it was going to look like that. Instead, I answered with, "He's a killer, many times over."

I put my hands on her knees after I crouched so our eyes were nearly level. "We can leave right now. I know what you want to do, but it's a hard, hard thing. There's something here you shouldn't see. Something no one should ever have to see."

Mrs. Powell never blinked. The merciless set to her face made me wonder for a second if *I* would be safe after she did her business.

"Okay." I stood and took her hand. She did need guidance in such an intoxicating setting and circumstance. As we approached the open door to the sisters' room, I said, "Stay at this angle and don't look into the room." I wanted her to see only Sarge sagging there against the wall.

She stepped in front of me, but I gripped the waistband of her Paige Adams jeans, my fingers curled inside, so I could restrain her if needed.

Sarge was still unmoving, slumped at odd angles. She looked at him a long time before taking a step forward. I held and her jeans stretched taut.

"Let me go, Myx." Her right hand gently removed mine. The reflected shine of the white room lit her face as she squared in the doorway. Those blue eyes were snapping from one point to another. She concentrated on each of them, and then the tears were falling without any sounds. Steady streams.

"They are …"

"Yeah, the five sisters."

She rested her bowed head in one hand, the palm covering her eyes. "Those poor girls … poor girls."

"They'll be getting home now. Finally." This seemed like too little to say, but it was all I had.

"The other case?"

"Next victim, I guess." No need to mention my refusal to

cooperate.

"Is he dead?"

"No. Drugged. Drugged just like they were."

Mrs. Powell walked with deliberate intention towards Sarge. The white latex gloves looked unnatural in combination with her short sleeves. But I guess everything was unnatural here. Maybe because I had them on so often, I considered mine to look kind of sporty.

Her kick was strong and well-aimed. He caught it in the ribs. The exertion forced a sound that was half grunt, half scream from her throat. Sarge didn't bother to respond.

"How should I do this?" She looked at me, but pointed at Sarge. I knew what she meant. She was asking how to commit murder.

This is where a boy should talk some sense into an emotionally distraught mother who has lost a child, gotten very little sleep, and then been thrown into an alien and frightful environment.

"You can hit him with that," I said, pointing with my chin to the broken chair leg on the floor. "I did."

She followed my cue and then looked back at me. "We could burn the whole place." I gestured towards the girls with my eyes.

"Or—he has a mean-looking knife and a bunch of guns upstairs." I sounded matter-of-fact. I waved, invited her into the hallway, then showed her the gas cylinder. "This is carbon monoxide. You can shut the door, turn this valve, and he'll never wake up again."

She put her left hand on the valve and left it there. She went back to the doorway and looked at him, then returned to finger the valve, but never turn it. I didn't speak.

After a time she looked up, away from the valve. "You knew, didn't you—that I couldn't do it? That I couldn't kill?"

"Yeah, but *you* didn't. You might have carried that with you a long time."

Mrs. Powell rested her head against the wood paneling and closed her eyes. "You're not just a kid, are you?"

Maybe I had graduated from being a little shit to her. "I guess nobody wants to be *just* anything." I took her hand off the valve, and led her towards the back door.

"Aren't I failing Shelly?" She had that sound you speak when comfortable in bed and saying your last thoughts before easing into sleep.

"You're proving she had a mother she could be proud of."

I guided her through the woods and held her close once when she stumbled. She stripped her gloves off before we left the protection of the trees and got in the Lexus. I left mine on—miles to go …

The driver's window came down after she started the car. I leaned in. The dash lights mottled her pretty face.

"I never fucked Scrappy Burnett."

"I know." My voice was white.

Her head was tilted up, lips inviting. I leaned further and kissed her cheek.

Before driving away, she asked, "What about him?"

Shelly's mother wanted closure—okay, she wanted Halpern dead, dead, and dead. My words (I made sure there were jagged angles in my tone) wouldn't disillusion her. I straightened up, softly tapped the roof twice, and said, "I got plans for Sarge."

Chapter Twenty-One

The woods tasted earthy on the way back. It had rained two days before; the ground was still damp in hollows and under fallen trees. My concentration had been centered on Mrs. Powell during my previous trips through.

I had left the back door unlocked. Time to get Sarge up.

The smell of burning hair made me scrunch my face and cough once. I played the flame from my lighter back and forth under Sarge's elbow until he jerked awake. In some small, overheated blast furnace of a cell in hell, maybe Malik was smiling. I rubbed my own left elbow as I reminisced.

He finally could say, "You bastard, you bastard!"

I didn't know who my father was, so I offered no argument.

"I couldn't find the $4000 dollars. Where is it? Give it to me and I'll let you go." You can imagine what my voice looked like.

His faced changed. There was hope, and a slyness too. "Let me go and I'll give it to you."

"No, you tell me first." This was my last negotiation before I caved into him—I wanted to appear at least a little bit convincing.

He shook his head. "Okay," I said. I held up the Beretta I had hidden in his office during Mrs. Powell's visit, flipped off the safety so he could see the motion, then slid his work boots to his free hand.

"Pull those on."

After reaching for the right one, he winced and let out a piercing groan as he felt the pain for the first time.

Through clenched teeth he grunted, "What did you do, kick me in the ribs when I was out and defenseless?"

"No." This was technically correct.

When he finished (and it was no easy task for him), I slid the handcuff key from its resting place near the doorway floor to just within his reach. I congratulated myself on a nice shuffleboard shot. He unlocked his bad wrist and staggered up, sliding against the wall for support. That thigh bruise was painful. Too bad.

"The money's in the office." When we got there, he said, "Turn around while I get it." He didn't want me to see his secret drawer. Old habits …

"Yeah, like *that's* gonna happen." I hoped I sounded smart and trendy.

"I got more than what I promised you hidden here. How do I know you just won't take it?"

He was making this harder than it should be. I had to be considerate of his position, though, and decided to play some more.

"A deal's a deal!" Just a naïve youth, that's me.

"I don't trust you."

"Picture this headline in the *Miracle Daily News*: Kid Kills Killer With Six Shots To The Face; Town Holds Big Parade For Him." I shifted the Beretta's trajectory from the center of his chest to his head. I was counting on him not suspecting I was too modest to be in a parade.

The drawer came out and apart. He split the money. I counted it, smiling, not with greed, but because I thought it was a nice touch. I even got a little too close and seemingly distracted to play the part. He didn't make a move on me though. Pain must make you more cautious.

"You ruined everything."

"Some things need ruining," I said.

"I have to take this stuff with me." He pointed to the rest of the contents of the drawer."

"You can take anything but weapons or the sisters' belongings." I wasn't playing here.

Sarge hobbled around, assembling his getaway kit into a small green nylon duffel.

"I need some time," he said, and then licked his lips in anticipation.

I pulled out my cell phone, saw that out here I again had a signal, and held it up to him. "I'm going to watch you leave. If I see you even hit your brakes, I call 911. I'll stay here for two hours, then I call 911 from your phone and leave. That's how long you have—two hours. You try to come back, get back in here …" I raised the gun, showed the profile of it to him, and then pointed it back to his chest.

He nodded. "That's enough."

He had a plan. That's okay.

It was barely dawn, not that light yet. He didn't touch his brakes even when rounding the corner in that black truck. Maybe he took driving lessons from Kat.

I put the keys on the desk, the Beretta upstairs, left the front door ajar, ate some more chicken, and exited through the back door with my backpack.

I knew he wouldn't return. I would make that call later, just not from there.

I stripped off my gloves in the woods, then jogged to Bindy's home. I hadn't run yet today. At first, it had been hard to keep track of the days as they went by without a sleep interval. Now it was natural to remember what happened when.

More than usual had happened in the past twenty-four hours.

I put my gloves on and was careful not to make any noise while climbing the stairs to Bindy's door. He was home; both his car and the van were here. I didn't exactly want to surprise him, but I didn't exactly want him prepared to try to kill me again.

I was a little disappointed I didn't need the key I had made— his door was unlocked. I listened before entering. No sounds of movement. There was enough light to move quickly. I went for Bindy's room, listened at the closed door, turned the doorknob, and opened it a sliver.

Bindy had told me he kept in condition by hitting the heavy bag that hung in his room, hooked to a beam.

I could see the beam. The bag was on the floor; Bindy had replaced it with himself.

I rushed to him, still making no noise, and started to lift his weight to take him down. But I could feel I was too late. His life had fallen past his body. I released him, stepped back from his swaying form, and looked into his open eyes.

The glow room?

The braided nylon cord he used was bright yellow, and made slow squeaking sounds as it rubbed over the hook in the beam. A human pendulum. I stopped the swinging with my right hand, and left it there on his arm a moment. He was still warm.

I searched his room, but found nothing that would give me even a hint to what he had been talking about. I looked at him.

Why'd you blame me, Bindy?

Miriam had the covers pulled up to her neck. She slept on peacefully. I stood in her doorway a long time, thinking that today was going to be the worst of her life. Her brain didn't know yet the tragedy that waited for her in the other room.

Maybe she was dreaming a happy dream. Maybe it would be better if she never woke up. I thought about that more than I should have before shutting the door on her last good sleep.

I stuffed Sarge's $4000 into an envelope and "hid" it under Bindy's socks in the second drawer of the dresser. Some were mended.

I wrote a note to Miriam at that same kitchen table where they had shared their meals. I had seen Bindy's writing often enough to make it perfect. What do you say other than you can't go on ... but that you love her? Miriam was a sweetheart—I hoped I said enough.

It was light now. I didn't want to be seen leaving, so I took an extra moment to feel outside before I went out the door. There's a pressure in my throat when someone looks in my direction. I can sense it before I'm recognized usually. I felt no pressure.

I kept hidden anyway until I was a few streets from Bindy's.

"This better be important." Kat's voice was throaty and angry. I had gotten her cell phone number when I went through her bag for the camera. (She carried two condoms, too.)

"Mornin', Kitty." I sounded more enthusiastic than I felt. I'm good at faking.

"Myx? Is it morning?"

Unlike most people you see on a cell phone, I was keeping my attention on my surroundings as I walked back to Martin Aubrey's computer at Blended Willows. Maybe because, unlike others, my surroundings could sometimes turn instantly harmful to a defenseless young boy like me.

"Wouldn't call unless I was desperate for your help. Need a big favor. And I thought to myself, why not ask the prettiest girl I know?"

"You're shittin' me, right?" She sounded more normal now.

"Too early for flattery?"

"Never too early. What do you want?"

"You know Worcester at all?" I knew she took dance classes there. The second biggest city in Massachusetts had a lot to offer that small towns didn't.

"Yeah, pretty good."

"I want you to drop something off at the Worcester Bus Terminal."

"That doesn't seem very exciting." She sounded disappointed. I think Kat had a taste for action.

"Important and exciting are sometimes different only because of time," I said.

"Kinda early for that Zen crap."

"Never too early!" I laughed; luckily, she laughed too. "Meet me outside of Blended Willows. How long?"

"Give me time to piss. Half hour. And Myx—cut the Kitty shit."

"Meowww." I hung up.

I made a fried egg sandwich with ketchup at Aubrey's apartment— it was good and buttery. I drank cold milk. I always tried not to leave dishes for my hosts.

I wanted to look at that text file Shelly had saved on the compact flash card. Its small size (only one kilobyte) told me there wasn't much on it. It was a Yahoo! mail address: username and password.

I surfed to it and looked. This was Shelly's new diary. She emailed herself a daily entry. Some had attachments.

One attachment, a set of two photos, was especially interesting. Kat had talked about seeing a picture that looked like symbols on wood. Here was the one she saw, and the one she didn't. It was Sonnet's key taken apart before it was destroyed. These pictures were neither blurred nor overexposed. Good job.

Now I knew what the fourth symbol looked like. I could open the box … I hoped.

I surmised Shelly went to this version of a digital diary after my intrusion on her privacy, after I pinched her into easing up on Miriam.

Miriam.

I hoped she still slept.

Shelly talked about teaching her father a lesson on Founder's Day, but didn't give any details. I had that feeling, the feeling like I already knew the details, but couldn't focus the impressions enough to interpret them. Was there something to what Sarge said about Sonnet's miracle clouding me?

Wake up, Myx!

I smiled. I would love to sleep again, even for an hour. It felt good to say those words even as motivators. What did I have to do to get past these blind spots in my memory?

I pulled the card from Marty's (I always called him Mr. Aubrey to his face) computer, and left. It still smelled good in there from the fried eggs.

Kat's Neon already sat in the parking lot. I got in. She didn't turn off the car and kept the heater on low. It felt too warm for me, but my circulation wasn't just getting started for the day, either.

"Interesting night?" she asked.

"I kept busy."

"Radio says somebody stole Sonnet's box last night. You didn't do that, did you?"

"What? Where?" I didn't have to fake my perplexed tone.

"At Sonnet House, where else? Somebody broke in and took it."

Kat sounded smug that she knew something I didn't.

Someone's got the fake box. "Anybody hurt?" I hoped Brass was either sleeping or at Elmira's when this happened.

"Didn't say."

She cleared her throat, hesitated, and then said, "Speaking of getting hurt, they say you can't be killed."

"Not yet." I reconsidered my words and decided they spoke more truth than I had intended. I just admitted to myself that I didn't take my previous experiences for granted and I didn't count on evading my final and permanent death in the future. Maybe the near future.

I unzipped the backpack and showed her the metal box. I didn't show her the porn (that would have been detrimental to my image, in my opinion). Some of the paint had been scraped off when it skidded on the pavement after hitting Bindy.

"This box goes in this locker," I said while I pulled the locker key from my right pocket and showed her the number imprinted on it. "Worcester Bus Terminal."

"What's in it?" she asked as she tucked the key in that same bag she had the night before.

I resisted quoting what that famous philosopher, Mr. Damianzo, had told me the previous day when I had asked the same question about the suitcase.

"What you don't know you can't tell."

"Don't you trust me?" She sounded on the verge of indignant.

"Kat, of all the people I know, I called you for help. This is important, and it's got to be done now—and it's got to be done right. Does that sound like I don't trust you?" That was my best answer without an answer. She didn't push it.

"What do you want me to do with the key?"

"Stick it deep in your trash when you get home. So nobody finds it," I said.

"Do you want me to wipe my fingerprints off this before I leave it?"

She was really into this. "Only for practice; it won't matter." I took her right hand and dabbed it on the box, covering it with her prints.

"Could I get in trouble for this?"

The real answer was "no." I said, "Maybe."

Her eyebrows cycled up and down. She smiled, "They'll have to catch me though." I was beginning to like her.

Kat hesitated, licked her lips, and said, "They say you can remember everything—you can see stuff like it's right there again in front of you."

I wondered why she cared. "You shouldn't be listening to *they* that much. And to tell you the truth, I've had trouble lately seeing certain things like I used to." Why was I explaining?

"I wouldn't worry. Maybe all you have to do is look a different way." She sounded sure, and somehow that made me feel better.

I reached for the door handle; it was cool and tasted sour with dull points. Kat stopped me by touching my left arm. "You going to Shelly's wake today? Closed casket."

I didn't like wakes. All that grief. I hadn't been to many, but maybe this was one I should attend. Kat, Mrs. Powell—would I make a difference? "Yeah, see you there."

I got out with my backpack, adding for her adventurous spirit, "Be careful."

She pulled away and out of sight, using all of her non-stopping skills.

Chapter Twenty-Two

Time to make my phone call; Halpern was probably Halders by now and scurrying for cover somewhere. I used the pay phone outside the library. It was on my way to the police station.

I'd been able to copy handwriting almost from the beginning of my synesthesia. The curves just felt right when I wrote them. Lately, I'd found if I could visualize a voice, see its form and force, I could constrict my throat in a way to kind of simulate it. I was getting pretty good at impersonation—both female and male. My best, in my opinion, were the new pope and Madonna.

The phone looked grimy, and the mouthpiece had flecks of food spattered on some of the little holes.

Shouldn't talk with your mouth full.

I used Madonna's voice for my call to the Fire Department. An anonymous call there was less suspicious, especially since there actually had been a fire inside Sarge's home. Beth Atkins, the dispatcher answered, "Miracle Fire Department, your call is being recorded."

"There's a fire at 247 Beverley Street. Hurry—fire, smoke—hurry! 247 Beverley Street! Fire!" I resisted singing some of the words, and just sounded excited.

Beth Atkins repeated the address, "247 Beverley Street. Please stay ..."

That's when I hung up. Firefighters would go in through the open front door and find the sisters, the police there to assist. Chief

Maldonato would find the gun and solve the shootings and the sisters' mystery all in one package. I would never tell that I wrapped it up and tied the bow. I could have been happier if that package with the bow satisfied me, too. Ramone killed Shelly and Dragon. Bindy killed Ramone, then himself. The murderers were dead. But it was still a mess. What had Bindy been talking about? He thought I was involved. Was someone framing me? And now, Sonnet's box was missing. I had the real box; it would take a lot of explaining if the wrong people (like the police) found that out.

Who had the fake box? It had to be Bindy who finally found the motivation to steal it. Who did he give it to? It hadn't been in his home or van or car.

I listened. Not a minute later, I heard the first blast of a siren. A fire engine. The second siren would be a cruiser. They were royal blue, those sounds—different shades, but the same color to me. They both got fainter and stopped.

I walked quickly and got to the police station before any news from Beverley Street reached them. There were three satellite trucks on Main Street. The press was here about the shootings. They were going to get more than that soon.

Sgt. Wayne looked the same as ever. I don't know if he ever slept or got tired, either. He shook his head when I walked in.

"Wish I could say I was glad to see you, Myx. Unless you have something special to add to this party, I'd advise you to keep out of the Chief's sight."

Sgt. Wayne looked down and then to me again. "You know Wallace Morton?"

He waited for my reaction. I gave none, and only said, "I call him Bindy." I didn't say "called," which would have given away what

I knew. "He's the newspaper guy and gives me rides at night. Good man." He may attempt to shoot you once in a while, but a good guy nonetheless. "Miriam. I go to school with her, his daughter."

The Sergeant nodded, and didn't look like he was going to add anything until I asked, "Why?"

"She found him swinging this morning."

"Nooo!" I had that sound of denial and disbelief we instinctively express when unpleasantly surprised by a death. So … Miriam was in pain already.

I shook my head and waited a moment before asking, "Sonnet House? What happened? Brass okay?"

Sgt. Wayne looked over his shoulder, making sure the Chief wasn't ready to chew ass. I could hear voices in his office. Was he trapped in there with reporters? He wouldn't like that much. Three unsolved murders brought a lot of attention and press. They would get a good story very soon.

Sgt. Wayne leaned on the counter and said, "Brass heard glass breaking, drew his gun, slipped and put a shot through a window, and hurt his back. He never saw who stole the box."

"He drew his gun?" I sounded impressed—and was.

Sgt. Wayne got that little grin I'd noticed when he caused someone discomfort. "Got word that a friend of yours wants to talk." He kept the grin and waited.

"I got a friend?" I was full of questions, it seemed.

"Johnny Bearcloud. Says he has something important to tell you."

The Indian.

I hadn't seen him since the trial. "Can't I just phone him?"

"Says face to face." The Sergeant was enjoying this.

"Hey—I'm not afraid of him … much! Will there be any 55-gallon drums close by?"

Sgt. Wayne laughed. "Want me to set it up?"

I nodded and he made a quick call. "Any time this morning. You know where Cedar Junction is? Walpole? Maybe you'll like it so much you'll stay. I know they're going to like seeing you there."

Why would hardened, long-term criminals at a Massachusetts correctional institute want to bother with a handsome boy owning a muscular butt like mine?

Just before the phone rang, Sgt. Wayne handed me a card the size of a store coupon. He had filled it out. "Show this; it'll get you in."

After he took the phone call, the one that I'm sure gave news of the sisters, I was forgotten by everyone. The station was electrified with the Beverley Street information.

I left as Sgt. Wayne told the Chief.

Not having a driver's license sucked.

I'd need a ride to Walpole, about a half hour away off Route 495.

I was still curious about Sonnet's box. The fake had been stolen, and I had the original. That would take some creative explaining if I got caught (which wasn't even last on my list of things to do today).

I might as well open it and be the first to learn the secret Sonnet had kept from us for 250 years.

There wasn't much traffic on a Sunday morning in Miracle. Mostly cars. No large trucks. Another siren had sounded in the distance. I could picture that Beverley Street was getting very busy.

I stopped at the All-Night mini-mart and bought some peace offerings for the Indian. I knew the clerk there. She had been robbed and beaten last year. The thieves threatened to come back and kill her. The police two towns over got an anonymous tip and found them asleep with guns and the cash and items they stole in a neat pile on their bed. I mean … that's what I was told.

Maybe I'd see them too at Walpole.

I didn't meet anyone on the way back to Miracle Self-Storage. This is where I had last seen Bindy alive. Since then, I had done all I could to keep him from being implicated in the murders—for his sake (he had been a friend), but mostly for Miriam.

I slid the door down behind me after flipping the overhead light on. The cement block smell inside sounded like a slow, continuous exhalation.

I took Sonnet's box from the Stop & Shop bag and shook it. No sound, no movement. It was heavy, as if solid wood.

Now that I had the four symbols from the key, this should be easy. I had seen the box before and had known all the symbols on it with one glance. But I had to look at it now to refresh my memory. Each of the six sides had a twelve by twelve parquet array. That should be so easy to remember.

What's wrong with you, Myx?

I realized now the key symbols were repeated twice on the box. Two of the six sides showed two key symbols apiece. The other four sides had one each.

I pushed them in all the different sequences I could formulate, and I formulated them all. I would have been frustrated if it hadn't been fun.

What if they all had to be pushed at once? One person could push four of them on three different sides. That meant I would need another person to push the other four. And that would mean I'd have to trust somebody to share two secrets: Sonnet's and the fact the missing box was in my possession.

I thought about this and threw Sonnet's box up with both hands, turning my wrists so it rotated swiftly in the air. I watched it revolve before I caught it and repeated the motion five times while thinking.

I knew who was going to help me open the box; I knew who I would trust.

But first, I had to get to Walpole while my pass was still valid. I also was curious: what could the Indian have to say after three years?

I dialed my cell phone.

"Red Top!"

"Cabbage! Road trip!" I said just as happily.

"No way, Myx."

"A friend of yours said you'd be glad to do it."

"And who's that?" Leo sounded as wary as he should have been. I've leaned on him a lot.

"Ben Franklin," I said.

"*The* Ben Franklin?" He was interested.

"The original. And, I'll buy breakfast."

"At IHOP?" He was hooked. The International House of Pancakes was his favorite. He loved their pumpkin pancakes with cinnamon sugar. I had to admit that sounded good to me too.

"Where are we going," he asked after giving the pancakes time to play across his mental movie theater.

"Scenic Walpole."

"Cedar Junction?" He was getting unhooked again. "You know I don't go near there since that … misunderstanding the state and me had."

"You can just sit in the car. Take something good to read. I have to talk with the Indian."

"Johnny Bearcloud? What if he kills you again?"

"I'll give you the hundred up front," I assured him.

"Oh, okay."

"Meet me at the Gibbs gas station in ten minutes." I hung up.

I took two hundred dollars in twenties from a green vinyl zippered case. It was a little bigger than a business envelope. Miracle Movement, the name of Bunny's dance business, was printed on the side. I usually took Ben Franklins from the suitcase and changed them for twenties at the Miracle National bank. I didn't want to cause suspicion by trying to spend hundred dollar bills around town. I hoped using the case helped the tellers believe I was doing business for Bunny. I was always cautious. Now that I knew it was Mr. Damianzo's money and he selfishly wanted it back, I was glad that I had been.

I left the porn. I didn't think the guards at the prison would accept my explanations about it.

The sun rose higher and glinted with a squeal off the red top of his cab. Leo was a little early.

"Where do you get your money?" he asked as I showed him five twenties, folded them, and jammed them into his upturned palm.

"Hard work and frugal habits." I left out "confiscating millions from dead guys."

He rubbed his thumb over the bills. "Nothing feels as good as money," he smiled.

"You're a virgin, right?"

"What?"

"Nothing," I said. "Let's eat!"

The IHOP was clean and crowded. Sunday mornings were busy for them. It was hot and steamy inside and full of family noises. During the week, there were more seniors eating. On weekends, parents gave the kids a sweet treat with waffles and pancakes and French toast.

Families, maybe after church before going somewhere together. And here I was with smelly Cabbage, on my way to a prison to meet a guy who had killed me once.

I had the Supreme Ham and Three Cheese Omelette. Cabbage ordered the Breakfast Sampler. Pumpkin pancakes on the side for us both. We drained the carafe of coffee the chubby waitress had left.

Cabbage looked happy for the rest of our trip to Walpole. But he usually looked happy. Although he had cleaned the cab a bit, it still smelled. One step at a time, I guess.

"Were you out last night," I asked. Cabbage either saw or heard about everything that happened in town.

"Sure, until about two thirty."

"See anything?" I didn't look at him, but could feel conniving circuits processing during his hesitation. He stayed silent.

We approached Cedar Junction, a maximum security facility. Rolls of Constantine wire topped the gray fence surrounding it. The little razor blades reflected the sun with high red sounds. There was hurt there waiting to happen. I thought about how to get over the fence, while hoping I never had to.

I gave Cabbage the card Sgt. Wayne had filled out. He showed it to the guard at the gate, who directed us to the visitors' parking. Cabbage all of a sudden looked greasier and more nervous than usual.

As I got out, I said, "Awful to be stuck in here, wouldn't it?"

Maybe he would be more talkative on the way back.

The guards checked my backpack before escorting me to the visiting area. We passed the exercise yard and that part of the general prison population who were scheduled to use it.

When they saw me, the calls and whistles started. Then they increased in number and volume as more attention came my way. I guess they recognized my jovial personality. I "accidentally" dropped my backpack and picked it up stiff-leggedly, with my butt to them. I got up and showed them an exaggerated, shyly embarrassed "Ohhh!" expression that I almost covered with the fingertips of my left hand.

That's when I remembered an article I had read about a guy at a Philippines zoo. He had been teasing a bear through the bars and left without his arm. I resolved not to drop anything else, if I could help it.

The guard escorting me laughed and said, "You want to meet some of your new friends?"

"No time today. Maybe next visit we could play some tag out there." It looked like most of them wanted to tag me.

He led me to a large room with four gray metal tables. The tops were a darker gray material. It stung with fresh disinfectant.

One guard stood in a corner. He looked bored but attentive.

Two men faced each other and talked at the table to my right. They were arguing in low tones. One was an inmate. The other looked like a brother.

I sat on the thin-cushioned plastic seat only a few minutes before another guard escorted the Indian to the chair on the other side of my table.

No more long hair. It was buzzed, not shaved. There was the dark shadow of where hair could grow, given the freedom. He had put on weight, but not fat. They allowed these guys to work out. Didn't that make them more dangerous? If I had a vote, I would pen them up so they'd be like veals when they got out.

He wasn't as dark as when I had seen him last. Must spend a lot of time indoors.

Seeing him made me think up ways to get out of there, if needed. I had wondered what I'd feel when I saw him. I guess I was a little angry, a little scared, and a little relieved. After all, he was only a man. I had been eleven when he pressed me down into that water. Until now, I had always remained eleven when I thought of him.

The relieved part of me started to take over.

He looked at me a long while; I let him. His dark eyes didn't move much and just rested. He gave off a low "wah wah wah" sound. Controlled power.

Finally he said, "My ass still hurts."

"I have that effect on a lot of people."

It took a moment, and then he coughed out a juicy laugh. "I bet," he said.

He was in no rush and kept a relaxed stare covering me. I knew he wasn't just looking; he was experiencing something, drinking something in.

"You've grown." His voice had the same bubbles I remembered from that day.

"That's what happens if you stay alive." I was surprised at the way I said it.

"You're angry. You should be. I held you until I felt your spirit leave." He looked down at his veined hands, which gripped the edge of the table. I wondered if I could tear myself loose from them this time. I hoped I would never have to.

He looked up and said, "You wonder now …"

Somehow he was reading me, maybe like I read others. "Yeah, I wonder how I would get away if you jumped over the table," I said.

"You would run?" The Indian had the start of a grin.

"I would fight with more speed and less guts this time." I felt pride that I wasn't as foolhardy any more.

"There was the girl then. You couldn't run."

"Yeah, I couldn't." Then I added, "But I wanted to," as if that made me smarter.

"What would you do differently now?" He was playing with me.

"Stab higher," I said.

He smiled, showing those stained teeth, and then straightaway began explaining the reason for his invitation. "I had three dreams this week. Do you dream?"

"I haven't slept since that day, that day with you. So, I just have daydreams." I guess I was still angry.

The Indian ignored me and continued, "I had a fever when I was ten. I was ill for many days. During it I dreamt of a wide stream that glowed. I stepped in and the waters flowed in both directions from me, as if flooding from below where I stood. Then I was aware of a figure who also glowed."

"Man or woman?" I asked. He had my attention.

The Indian shrugged and shook his head. "It drew water from the stream in cupped hands and I drank from them. Then I awoke with no fever; my mother was bathing my face."

He seemed in no hurry although I knew we had a limited time here.

"After that, I had dreams of nature, of symbols. My people told me the spirit was talking and wanted me to tell my dreams, that it was important to interpret them for the tribe's good. This scared me. Scared me so much I lied. I said the dreams left. They didn't, not for a while. Then I dreamt the water stopped flowing. It sat there, dark and full of debris. My last dream showed no water; it had dried and left a dusty furrow."

He took his hands from the table and rested them in his lap. I hoped he wasn't reaching for anything in his clothes. The rhythm of his voice was soothing me into a relaxation I couldn't afford. I drew myself back and asked, "And this week, dreams again?"

Just a small affirming motion of his head, "After twenty-five years. I had said no to the spirit and it left me, left me to this life." He waved around us with a sweep of his right hand. "This is only meant for me because I abandoned my call."

I was curious … and surmising. "The dreams were about me?"

He looked up to his left as he spoke. He was remembering images. "The first one, my stream was still dry but another trickle of water poured from the horizon to my feet and stopped there. A figure with a staff walked toward me. A serpent attacked and he struck it with the staff."

"Was it me?" I asked.

"It didn't look like you, but I know it was your spirit, the one I felt that day, and the one before me now."

"Do you know what it means?"

The Indian shrugged and his shirt stretched around the muscles of his shoulders and neck. "The second dream is dark. The same figure must climb into deeper darkness, into a womb where life ceases until reborn in light and worth."

"I'm staying out of where my life ceases if I have a choice." I thought I sounded very sure of myself.

"Spirit gives a choice but makes clear what the right direction is. I didn't follow it. I knew, but didn't follow. My life was never the same because I wasn't true to my gift," he said leaning forward. This was the first time he exhibited emotion. His words were green and red, but of a light shade showing me he believed them.

"The third dream, I'm looking up, the bluest sky. Two specks become larger. Two eagles flying, one larger, one higher. They fly together then clash." He put the palm of his right hand down onto the back of his left and gripped hard. "One falls, the other catches it."

"Any ideas?"

He shook his head. "I feel now I've done what I needed. You must do the rest. You must live the life you know. I continue this." He obviously meant the prison, but which one?

"In the last dream, where did you stand?"

The Indian frowned and said, "My eyes were in the sky."

"That doesn't mean you can't remember more," I said. I knew all my senses worked even when I concentrated on one of them. "Can you look down in your memory?"

"No, my eyes are raised."

"How about sound?"

His eyes shifted to his left. He was listening to the dream. "Yeah, yeah. There's wind and something else."

"How about feeling. Can you feel where you stand?"

Johnny's eyes went to his right and lowered to the floor. Feeling this time. "It's water. I'm standing in water. The sound is its flow. I'm in the stream." His eyes were glistening.

I knew we had both just learned something, I could feel it in a dozen different ways that didn't make much sense to me yet. Johnny

Bearcloud was still in a prison of concrete and metal bars, but freed from confines of less substance, yet greater strength—his spirit. I too felt a letting go, but decided to give myself room to translate that into something useful.

"Time's up, Johnny," the guard in the corner called out and rapped on the door. Another guard, his escort, came in and over to the table.

I lifted my backpack, showing the guard. "I have something for him."

The guard looked inside first. "Okay."

I pulled out three cartons of Camels, no filters. That's what he smoked on that day. He still had the smoke on him today, so I knew he hadn't quit. Then I took out a Snickers, large. Finally, a bottle of Polar Spring water.

He looked puzzled for a second, and then laughed, "No pussy plugs?"

He gathered his things off the table, threw his head back, and whooped loudly that same sound I had remembered every day since he killed me. It startled the guard.

My hair stood on end.

Chapter Twenty-Three

I blew kisses to the inmates on the way out. What the hell! The guy in the Philippines had lost only one arm.

Cabbage was reading Kafka's *Metamorphosis* when I got back to him. What was I missing?

He looked up, tucked the book under his seat and said, "I thought about leaving you here twice."

"That all? You wouldn't have gotten far without this." I handed him the card I had used for entry. It had a timed red stamp and a signature on the back now. We needed that to escape.

Leo was calmer on the return trip to Miracle. Distance from the prison agreed with his disposition. I wanted to know what he had seen last night; now seemed the right time to ask.

"So, you were out late." I'd circle it a while, if I had to.

He tapped the steering wheel while thinking, and then asked, "Ben Franklin got any friends?"

Bless his heart. He was trying to squeeze me. "Sure, but so do I," I said. Such a simple statement. Anyone who reads Kafka should be able to wrest all the subtle implications from it.

"Okay, okay; no need for mean." He did understand. "I saw a blue Neon that was speeding. Young girl driving."

That would be Kat.

"Let's see." He was thinking. "There was a fender bender on East Main. Nobody I knew. They didn't call the police, so it couldn't have been much. And I saw Bindy's van a few times. Funny thing is, he's never out on Saturday night, at least not in the van."

"You know Bindy's dead, right?" He didn't and I felt it, but it felt kinder to ask the question instead of pelting him with it point-blank.

"What?" He looked at me, his mouth open. There's that disbelief. Cabbage and Bindy were divers of the same depths beneath Miracle's surface. I was down there too. "How?" He was managing single words now.

"Looks like suicide." At least that's what I had decided when I watched him oscillate on that hook.

"Oh man, not Bindy." There's the denial. "Just last night, there he was, and he's gone. You're not shittin' me, are you?" More disbelief.

"No. Where'd you see him?"

"Driving on Main Street a couple times. Then he was parked in back of a blue Buick Regal. That was on South Street."

Blue Buick Regal. I saw one the night before. I didn't list it, or Bindy's van, at the police station.

Why not?

"What time?"

"Late, Myx. Just before I went to sleep."

I asked about the Sonnet House robbery. He didn't know any more than I did, and much less than I suspected about it. I didn't mention Sarge or the five sisters. He'd find out today from his usual and varied sources, as would the rest of Miracle through more conventional means. There should be lots of reactions. Miracle had become the center of a regional, and most likely a national, story of fear and sorrow.

Cabbage stopped the cab in front of the pawn shop. Home. I got out and handed him another twenty through the passenger's window. "Thanks," I said.

"What's this for?"

"Books ... and cologne," I said. I thought saying "deodorant" would have been too direct.

Benny and Bunny were out. They usually had Sunday brunch at the Bella Vista Ristorante in Framingham. That gave me time for a nice hot, leisurely shower.

Seeds. The water felt like seeds. I could feel each one in succession, warm and hard before they broke. The steam reconstituted the smell of the fire that had been trapped there in my nostrils. "Sorry," I said again, picturing Laurie Augdon, the sister I had kindled. I recognized them all from the news when they each disappeared. I had a lot to wash off since the last time I had cleansed.

I didn't bother trying to relax on my bed. I had a feeling I wouldn't be thinking of *that* day and the Indian as often now that I had seen him again. Maybe I finally could settle during my relaxation exercises. Not today, though—Shelly's wake.

Instead of my usual uniform of black jeans and a T-shirt, I put on a blue short-sleeved dress shirt and a pair of navy Stressfree classic fit pants from the Gap. I debated a bit before completing the outfit with a tie. The black Tube Moccasins I had gotten from Payless felt hard on my feet. I liked my New Balance running shoes more—not only for comfort, but for safety. Maybe I wouldn't have to run, jump, climb, evade, or scurry while I had these shoes on today. I hoped not.

Bunny kept a box of assorted cards in her bedroom dressing table. As I sat there and wrote out my sympathy card, I heard my adopted parents get home. Bunny's low voice was reprimanding Benny for something, no doubt deservedly. Benny would be perfect by now if he had heeded all of her advice and direction.

Benny wasn't perfect and never would be.

I didn't bother moving and finished. I wasn't allowed in here.

"Didn't I tell you not to come in here? I don't want you in my things." Bunny had her hands on her hips, and a tiny squint that went perfectly with her frown.

I sealed the card, got up and said, "Shelly Powell's wake. Needed a card." I walked past her and into the hall.

"Wait," she said with her clipped commandant tone. I was ready for another lecture. I knew I wasn't supposed to be in there; I could have left in time; I hadn't bothered.

Before I could pivot, I felt her fingers tucking the back of my tie further under my collar. She turned me around and made one more adjustment to my shirt, and then tightened the tie a little. She patted it flat.

After one last inspection, she said, "You look good. Go." When I hesitated, she again said, "Go." This time with a graceful curling gesture of her arm and hand that showed me the way out.

I went. It was the first compliment she ever gave me. It felt better than it probably should have.

Calling hours at the Saybrook Funeral Home were from 11 A.M. to 2 P.M. By the time I walked there, it was a little past one. There were a lot of cars parked on the street. Shelly would draw not only family, but also many from the town because her father was a Selectman.

It was bronze-colored, the closed casket. I think Shelly would have liked it. There were lots of pretty flower arrangements. Their smell mingled and would have been pleasant if not for the occasion.

Mrs. Powell sat closest to Shelly, the first in a line of chairs against the wall on the right. The rest of the family filled out the row. Two of her sisters were there, and although they were younger, neither had the same beauty.

I stood in line and took my turn kneeling before the casket. I didn't pray but wondered silently instead. After a moment, I got up, placed my card in a tray on the right, and waited to work down the line of family. One of Mrs. Powell's sisters dabbed at her eyes with a tissue. A handsome man with dark, shiny hair patted her back. Husband, I assumed.

"Sorry." I was saying that a lot today. Mrs. Powell grasped my hand with both of hers when I shook it. She remained seated for a second then got up, pulling me to a deserted corner of the room.

She bent close to my ear and whispered, "They didn't find him."

I tilted my head, raised my eyebrows in an exaggerated *what-do-you-think-happened-to-him?* look and said just as softly, "They probably won't."

Her face hardened and she watched my eyes for longer than I would have liked. I made an effort to make them show what she wanted. She finally nodded. I'd let her assume whatever freed her to feel best.

"Thank you," she said, leaned and kissed my cheek, then walked to her seat. She said a few words to her husband, who glared at me.

If I had my New Balances on, I could have scurried away in time. That's what I told myself anyway. As it was, I stayed there in the corner as Mr. Powell got up and came at me with his lips tight and right hand clenched. I wasn't going to get socked here, was I?

Close to my ear, he gritted out, "You have a lot of balls coming here."

"Thanks. Paying my respects." He was angry, grieving—and my

presence wasn't helping. We didn't like each other. I should leave.

"You're messing where you don't belong. I don't care what Patty says, things are going to get very unpleasant for you."

I didn't know what that meant or why he had taken such an active dislike to me. This is where I should offer some kind of olive branch, spread some oil on the water.

"I know you get off on uncircumcised cocks—just like Hector Ramone's missing one," I said calmly with just enough volume to ensure only he would hear.

He wobbled and might have drooped against the wall if I hadn't steadied him with my hand on his elbow. He recovered nicely though and tore his arm from my grasp.

"What part of 'go fuck yourself' don't you understand?" he asked a little too loudly.

"The 'yourself' part," I said more quietly. I think he did hear that before he hurried back to his seat. He and Mrs. Powell had a few words before she looked up at me.

I looked back and shrugged with an exaggerated puzzled look. I think I did an adequate job of appearing innocent.

Well, that was unpleasant, more for him, I'm sure, than for me.

I heard him come up behind me long before he pinched my neck in his big hand. He shook me a little, like it was a friendly greeting, but he wanted it to hurt. I admit it did a bit in that second before I turned in a way that let me slip easily out of his hold. Break towards the thumbs is my motto.

Artie Akavelian had been the starting right defensive tackle for Miracle High all four years. He had been Cyndi Bellacqua's boyfriend the last two.

"Hi, Artie," I said with more up-beat than was called for. This was the first time we had ever spoken. But Artie and the jock table had murmured some comments and laughed when I went by in the cafeteria several times. Passing judgments and enjoying them was a good way to get through the lunch period, I guess.

"Outside," he said with a tight, and maybe I was reading too much into it, mean grin.

Cyndi had appeared behind him. "Come on, Arts. Not here. Don't be like that." She looked good in her straight, dark blue dress. She also looked either worried or scared; I didn't know her well enough yet to tell for sure. I concluded we both didn't know.

Maybe he didn't hear her pleading. I'd help by repeating, "Yeah, Arts. Not here. Don't be like that."

He obviously heard me. His face reddened and he showed his teeth when he said again, "Outside."

Billy Westlake was the team's quarterback and Kat Andrews' boyfriend. He walked close, put his hand on Artie's shoulder, and leaned towards me. "Let's go and talk." Kat was behind him. She didn't look worried or scared. She gave me a big smile and thumbs up. She had completed her mission successfully.

How dare she not be concerned about my welfare here!

I waved goodbye to Mr. and Mrs. Powell before my new friends escorted me out the door, through the parking lot, and onto the grass behind the funeral home. The girls followed.

"Cyndi told me about what you did," Artie said as he gave me a push on the chest that sent me back a step, "that you like to take pictures."

"Oh, that's just a hobby—I'm not a professional or anything." I smiled. This admission didn't calm Artie down in the least.

He looked at Billie and said, "We have a real smart guy here. He's gonna be a lot smarter after I teach him about never taking pictures again." He grabbed my tie, pushed my chest with his fist, and then yanked me back yo-yo–like when I reached its length.

That's my good tie!

"Never?" I asked. That must have been the wrong question. He got angry and repeated the push and jerk of my tie.

Other than the Indian, I'm the quickest person I know. Maybe even quicker than Johnny now. I had been stuck at eleven years old when thinking about him, until today. My synesthesia kinesthetically coordinates my body. The same reflexes that allow me to move in silence also let me pinpoint my strength. I coordinated planting my left foot, turning my hips to the right, and swinging my left fist with the return force Artie gave me by his pull on my best tie. I caught him exactly where I wanted: under the jaw on the right side of his neck. A chart I had seen called my target the sternocleidomastoid muscle (the big one on the side of your neck; the one that tries to protect your carotid artery). Hitting bone only hurt your own hand; I had learned that and found other more effective methods of retaliation.

I heard Cyndi give a little scream.

His head folded to his shoulder, sandwiching my hand briefly. Before he sat down, I pulled the length of my tie like a handkerchief out of a magician's hand from Artie's ever-loosening grip.

I could have run away on the way out, and seeing him there made me regret my decision not to. Maybe I was just showing off for Kat. But here I was, so I continued.

Billie had taken a step in my direction. I pointed at his face and said, "Don't try it." Something either in my tone or expression made him stop.

Artie's mouth was wide open; his hands splayed on the grass

steadied him. He would try to get up in a moment.

"Artie, can you hear me?" He looked straight ahead with unblinking eyes. I decided to just go ahead with my speech. "Artie, you try to get up and I'm going to kick you in the face. I'm going to make sure you don't get up. You understand?"

I think I saw a small nod. I gave him credit for it anyway. Having a good memory pays off sometimes. Well—all the time (which is why my recent lapses were a bummer). Chief Maldonato's computer, which I had harvested the day before, held an interesting file about Artie. Obviously, like a lot of things in a small town, it got suppressed.

"Artie, you rest there while I talk to you. You have a full football scholarship to Boston Catholic University. That's worth almost $200,000 for four years. You don't want to lose that. Three months ago, you were caught selling pot to an undercover cop. Nobody but our friends here," I waved at the other three, "ever has to learn about that—especially Anne McNamara in admissions." I had to go through her records one night last year when I was trying to find Thomas Alva (too many security cameras there for my liking). I talked to her that day when she told me all student information was confidential.

Artie looked like he understood. I'd finish up. "You don't want to have to work at your father's fruit stand the rest of your life, do you?" Artie's eyes now focused on me. He shook his head.

I stepped forward and extended my hand. He hesitated a second and reached out. He was a big mutant of a guy, over 290 pounds. I easily pulled him up.

"Tell you mother corn syrup gets out grass stains." I had read that but never tried it.

I looked at Cyndi. She had spilled my beans about her ass. Some girls can't keep a secret. Guys get jealous; it's the law.

I walked back to the parking lot. The others followed. It was Billy's turn. "You got nothing to threaten me with. I'll make your life miserable," he guaranteed.

A passing car almost masked a small tinkle from the asphalt. Kat had taken a chain from her neck and dropped it there. A class ring was attached.

"Don't bother, Billy. Go home." She marched over to me, took my arm, and we walked to the front door before she let go. "I didn't get a chance to say what I wanted to say to her yet."

It didn't matter much to me if she meant Shelly or Mrs. Powell. Probably Shelly. "Don't get caught for the Rosary."

"I know," she smiled.

"I need your help this afternoon," I said.

"Is it something mysterious, dangerous, and illegal?" she kidded with that eye-widening playful look I was getting fond of.

"Yeah," I said, raising my own eyebrows in response. My voice was white.

She started to go in, hesitated, turned back and said, "Last night, I dropped you off right near where they found those bodies today."

News travels in a small town. "Coincidence. Scary. You never know, do you?" My voice was no longer white. "I'll call you in an hour and a half."

"Should I dress for action?"

"You'd better," I cautioned.

Chapter Twenty-Four

The shadow of Saint Eulalia's Church felt cold as it covered me. I stopped so my face remained in the sun, and enjoyed feeling the difference. One was a taste of gritty chocolate and the other a thin saltiness. I moved back and forth a few times along the shadow's edge, immersing and emerging.

The church was only a few blocks from the Saybrook Funeral Home. I hadn't dropped in for a while. It was a good place to think at night, but I needed to think now: think about Sonnet's box, both the real one and the copy. I wanted to know what was in the box. With Kat's help, maybe that would happen very soon. Whoever had the copy, whoever Bindy had given it to, whoever drove that blue Buick Regal—by now it should be obvious to the new owner that the only secret it held was that it held no secrets. That would be disappointing to anyone who had gone through all that trouble to get it.

Maybe that disappointment would turn to something I could use to tie this all up.

It wasn't over.

I had days and nights strung together, without interruption, to devote to this if I needed them. Some things aren't meant to be found out. Those must be the things that aren't brought to my attention.

The church was huge, made of tan brick and limestone trim in a Romanesque style with a tall Lombard tower housing the bell (I loved the sound of that bell; it tasted sweet and creamy). I climbed the pink granite staircase and found the main door locked. Even churches needed locks now to keep the more active sinners out. I kept a key buried under the hydrangea near the side door. I let myself in there.

Some Catholic churches are built in the shape of crosses. The nave of St. U's was eighty steps long (I had walked it off a lot), that's about 200 feet. Perfect for those long processions down the Italian marble aisle while organ music sounded and choirs sang. The transept, the shorter piece of the cross, was thirty-six steps long and intersected the nave just before the altar.

It was empty. Good. My hard shoes made echoing sounds on the stone floor. I stopped halfway down on the left side of the aisle, shuffled to the middle of a polished wooden pew, and sat. The lights, hanging on thick black chains from the forty foot ceiling, were off, but stained-glass windows on either side let painted sunlight in.

For two dollars you could light one of the votive candles at the front. There were banks of these: some lit, some not, some burned all the way down. Air currents made the flames and shadows move in interesting ways. To me, they felt pliable and sounded like the wind in a field.

I could feel the weight of the air here, I think because it's enclosed, contained, stagnant. I could smell the evaporated wax of those candles and the lingering charcoal and incense from past ceremonies.

It was a good place to meditate.

Footsteps coming down the aisle told me meditation would have to wait.

"I could call the police, you know," said an imperious voice.

I turned to see the Pastor, Father Bernicci.

"Then where would we be?" I answered.

He genuflected, and as he sat down next to me, he said in a

confidential tone, "Up shit's creek."

We both laughed. It sounded good in here.

"I must have missed you at Mass today, Myx."

"So many faces out here. How can you see everyone?" I said. He knew I came here on my own schedule.

He looked ahead, straightened his black jacket and asked, "Did I ever thank you for clearing up that little matter?"

"Only every time you see me."

Richie Lorenzi was thirty now. He accused Father Bernicci of molesting him eighteen years ago when he was an altar boy of twelve. Tried to blackmail him. I paid a sundown visit to Richie's place and what I found convinced him that he had been mistaken. Father Mike wasn't guilty of *that* one.

"Can never be too thankful. What brings you here today? Confession?"

"You don't have that kind of time," I said.

He reached into his inside breast pocket and pulled out a four-ounce black leather flask. "My sister gave me this."

"A true sign of love," I said.

He unscrewed the top, flipped it open with a practiced hand, and took a drink with an approving "Hmmmm." He offered it to me.

"Gave it up for Lent."

Before he took another drink, he said, "And your sacrifice won't go unnoticed—especially by me." He screwed the top tight and put it back in his pocket.

"Tell me of the angel again." He turned to me, giving him diagonal room enough to cross his legs without hitting the pew in front of us. The smell of whiskey was not unpleasant as it blended with the other scents in the church.

"I always remind you that it wasn't an angel. It was like a dream. I can't explain it any better than that. It glowed and I couldn't tell if it was male or female."

"A-ha! Go on." The good Father was enjoying this.

"Both times it was the same room with the same figure there with me. It opened doors. That's it, end of story. It was like a dream, nothing else. I don't think about it much." My voice was cloudy. I don't think about it until I see a dead person. Then I have to look in their eyes and try to validate myself. I decided not to tell him about Johnny Bearcloud's fever dream.

He let me be quiet for a while before asking, "Now, Myx, why are you really here? Is it the Halpern thing? He'd done work in here. You involved there at all?"

I think my shrug deflected the truth enough. "It's not that. Everybody's got secrets. Why do they have to hide them so deep?" In dealing with people—visiting their homes—I had found so many little shames, so many of them alike. Everybody thought they were the only ones who had to conceal them so they wouldn't be judged. I guess after asking the good Father the question, I realized most of my unknowing hosts' guilt and anxiety over their little "sins" was a useless waste of energy.

"That's what the Church is for, my son. We have invisible absolution for imaginary ills. We shine a light on those dark places people make for themselves. How could anyone feel clean if we didn't define the filth and offer a way to purify it?" He had been reaching for the flask again, but let his hand drop from inside his jacket, maybe intoxicated now by his own words.

"But the guilt. Why does it have to be like that?" I thought of Miriam, now without Bindy, and all because he had somehow ... if I only could remember.

"Every *why* we ask questions the grand design. Only God knows how all the pieces fit and when they're to be put in place. Light and shadow, we need them both. Where there is darkness, shine a light on it," he said. He patted my knee twice and left his hand there. I knew our "audience" was drawing to a close.

"You're a handsome boy, Myx." The hand rubbed in light repeated motions. I didn't move. Maybe this was a special blessing. He finally got up, and before he left said, "You should iron that tie."

I got back to my thinking there. The ceiling, the smells, the light, Shelly, Miriam, Bindy, the sisters, my memory.

Why couldn't I remember certain things?

I could only see fogginess in certain areas. Kat had told me to look at things another way. Could I do that? Could she be onto something by luck?

I tried looking in a different color. Nothing. I tried looking from far away at these images. Nothing. I tried looking microscopically close at them. Nothing. I tried looking at them on a time line. There! They were black marks in the time line. I could tell when they occurred. I could remember where I was then, and who I had been with.

What's under the marks?

Father Bernicci had just said to shine a light. What light could I shine on them? the light of reason? the light of hope? the light of logic?

What finally worked was the light of continuity. I could see what happened just before and just after each of the memory lapses, those black marks. The edges there weren't impenetrable, and I could carve away at them by using associations of what had just occurred to what had to have followed. I kept staring in my mind at one until it melted. Then it was easy for me to make all my memories available again.

I brushed my hair back with both hands, brought them around to my face and covered it. I lowered my head.

For a long time, in the painted sunlight, I wept.

Chapter Twenty-Five

I felt better. Not good, but better. After locking the church, I took my time getting home and changing clothes. I ironed the tie before hanging it on my tie rack (which had exactly three ties on it, two of which I bought).

From the sounds coming from their bedroom, I surmised my parents were too busy to chat. I used the cheap laptop Benny kept in the shop to get on the web and print photos of the key to Sonnet's box on plain paper.

I called Kat.

"Billy?" she answered.

"One more guess," I said.

"Myx. He's been calling me every five minutes. He's driving me nuts. He can't believe anyone could dump him."

She sounded like she was going to continue about Billie, so I interrupted with, "Can I trust you?"

"Trust me? What do you mean?"

"I assume Cyndi told Artie about last night. I just want to be sure you can keep things to yourself." No sense going any further with Kat if I didn't think I could count on her.

"Cyndi's a jerk like that," she said with some anger.

"And you?"

"Oh, I'm a jerk in other ways."

Kat's voice looked good. "Pick me up in front of the pawn shop as soon as you can. We have something amazing to do." I thought that would get her going.

"Be there in five." She hung up.

I wondered for a second how she could make it here in five minutes. Then I debated whether to have something to eat.

I won the debate and my prize was two bananas and a piece of Boston cream pie I found in the refrigerator.

Kat was waiting, parked on the wrong side of the road, by the time I got to the curb. She had her hair tied back in a short ponytail, and wore jeans, a sweatshirt and sneakers. She was dressed for action.

"Did you hear what happened to Mr. Powell?" My butt hadn't even touched the seat yet when she asked.

"Tell," I said.

"When I got back in there, right after you left, he tried to stand up, and then collapsed back down. They took him to the hospital with chest pains. Now, I knew you'd want to know all about it so I made a call to Sammy—you know Samantha Keenes, don't you? She's a junior who ..."

"What did Sammy say?" Kat might need help telling her story. I was willing to provide that.

"Well, she volunteers at Miracle Regional two weekends a month and she was there and said Mr. Powell was okay, but they were keeping him overnight."

"Good work. I hope he's all right." I meant it.

Kat smiled and drove off across the street without looking either way. At the end of the street, just before she had to make an on-the-go decision about our destination, she asked, "Which way?"

"Miracle Self-Storage," I said and then braced myself as she turned left.

"Be there in no time."

"No doubt."

She licked her lips, looked like she had her own debate, and finally said, "That thing with Artie today."

This is where I should impress her and tell her I can kick the crap out of anybody. "Yeah. I was wrong about that. I could have gotten away and it never would have happened. No guy should get beat down in front of his girl. I think I did it because you were there. I'd do it different if I had to again."

"Because I was there? How come?" She knew how to milk compliments.

"Hey, you're pretty, popular, and got a great ass. Why wouldn't I show off?"

"I do thirty lunges every day."

Good ol' Kat wasn't going to let false modesty dispute anything I said.

I was gaining a little confidence in Kat's driving by the time we reached my storage unit. "Wait here," I said.

She didn't and followed me, looking around in the few seconds it took to retrieve the bag holding Sonnet's box. She leaned against the pressure of my hand, giving playful resistance as I pushed between her shoulder blades, forcing her out of the unit before I lowered the door and locked it again.

"This yours? You got lots of stuff."

"All junk I've collected. Nothing important." More important to the people I'd collected it *from*, I'm sure.

"What's in the bag?"

I showed her and watched her face. Her mouth made that little silent "oh" shape, and her eyes widened.

Finally she whispered, "Sonnet's box. Did you steal that?"

I had made up a good story to tell her, one that made me the hero. Instead I simply said, "Yes, but not from Sonnet House."

I expected questions about if we could get in trouble and suggestions about how we should give it back right away. Instead, Kat said, "Where to?"

"Miracle High School."

"It's Sunday; it's closed."

"Institutions of learning are always open to those with a thirst for knowledge." I tried to sound like I was quoting somebody smart.

"We're breaking in?"

"When you have a key, it's more like a spontaneous visit." She nodded like that made sense. I had her park a few streets over and we walked to the janitor's door near the dumpster. There weren't any outside surveillance cameras here. This was my favorite way in, in spite of the smells from the dumpster. Kat gagged once.

Now that I had my memories back, I suspected we needed a good-sized space, a floor that had a dark carpet, not tile or wood. I picked the teachers' lounge. Another key got us in there. It smelled of stale food and coffee. They had sharp edges and blue streaks.

This room was off limits to students. "First time you've been in here?" Why was I asking?

"Second. Mr. Broderick took me here once."

I stared at her until she said, "A girl should know when to keep her mouth shut."

"I hope you did," I said and we both laughed. "Help me move this table."

Kat and I cleared the center of the floor, leaving it empty except for the shadows the windowpane dividers threw. The sun was going down, and I wanted to get this done without turning on any lights.

I took two pairs of gloves out of my back pocket. "Put these on so we don't leave fingerprints."

"But our fingerprints are all over here."

"I'm only worried about the inside of the box."

"We're going to open it? We'll be the first ones to open it?" Kat just realized what we were up to. Opening Sonnet's box was a big event for Miracle. Everyone growing up here had heard about it all their lives, and looked forward to it. It appeared that thinking that she was going to be part of it overwhelmed her for a second.

"Unless you want me to do it on my own?" I played with her.

She snatched the gloves from me, put them on, and held her hands vertically in front of her. "Ready, doctor," she said.

I held Sonnet's box in my own gloved hands. Kat had a moment of happy surprise. "Hey, there's the one on my butt," she said, pointing to her symbol on the box.

"Refresh my memory," I said. She gave me a sly look.

"Shelly told us something about what my tattoo meant or where it came from the night she dragged us to Skin Sins. But we were so drunk …" Her voice got lower as she stared off. Her eyes defocused and I knew she was looking at some scene in her mind. She continued after clearing her throat, "It seems stupid now that she's gone, but Shelly could always make us do whatever she wanted and make it seem like the greatest idea we ever heard."

I positioned the box in the upturned palm of my left hand. I wanted to do this quickly because of the weight. "I'm going to point, and you put a finger on that symbol."

She nodded. Then I pointed to four symbols. It was a bit awkward, but finally, between the two of us, we had the eight widely-spaced symbols under our fingers. An added benefit was Kat's contribution to supporting the box's weight.

"Okay, push," I said. Nothing happened. Maybe they needed to be pushed in sequence. "Must be some combination."

"I wish I paid more attention in my statistics class. That was all about how many combinations there are."

She was talking about permutations. With eight symbols to be pushed, there could be over 40,000 combinations. I didn't think Sonnet would be that cute. If we pushed the same symbol in pairs, that would mean only twenty-four combinations. I decided to try that instead.

On our eighth try, the box opened for the first time in 250 years. Actually, the side facing Kat released from the rest of the box by less than a tenth of an inch and stayed at that distance.

Kat squealed and almost lost her grip. "Easy," I said. "Let's put it down." I guided it to the floor with the loosened side on top. Once she let go of it, Kat danced her own victory celebration while I tugged gently at the newly identified lid. It wasn't coming off.

"Is it stuck? Here, let me pull it." Kat bent down and would have applied excessive, overenthusiastic force to the wooden case.

I caught her hand in time and patted it. "You stand there for a minute and look pretty while I figure this out," I suggested.

"You like my hair this way?" She shook her head so the ponytail wagged.

"I can't think how I wouldn't like it," I said and didn't look up. I tried to peek in the crack to get a clue about opening it, but it was too thin and inside was too dark. I pulled up harder with no better results.

I was thinking about pressing the symbols again when Kat said, "Maybe it unscrews." This seemed unlikely to me, but I tried it. Counterclockwise only made the whole box turn on the smooth carpet.

"Kat, hold the box while I turn the top."

She knelt down, framed against the windows. Dust particles floated in the sunlight, some landing on the edges of her illuminated hair. She was close and smelled good.

"Righty-tighty, lefty-loosey—that's what my dad says." She nodded "yes" repeatedly as if that was the solution we had been waiting for.

I applied more force, but the lid didn't move. "Try it the other way," she said.

"What about your dad?"

"Oh, he's always wrong," she laughed.

The other way worked. It did unscrew. It took five revolutions to disengage the top from the wooden spindle with the threaded tip.

Now that I had regained my memories, I had guessed what would be inside. Sonnet's writings, those in the library at Sonnet House, had hinted at it. I wondered if Sarge suspected. If his other interpretations were any sign, I bet not.

The box was stacked tight with square wooden chips. They were in a twelve by twelve array. I picked up one chip; it was about a quarter of an inch thick. That would mean 6912 chips in total. I pushed down on the top layer and felt a springy resistance. That's why you could shake it and nothing rattled: the lid compressed them against some resilience on the bottom.

Kat looked vaguely disappointed and made a grab. "Let's dump them out."

I stopped her, "Let's keep them in order. We have to put it all back together again, you know. This will take a while."

"This isn't the fun part, is it?"

"It's all fun if you think we're going to know the secret real soon." That's as much of a pep talk as I was going to give, but it was plenty.

With one short sudden lunge, Kat leaned close and kissed me on the lips. It was brief and light, but it was definitely a kiss. "What can I do?" she asked. "I can look pretty while helping." She teased me with my own words.

I wanted to just look at her and taste the kiss while it lasted, but heard myself say, "We have to spread these on the floor. But keep them in order, and don't rotate them." I didn't know if rotation meant anything yet.

Each chip had a shiny finish. Some had lines extending across the whole length; some were blank. There were marks on both sides. But in the afternoon sunlight, the reverse sides looked reddish to me, raspberry tasting. Kat couldn't see the difference.

Sarge had said it, "Lacquered in blood." I knew it now. There were two secrets here. The second one needed the map in the Sonnet House. That would be harder. Maybe Sonnet had never wanted that one found or deciphered.

After looking at both sides of the first thirteen chips I said, "I changed my mind—dump them out." Sonnet had carefully packed the box with the blood-lacquered faces down. Maybe others needed his orderliness, but not me since his blood whispered a soft "sssst" each time I saw a coated square.

"Now you're making sense." Kat didn't need any other encouragement. She tipped the box on its side and the wood wafers slid out with little clacking sounds. It was a puzzle, a big one.

"Spread them all out, and then I'll look at it."

"This is impossible. Look at all these. They're just little lines."

Kat sounded discouraged, but I wasn't. Those little lines had started singing to me, telling me their story and how they related to one another. We got them spread out quickly, but lots of them had that redness to them; they were the reverse sides.

"I have to turn some over," I told Kat.

"How do you know?"

"They look funny." I was happy she accepted that and didn't make me explain further. I turned all the "red" squares face down. This took a while. Then I concentrated on the puzzle in front of me.

I didn't bother physically putting it together, but mentally moved them all closer to completion. I just stared, barely blinking, while doing this. Kat sat quietly cross-legged.

After a few minutes, I said, "I got it."

"You're shittin' me." Kat's disbelief lasted only a moment because she asked, "What's it mean?"

"What we're doing here is what Shelly planned to do. She wanted to be the only one who could open the box, and she wanted to do it in a shocking and spectacular way in front of the whole crowd on Tuesday. This was to get back at her father. Did you know she was that mad at him?"

Kat took in a deep breath. She had forgotten about Shelly for a while, and I brought it all back. "How do you know about this?"

"I looked at her diary when I was at her house." I let Kat assume this was recent and not last year. I could finally remember all that was in her diary now.

"I guess she loved him still, but never got over what happened when she was young. But there was something else that was going on with him that she wouldn't tell us."

Maybe she had found out about her father and Hector. I wasn't going to tell Kat that Hector had both Sam Powell and Bindy as lovers. Shelly, maybe out of spite, had seduced him away.

"I think Shelly was going to have you, Cyndi, and Hector show your tattoos when they found the key was damaged. Along with her own, she figured it would embarrass her father while making you four the center of attention and talk for a long time."

"That was a bad plan," Kat said.

"Lots of bad plans work. Some have bad results."

"I wouldn't have showed my ass in public." She crossed her arms.

"Not even to be famous and open the box?"

"Hmmm." Kat unfolded her arms. "So what's it mean?"

"There's an outline of Miracle's boundaries. This is contained in the shape of a heart. Inside all that are the words 'Whosoever enters here finds Forgiveness.'"

"That's it? That's all? That's the secret that's been locked up in that stupid box?"

That's one of them.

This was Sonnet's revelation. This is what had meant so much to him and changed his life. But it was personal and looked ordinary from the outside. Kat was on the outside; it meant more to me— especially now I knew why Bindy had accused me.

Instead of explaining, I said, "Turn all the pieces over." We did this in silence. Kat probably anticipated something more exciting to come.

The sunlight showed each to have that same flavor. More lines, little edges and shapes, I knew I could remember them all. It felt good to have faith in myself again.

Kat put her head on my shoulder while I looked. "What's it mean?"

"Beauty is its own reward." My voice was dark.

"That's so true," she said.

It took a half hour to stack the chips neatly back into the box (red side down), screw on the lid, and press it into the resistance. It clicked shut again. This time, not for 250 years, but for only a few days.

"Shelly never would have gotten it open, would she?"

"Never is a long time," I said. "I don't think they'll be able to figure it out on Founder's Day, either. You want to help if they need it?"

"We're giving it back now? What should I wear on Tuesday?"

I let Kat run her clothing choices by me while I put the box, the key, and the photos in school locker #172. It was an empty one and partially damaged. It would be a safe home until the police got there. I wiped any stray prints off the surfaces.

I stripped off Kat's gloves, and then my own. We left the school by the same entrance, and Kat held her breath this time.

I had her stop at the library after driving by once. There was no one watching. "Don't talk while I'm on the phone," I said before I got out. I didn't need her making noise in the background. It only took a minute to give the location of Sonnet's box, and I wondered if they would even realize it was the pope's voice.

"You can drop me off at Sonnet House," I said.

"Want me to come in?" Kat was hungry for more excitement.

"No, just going to look around before I go home."

"All I have to look forward to is a boring supper at home." She gave me an exaggerated pout.

Supper sounded good to me, but I didn't have time for it now. "Maybe you could try on outfits for Tuesday?"

"Ohhh!—that's right." She looked happier.

A police cruiser sat in front of Sonnet House. It belonged to Sgt. Adriano, the oldest (also the fattest) officer on the force, who was due to retire in a few months.

Kat drove by without my telling her. She stopped at the end of the street. "I'm getting used to you," she said.

"Thanks for helping me today. It sounds stupid to say I couldn't have done it without you, but you can see it's true."

"It was fun. What happens now?"

"Waiting for the big celebration and letting the whole town know what Sonnet said." I left out the part about how the killers still had to pay for what they did.

"You're not telling me something. You going to be okay?" She lost that smile I was beginning to like so much.

Kat was reading me. I wasn't doing a good job in front of her, so I faked harder. "You kidding? I'll call you later just to show you." This was a good time to give her a last kiss.

Instead, I got out of the car and waved before she drove away. Rather than watch her go, I pulled out my cell phone and dialed. I got an answering machine.

After the beep, I said, "I know everything."

Chapter Twenty-Six

I knocked at the back door and called "Sgt. Adriano," a couple of times before he looked through the glass and saw me. One hand rested on the butt of his gun and the other rubbed the sleep from his face.

He unlocked the door and said, "Amens, visiting hours are over." But he turned and let me follow. I closed the door and locked it. "Now that I'm up, let's take the tour." We started to check all the rooms; it would only eat up a few minutes.

"I heard Brass had a scare last night. Came to see if he's okay." My voice was cloudy.

The Sergeant pointed to the broken glass in the case where Sonnet's box had been. The fake box. "He'll be out all week. His back. They got the box. That's all that was taken. Chief has me here babysitting while all the excitement's down at the station. You must have heard about the sisters?" He put his face close to a West Room window and looked out both ways along the edge of the building. The pane next to him had a piece of plywood over it. He pointed to it and laughed, "Brass had some target practice."

"I heard. Must be quiet here now."

"You're the only person I talked to today. They're all buzzin' on Main Street, so no relief. It'll be a long night. Babysitting, that's all; this is because of the robbery."

I looked at the uniform stretched over his 250 pounds. "You must be hungry. Isn't Sunday night clamcakefest at the Chowder House?"

He knew what I was talking about. He took his family there at least twice a month and bragged about getting his money's worth when they had an all-you-can-eat special.

Sgt. Adriano looked out the window again in the general direction of the Chowder House. He was as still as the woodwork for a while. I thought I heard his stomach, but it might have been the house settling.

"You come here a lot?" he asked.

"I keep Brass company sometimes and even watch the place when he wants to make a run to Wendy's."

"Wendy's. That sounds good too, and it's only a few minutes away."

Shut up, Myx—wrong choice!

He was weighing alternatives, but I needed him to be gone for more than a few minutes. I had to tip the scales toward the twenty-two–minute one-way drive to the Chowder House. That would mean I'd have about an hour to myself here. "Their clamcakes aren't greasy at all, and the chowder is so thick and creamy," I said. I tried for wistful.

"Too bad you don't drive."

"Yeah—that sucks. Guess I'll get going."

Before I even started to turn away from him, he asked, "Want to do me a favor?"

"Do I get to keep all my clothes on?"

He laughed and said, "What you do while I'm at the Chowder House is your business. You mind watching the place while I make a run?"

"Sure, go ahead. I'll read in the library. Give me your cell phone number, and if I even hear a squeak, I'll call you faster than a gal can change her mind." I didn't give Brass credit for the quote.

He was barely out the door before I was standing in front of the map in the West Room. The final rays of sunset showed me again which bits here were lacquered in blood. They had never sung to me before because they didn't fit. But now, when I added the raspberry-tasting pieces from the box, the song swelled in volume and harmonized.

I moved and rotated the chips from my memory to hook and join with those in front of me, a puzzle with thousands of pieces that I had to keep straight as a visual image. I found it easiest to keep renewing the partially completed image as a separate picture instead of adding to it continually—just one of the shortcuts that had taken me months or years to learn while adapting to my new mind after my deaths.

After a few minutes, I laughed out loud; I was sweating with the effort as I stood there motionless in the comfortably cool room.

After five minutes, it was complete: the second and more obscure part of Elbridge Sonnet's 250-year-old message. The tiny lines, bits, and swirls had come together to proclaim, "Whosoever enters here finds only Mammon." A diagram showed three five-pointed stars beneath the words. These targeted spots on the paneling to the right of the map's frame.

The scrollwork there presented a long, narrow S-shaped snake.

The puzzle stars covered the head, the tail, and the middle at the inflection point. On the actual panel, I pressed each of these separately. Nothing.

It took a minute to finally find the "middle, head, tail" combination. I had to hold each (the tail with my foot) to get it to work. And by working, I mean that a two-foot-wide by five-foot-high section of the wall sprung out an inch. Molding had hidden the seams. Identical molding repeated in patterns around the room. This one hadn't distinguished itself to me before in any way.

I pulled gently on it and it didn't move. I ran my hand along the inside of the molding and found fingerholds. There was a duplicate set on the other side, both a little less than shoulder-high (people were shorter in Sonnet's time). I set my fingers into them and pulled hard, and when that didn't work, pulled harder. It moved, it slid, it was heavy (were people stronger back then?). Like a defiant solid wood drawer on its tight tongue and groove base, it fought me for every inch as I pulled it out about four feet into the room; now I was sweating for a real reason. The bottom support in the wall held the projection an inch off the floor. Unfinished oak, I could smell it as it squeaked and burned with friction. It stopped and no amount of force would make it go farther.

Three feet of it seemed to be solid wood, and would have made this section seem as dense as any other part of the wall. No wonder no one ever found it. The inner end presented a carved handle, I surmised so it could be pulled shut from the inside. I put that on my list of things I never wanted to do. A black opening called to me from between the two top and two bottom runners. This was a small passage into the wall. An unfamiliar odor came from it. I coughed. The air felt jagged and smelled purple.

I needed a flashlight. I knew Brass kept one in the office desk, but it was locked. The key was under the blotter and a minute later I directed the Mini Maglite beam into the wall. It showed a corridor two feet longer than the piece I had dragged out. There was an oval hole, the edges sanded smooth, on the floor in those extra two feet. The smell came from there.

It was a diagonal chute angling downward about fifty degrees. I leaned as far as I could into it and saw only smooth wood sides. It was about as wide as my shoulders, and seemed to get gradually narrower with depth. I slid the flashlight into my back pocket.

Ever since I had been stuffed headfirst into that 55-gallon drum, I have hesitated about rushing into situations like this. The smart thing to do would be to lower myself cautiously feet first.

I extended my arms into the black tunnel and dove. My breathing sounded loud in the confinement. The farther I went, the tighter it got. Could I get stuck here, head down? That would be, at the very least, embarrassing—at the most, deadly.

I wiggled down using my elbows and finally my toes when I got my body all the way in. I was breathing heavily now with the effort. The sides squeezed more as they continued to narrow against me. The darkness seemed to squeeze too. I finally stopped, wedged. I couldn't even take a deep breath.

Breath.

I exhaled as much as I could, and when the tunnel loosened its hold, I swam downward on that one expelled breath for as long as I could. The exertion made me want to pant, but I needed to keep my momentum. I might not be able to start again.

The inches I fought for turned into feet. I figured about twenty feet total before I fell out of the channel and into the darkest space I had ever known. I managed to flip my body a quarter turn so that I landed on the bottom of my shoulder blades. If I had any air left in my lungs then, I'm sure I would have made a sound. I landed silently except for a clatter from the floor; it had moved with my impact.

I bounced to my feet but stayed in a crouch. I had only fallen about four feet and didn't want to bang my head on the ceiling. I reached up and felt rough beams. That would have hurt.

A deep breath brought a series of coughs. A bitter mustiness saturated the air here. I remained motionless, both listening and trying to gauge any lightheadedness. If this air wasn't breathable, I had to get out quickly. A second or two of sniffing told me it was okay to stay. Even the pain in my back was starting to lessen. I grinned in the blackness.

I kicked at the floor with my left toe, and dug a furrow as it yielded with little clinking sounds. They felt like small smooth stones. I knelt down and felt. They weren't stones; each had a rounded body smaller than a pea that curved and tapered to a point at one end.

I pulled the flashlight from my pocket. It showed me the floor's makeup. The reflected light hurt my eyes with shrill notes and needle-pointed pricks.

It was gold. The whole floor was gold, shining gold. I scooped up a heavy handful of it and let it trickle and tumble through my fingers.

They were tears. Golden tears falling. Each had been cast and molded and then shed down the passage that led me here.

I scooped a hole, trying to estimate how deep the gold pool reached. I stopped at a foot and a half, but it didn't. I wondered how far it went. I don't think of myself as greedy, but I was breathing very hard for no reason other than the sight in front of me. (Maybe my airless crawl was part of it too.)

That's when I felt it, that pressure I get when someone's eyes are on me. I turned and pointed the flashlight at the wall behind me.

The glow room?

He had no eyes, just two dark sunken holes—but I looked and asked anyway. All in black except for the white linen shirt showing through the tattered waistcoat and white stockings below his breeches. A folded hat was on his lap.

An involuntary, "Uhh," squeezed out of me when I saw him sitting against the wall in that simple and sturdy wooden chair. Sonnet, it had to be Sonnet, desiccated and mummified, waiting for me, the solver of his puzzle.

This chamber must have been nearly airless for these centuries—he was well-preserved. Strands of gray hair hung in clumps from the taut crust that was once skin. The cheeks were wrinkled and hollow. I shined the light into his mouth, which had fallen open with death—the tongue was a dried, black sliver, and the teeth showing past the withered lips glared yellow and brown. There were some missing. One hand had fallen to his side; the other was in his lap, near the hat. It had a signet ring on the index finger. The same serpent "S" that had opened the passage above showed on the ring's face.

That handle—he had pulled it shut from the inside and slid down here to sit and die.

Why?

I looked at his writings again in my mind (they were available to me now), and then whirled the flashlight beam to the opposite wall. There were five evenly-spaced words carved across the top in large letters. The deepest reaches of the intaglios glimmered with gold. They were the five princesses of light: Prudence, Fortitude, Temperance, Humility, and Charity. In various volumes, he had referred to himself as "born of woman" then "born of sin" and finally "born of grace." Sonnet himself was the thrice-born dark prince. He had completed his ritual, his miracle of forgiveness, while watching the princesses. Here he was, his final rest on this bed of tears, just like he wrote.

I looked at him and asked, "What did you do to force you here?" Same response as I got with my first question. And without having any real authority to do so, I stated, "Mr. Sonnet, you're forgiven." I got a bit closer to the chair than I had intended, and bumped it. This gave Elbridge Sonnet his first movement in centuries. If I hadn't caught him, he would have leaned off the chair. He felt like a bundle of sticks.

The candle beside him, thick with drippings and topped by a blackened wick had extinguished centuries ago. I thought about lighting it, but didn't want the odor to drift up into the house.

I checked the unfinished wooden walls for another exit; there was none. That slanted shaft was the only way in or out of this ten-foot-square pit. Without looking at him this time, I said, "It was a lot easier for you to get this gold in than it will be for me to get it out." My voice sounded so strange in the cell that I decided not to make any more unnecessary sounds.

That's when my cell phone rang and made me jump. As I answered it, I could hear my heart beating. "Good evening," I said. I hadn't bothered to use star 67 as I usually did on my outgoing calls. That hides your number from caller ID. I wanted this call, and was waiting for it, but had been distracted by Sonnet and his gold.

"You seduced me, Myx." The voice was even, low, and familiar.

"I can do that?"

"You made it always sound so easy. Your plans, they work so nicely. You said a good plan is like the right key to a lock."

Living with Benny must have made that seem like a good metaphor when I said it. I'd continue with it. "But sometimes, you have to jiggle the key to make it open."

"Ahh, the jiggling. That's what I wasn't prepared for. Looking back now, I can see how you were able to instantly adapt to so many situations by adding little touches that are beyond my limitations. I appreciate you even more now."

The flashlight started to dim, so I turned it off and sat down in the dark, on the gold, with my back against the wall, next to Elbridge Sonnet.

Sgt. Adriano would be back soon. I didn't want him finding my gold, but I relaxed and continued the conversation.

"Your box didn't work," I said.

"That was disappointing after all that effort. Do you know why?"

"Wrong box. You got the fake. And you only had half of the key." I pressed my lips together, determined not to say what I was thinking, but then added, "The four lives it cost was more than just an effort." I was surprised at my anger. After dying twice, I had been more able to put things into perspective without much trouble. I guess some things didn't want to be perspected.

"Now, now, Myx. That's not like you at all, is it? Wrong box— that hints that you know where the true box is."

"I do know; the police have it."

"But not before you opened it," he said calmly, deducing correctly.

"Not before I opened it and figured out its two secrets."

"One of which was some meaningless subjective value that gave Mr. Sonnet that oceanic feeling of being in touch with the universe and thereafter some personal epiphany. That part is ordinary, and although perhaps interesting, not of any use to me. I want to know about the map. Did the map show where the treasure is?"

I weighed whether to tell him. "Tons of gold under the house itself. I'm sitting on it. It's going to be very difficult for me to get it all out." I weigh fast.

"Which would make it …"

"Impossible for you." I had finality in my voice.

"Doesn't sound very portable, which is what I truly need at this juncture. So, Myx, I will do what you called jiggling the key. Instead of the treasure, I must be satisfied with the suitcase you were so proud of. That I can carry, and be off to my new life."

How dare he want my suitcase! Especially now that I knew who the true owner was. "That's not going to happen," I said. I felt that more jiggling was about to happen, and I wasn't going to be initiating it.

"I could let the police know about so many of your little indiscretions, but I don't think that would work very well."

The next thing I heard was a scream. A woman's scream on the phone.

"This is very unlike you," I said.

"Yes. Unfortunately, it's required. You know who that was, of course. With your powers, it should be so easy."

"Mrs. Powell. Don't hurt her any more," I said in total darkness while propped next to a 250-year-old corpse.

"Loyalty is a strength, but, sadly, a weakness when exploited. I'm exploiting." There was no smugness, just an objective assessment.

"You'll let Mrs. Powell go, let us both go if I give you the suitcase?" I asked as a formality.

"Yes, of course. I only need the money to make use of my exit strategy and live the life I deserve." The voice was dark, but I knew it would be. "Myx, I didn't intend this to happen."

"Results and intentions are different things. We have to live with results and rationalize intentions," I said.

"You're quoting me; that's flattering."

"How do we do this?" I wanted to hurry now.

"I have a gun which I barely know how to point. A person in an unfamiliar situation, facing grave consequences is …"

"… dangerous," I finished, quoting again. I got his meaning. "Orchard Street is a dead end. No street lights. I'll meet you there in an hour." I gave the simple directions and hung up without saying goodbye.

While on the phone, I had heard the car drive up. It was barely audible down here, even for me.

The sergeant was back and I had to hustle if I wanted to keep my gold. I turned the flashlight on, but it died in a few seconds, leaving me in the now-familiar shroud of blackness. But I knew where my exit was. Once I got to it, though, I found it was too high for me to get into it. I could get my head and arms in, but couldn't jump high enough to start slithering up.

The quickest way would be to appropriate Sonnet's seat. I rushed back to him, put my hand on the chair and stopped. I discovered I didn't want to dethrone him and leave his body discarded.

I'd do the next quickest thing: use the gold itself as my step. I knelt and scooped the heavy metal into a pile beneath the shaft.

I tried twice before it was high enough to shoot me up until I was scrambling, breath exhaled. It actually was easier going in this direction once I had forced my way past the narrowest section. I was racing with Sgt. Adriano. He had opened and slammed the door. "Myx?" he called.

I reached the main floor, pulled myself out of the hole, and scooted in a crouch back into the West Room. The air tasted sweet out here.

I put my palms flat on the extended wall section and pushed. Nothing. I bent low, put my shoulder against it and drove with my legs—it squeaked and moved. I kept shoving until it clicked perfectly back in place.

Then I dropped to the floor and started doing pushups, just as the Sergeant walked in. When I got up, I was covered in sweat.

"Nice work, Myx. Good guard you are. Somebody could have stolen the whole place. Any trouble?"

"Quiet as a tomb," I said, smiling at my apt cliché.

He held up a large white paper bag with a few dark stains on it. The blue lettering, a Zapfino font, said Chowder House.

"Let's eat," he said.

I had just found millions in hidden gold, discovered the centuries-old mummified founder of our town, talked with the person behind the recent killings, and made an appointment in less than an hour to exchange a fortune in cash for the life of a captive woman—this was hardly the time to think about food.

The clam chowder needed a little salt. After I popped the clamcakes into Brass's microwave for a few seconds, they were as tasty as if just served at the restaurant.

264 ■ DAVE DIOTALEVI

Chapter Twenty-Seven

I made two calls while running to Miracle Self-Storage.

The second was my promised one to Kat. I had made the promise, but hadn't intended to keep it. Now I wanted to hear her voice again, maybe for the last time.

"Hello." At least she wasn't still saying "Billy" when answering. Maybe he gave up.

"Meowww." Although I was running at a good pace, I was able to keep my speech even and without breathlessness. I cushioned my steps a bit more so there wasn't any impact on my voice.

She let out a sigh and then laughed. "I kinda like when you say that, Myx."

"Told you I'd call," I said. What I wouldn't tell her is that since seeing her last, I had found a fortune and negotiated with the person behind her friend's death.

"I was just trying on outfits—yanno, for Tuesday when we open the box. I was thinking … you made it look easy … figuring it out. Do you think they could have opened it on their own?"

"It probably would have taken them longer," I said. Lots longer; even if they didn't mix up the blood-lacquered sides with "forgiveness" sides, they would have a puzzle of almost seven thousand pieces to put together in front of a crowd. That would be a letdown for them all. Sonnet had hidden his vault so artfully—I don't know if he ever wanted to be found. Some shred of fair playfulness made him leave those puzzle clues. Leave them for me.

"Did the police get the box?" she asked.

While eating, Sgt. Adriano had mentioned they had found it and thought the robbery had been a kid's prank. They weren't happy about the damaged key, though. I was glad I had wiped our prints off everything (I usually was).

"Yeah, they got it and the ceremony will go on. You remember the message it held, right?"

Kat thought a moment and said, "Something about forgiveness."

"Whosoever enters here finds forgiveness," I repeated for her. "And the heart and the town," I reminded her. "If I don't show up, you tell Chief Maldonato that's what the message was. Tell him I said so. The people in Miracle should hear it on Founder's Day. That's what Sonnet wanted." I pictured Elbridge Sonnet sitting there still; I felt I owed him something now.

"Why wouldn't you be there?" Her voice was very soft.

"How are you wearing your hair on Tuesday?"

"This isn't over, is it, Myx?" I wasn't throwing her off this time.

"Thanks for your help, Kat."

"Kitty," she said.

"Kitty," I said back before I hung up.

There wasn't much traffic on a Sunday night in Miracle. I was thankful for that. I had to carry the suitcase from Miracle Self-Storage to Orchard Street in about a half hour. Not having a license sucked, and I didn't want to "borrow" a car or bum a ride for this trip. The suitcase full of money weighed just under a hundred pounds. This would be interesting.

It was completely dark by the time I left my unit with my Louis Vuitton (at least it was mine for a little longer). Unfortunately, this was a very old model, one that didn't have wheels. I had thought about using my skateboard under it; that might look even more suspicious than I needed.

So I switched hands often, took the most direct route I could, got off the sidewalks whenever a car approached, and arrived early enough to have my shirt start drying before I saw the headlights coming toward the dead end on Orchard Street. I sat on the suitcase, close to the wooded lot, just on the street. Although they had cleared the remains of the fire, I could still smell the bitterness coming from the open cellar hole and foundation. This suitcase had come back to where I found it.

The blue Buick slowed and carefully parked. It remained running, but the headlights went out, leaving the parking lights glowing amber and making this scene taste sour and dull.

The driver's door opened, and he came out with a gun, a Smith & Wesson Centennial Stainless Model 640, which seemed in no hurry to point at me yet. Finally it did when I stood up, and we faced each other.

"I trusted you," I said. This surprised me. I hadn't planned on saying that.

"You had good reason to, until now."

"Yeah, until now," I repeated. "The hypnotism worked."

"Oh, not that well, Myx," said Dr. Zylodic. "I could get you to talk and forget, but I could never elicit any action from you. That would have made it so much easier for me. I couldn't get you to do the simplest thing, like draw those damned symbols. I knew very soon you would see through it all. Your memory, your thinking have so many redundancies.... This was just too soon." He adjusted his black-framed glasses with his free hand.

It was the first time he ever swore in front of me. He was not comfortable here. "I've never seen you outside your office. It's strange," I said. I moved slowly one step to my right. The gun only vaguely followed, but in his untrained hand, it felt more dangerous than others that had been aimed at me by far more competent threats in my past. I really couldn't predict where his bullet would go. There was no peppery smell here. I doubt he had ever fired this gun.

"This has been a trying few days for me. I've been here in Miracle several times. My hypnotic suggestions to you have kept much of this invisible. Very stressful. Which is why I used your acquaintances to do those things that I knew I wasn't qualified to accomplish. As you say, I 'pinched' them."

"Bindy and Hector. Under hypnosis I told you about their secrets, and you used them. I remember it all now. I told you about Sonnet's treasure, how he hid some clues in his books."

"I mentioned that you seduced me, Myx. It started with Shelly Powell's diary all those months ago. Her plan to open Mr. Sonnet's box to shame her father. She's a spiteful girl, Myx. She even took away his lover, Hector Ramone."

"*Was* spiteful," I corrected.

"I chose inferior instruments in Bindy and Hector. Their homosexual love triangle with Mr. Powell seemed an elegant tool. They ultimately proved very unsatisfactory. But they were all tied together. You had found that out. I thought the leverage would be powerful and effective."

"Secrets are a responsibility, even when you steal them," I said. "You used me."

Bindy had been afraid that his daughter, Miriam, would discover he was bisexual. I had caught him and Ramone many times late at night during their "secret" meetings. One time he saw me and knew that I knew. No wonder Bindy thought I had betrayed him after Dr. Zylodic made him part of the plan. I did betray him, during a session, then forgot. Hypnosis was no excuse, not considering the results. Shelly, Bindy, Mr. Powell—Ramone connected them and I had handed that to Dr. Zylodic.

"I used Ramone's greed. He believed I would give him half of what I found. All Hector needed to do was get the key to the box, the four symbols. I knew there were four, Myx. You had told me that. But, sadly, Ms. Powell would not cooperate. She had used Hector against her father and that had probably blinded her to the reaches of his vicious nature. He shot her and took the symbol, her lip, with him." Dr. Zylodic moved back a step when I shuffled forward a few inches. "I never intended for there to be any violence." His voice was white.

"He would have killed you too. You must have known that," I said.

"I know human nature and try to control dangerous situations," he continued. "Hector made several mistakes. Killing Shelly was only the first. The second was getting caught by poor Mr. Steinsaltz, whom you have called Dragon. He shot him at the tattoo studio and took the designs recorded there. All four of them."

"Hector didn't like to lose. He jiggled the key, Doctor. Maybe if he went to Dragon's place first, it would have been different." I was hoping the time we spent talking would be enough.

"He killed him, though, and it continued to go wrong after that. I'm sure, as you assessed, he would have killed me too if I wasn't just an anonymous voice on the phone threatening him about his petty drug trade and luring him with thoughts of riches."

"Bindy didn't steal the box that night. That was his part in your plan, right?" Bindy often stopped at Sonnet House at night to visit Brass and give him a paper. This was another thing I had told the doctor under hypnosis and then had forgotten.

"He was to have given the box to Ramone, but he couldn't bring himself to do it. You can imagine after killing twice already that night, Hector was not to be denied. But he underestimated Bindy; he threatened him, his daughter, and then unwisely showed Bindy the severed lip. In the ensuing struggle, Hector himself was shot. I abhor the loss of human life, but feel very little compunction about that."

"I know Bindy. That's not how he felt about it, after he did it. Ramone pushed him the wrong way. About Miriam," I said.

"Yes, I recognized that and exploited it. When I couldn't contact Ramone, I called Bindy. He was understandably distraught. I have to admit, I was too. It had all gone horribly wrong. But I've dealt with many overwrought patients. I gathered my wits and got the whole story from him and then pointed out that unless he got the box for me, Miriam would be alone when her father was in custody. That persuaded him. Myx, you intruded and he lost all will and courage. It wasn't until last night that he succeeded.

"That's when I hitched the ride. I felt something was wrong." The blood on his hand—it was from the fight with Ramone. The gun, it wasn't in the van then; I was probably lucky. Lucky too that Miram was there when I visited Bindy's home. Hard to think about being lucky when a gun is pointed at you.

"Three deaths, Myx. All for nothing. I had to actually meet with Bindy and use this gun as a threat. It wasn't pleasant. The box he finally gave me didn't open, as you know."

I thought about Kat and me in the teacher's lounge earlier. "It wouldn't have been that easy, even with the real box."

"You're a clever boy, Myx. My favorite, and I have *many* interesting subjects." His finger tightened. We were getting close to the end. "I had hoped you would just leave the suitcase. I know you. That would have meant one thing, my freedom, that you were allowing me a graceful escape. When I saw you here, I admit I felt disappointed. But only slightly. I knew this had to end, that I wasn't a match for you here in your element. Was it Mrs. Powell? I never hurt her much; it was just the use of a pin to make her scream like you had told me once."

"More Miriam … and Bindy. I didn't think you would kill Mrs. Powell. She's in the trunk, right?" I had heard little scufflings coming from there. That meant she was more or less okay for now.

"I would have let her go. One of my subjects is unusually skilled at arranging flawless escapes for unsavory characters. I already availed myself of his services and would have been gone. It's changed now, hasn't it, Myx?"

I ignored the question. "The other reason I'm here, Dr. Zylodic, is to thank you. It all made sense because of you, my synesthesia. I never told you how much I appreciate what you've done for me. How much you've meant to me. How much you've taught me—about dying, and about how to live. Four years is a long time."

He nodded. The gun was getting heavy for him. "It was very interesting. I wonder now what you would have been like as an adult, fully developed. It's time, Myx. We must play to the end. Goodbye."

"Goodbye, Doctor."

I was twelve feet from him, far past my eight-foot rule when I lunged for his gun. The shots sounded loud, round with black tendrils that tasted bitter.

A buzz and a hiss flew close to my left ear, like an insect too busy to stay and sting. Two dark spots appeared on the breast pocket of his white shirt, to the right of his blue tie. I caught him before they turned red at all. I lowered him to the ground, sat and cushioned his upper body in my lap, and kept my arms around him.

His eyes were still open when I asked, "The glow room?" And before they closed I had my answer; I wouldn't have to ask again. For the second time today I felt I had a right to say it. I said, "I forgive you."

I heard light steps behind me, sure and coordinated, like a dancer.

"How'd you get so close?" I asked without looking.

"Some people think it's all about aiming." Rico bent down and took the gun from Dr. Zylodic's limp fingers. He had been the first call I had made on my way here. "Who's this again?"

"Sarge Halpern's partner. After I took the suitcase from his house and called the police, Halpern got away. He must have called this guy, who tried to get it back." I bleached my voice just enough.

"He didn't do a very good job, did he?" Rico had the same calm tone as usual.

Headlights got bigger as the Lincoln pulled up. Guy got out. Rico must have come through my shortcut.

"Remember this place, Rico?" Guy pointed to the missing house. He didn't need an answer. Then he went to the suitcase and opened it.

"Did you look in there?" Rico asked me.

I carefully laid Dr. Zylodic on the street and stood up. "You want the lie or the truth?"

"I think Mr. Damianzo would like the lie better," said Guy.

"Then ... no."

"It's light, Rico." Guy could tell money was missing. Then he found the duct tape, and threw Rico the key.

Rico caught it, turned it in the glare of the headlights, and held it up to me. I shrugged. He put it in his pocket.

These guys never gave up. I had needed to transfer my debt to Sarge. That key would lead them to the box Kat had deposited at the Worcester Bus Station. In it they would find the invoice I had forged for repairs on the house at this address. That was, I hoped, enough of a link to the suitcase. Also in the box was money and enough information to track down Sarge (including a finely-crafted letter from his father in an original envelope with a return address). One day, there would be a knock on Sarge's door which would be the last one he would hear.

These guys never gave up.

Guy closed the suitcase and easily picked it up. When he got to Dr. Zylodic, he bent down, grabbed his belt and easily carried him and the suitcase to the trunk of the Lincoln. He threw them both in.

"You seen too much, kid. You know what Mr. Damianzo calls people like you?" Rico asked.

"Loose ends?" I remembered how Mr. Damianzo had said it.

"No loose ends. It's a rule."

For a second I thought about Kat and the kiss she had given me.

"On the other hand, Mama is making eggplant parmesan on Friday. She wants you there. We'll pick you up at six." Rico got into the car.

Guy called out from the driver's seat, "The eggplant should be good. Don't hang around here too long."

He drove away.

Chapter Twenty-Eight

The trunk overflowed with her scent. She lay there, furious and struggling, illuminated by the small bulb. She squinted; the sudden brightness hurt for a second. Dr. Zylodic had used two kinds of tape: duct and masking. The masking tape held a clean, wadded handkerchief compressed hard in Mrs. Powell's mouth. Considerate of him. Many turns of duct tape bound her wrists together behind her. More turns did the same to her ankles, and a short length of rope bent her knees backwards, connecting wrists to ankles. It looked painful.

"I need your help," I said. She glared back eloquently. I think I guessed correctly at only a couple of muffled words she mumbled through the gag.

I cut the masking tape with my knife and carefully peeled it counterclockwise. I lessened any discomfort by drawing it loose at a downward angle, not pulling her hair much. I took the wet handkerchief from her mouth and wiped around her lips.

That's when she thanked me: "Get me out of here, you little shit!"

Little?

I held her ankles so they wouldn't spring when I cut the rope. She groaned when they released. She had long sleeves on; that made removing the duct tape easier and less painful.

"Stay there a minute and rub your wrists." I massaged her calves and ankles. Her muscles yielded under my kneading.

"Who was that awful nerd?" she asked as she attempted to get out of the trunk. I held her right hand and pulled with a steady pressure.

"Watch your head." The blonde hair felt warm as I guided her past the lip of the trunk. "That was a bad man."

"I could barely hear anything. Who were the other voices?"

"Badder men," I said. If she had any questions about the gunshots, her own imagination provided the answers.

Her legs weren't fully recovered, and she swayed. I caught Mrs. Powell and held her against me for a while. She rested there and finally said, "Is it over now?"

"Almost. You have to follow me to Belmont and then give me a ride home."

Mrs. Powell pulled her head off my shoulder, looked into my eyes, nodded and said, "Whatever." She eased her head back down and we stayed there for a while.

I drove Dr. Zylodic's car to her home, and she followed me in the Lexus to Belmont. The thought came to me that my longest driving experiences came in dead men's vehicles. That probably wasn't as surprising as it appeared since they were no longer in a state to drive them when I needed transportation most.

I stopped in front of the Belmont Dunkin' Donuts on Church Street. She stopped behind me.

I got out and said, "Wait here for me; I'll be back in a while." As I drove off, I saw her pull into the parking lot.

It took only a few minutes to reach Dr. Zylodic's home. He lived alone. I pushed the automatic garage door opener and parked his car there. His house/office was cluttered with papers. I looked at all his files in the cabinets, and then copied everything useful from his computer. Later, I'd check the keylogger I had put on there last year. There was lots about me, lots that I had told him under hypnosis, lots that the police didn't need to know about. I formatted his hard drive, and then took a hammer to it.

I put gloves on even though I regularly had appointments here. My fingerprints should be here, but I was being extra careful because of what I was about to do.

I punctured the oil tank in the basement and sprinkled gas from a five gallon can I found in the garage. I covered both floors, stairs, and the interior of the car. Malik would have been proud of me.

The house was starting to glow as I ran towards Dunkin's. No one saw me.

When I got into her car, Mrs. Powell handed me a bag. It had a butternut and a cinnamon donut in it. A large coffee sat in the cupholder.

"Extra light, extra sugar," she said.

"How did you know?"

"I'm a good guesser. By the way, you smell like a gas station attendant who's been to a luau."

It's hard to torch a house and go totally unnoticed. "Can I use your washer?" No use letting Bunny and Benny puzzle over why I stank.

We drove back mostly in silence. I thought of a 1917 patent I had seen. It was owned by a guy who was thought to have been a crackpot at the time. He invented a hand pulley system that formed a makeshift conveyer belt. He never got it to work right. I saw his flaw and knew it would be perfect for me to get my gold out of Sonnet's vault through that narrow passage. I bet I could move a ton an hour with it.

"Brass Harkins hurt his back at Sonnet House. Think you could get the Chief to let me fill in for him this week on the night shift?" That would give me plenty of time to do my banking.

"The Chief will do what I tell him. But why would you want to do that?" she asked.

"Well, it's Founder's week. It's like being part of history." I didn't mention that I was making history. After the gold was gone, I planned to leave the secret entrance sprung so that Elbridge Sonnet would finally be found.

I already had ideas about where to "borrow" a truck for the week and where I was going to store my gold. On Friday, I'd find out who Mr. Damianzo's gold contact was in Miracle.

Mrs. Powell said, mostly to herself, "Shelly. Shelly's gone, and now I'm alone."

"You know that Bindy Morton died today. He has a daughter Miriam—she's alone now too." I left it there for her to think about.

By the time we got to Mrs. Powell's house, she was dragging. Not much sleep in the past few days. When we got inside. She sat on the big sofa and stayed still. I untied her shoes, took them off and pushed her shoulder sideways. She sank into the softness, her head on a pillow, and curled up. I took the blue fleece throw hanging over the back of the couch and covered her. She snuggled in it briefly, and then was asleep.

I sat in the kitchen and ate a roast beef sandwich with mustard and horseradish while my clothes percolated in the washer (I wore Mr. Powell's running shorts I found near his gun). A cold glass of milk cleansed my palate of the oil and smoke.

After transferring my clothes to the dryer, I headed for the shower to relieve myself of any other lingering traces of Dr. Zylodic's symbolic pyre.

Seeds. The water felt like seeds pelting me. The pressure here was lots better than at home. It felt good. I braced my hands against the wall and kept my head in the hot stream for a long time.

Then I heard the bathroom door open. "Did you find a washcloth and clean towel?"

"All set, Mrs. Powell," I said while keeping my eyes closed.

For a few moments there was a rustling sound, and then the shower door to the rear of the tub slid open. I remained still as Mrs. Powell got in and got close. She put her head next to mine under the water. I could feel her soft naked breasts and hard nipples against my back.

I thought of first seeing her at the police station just forty-two hours ago. Shelly, Dr. Zylodic, the sisters—so much had happened.

"We did it," I said into the spray.

She put her lips next to my ear and whispered, "I bet in a half hour, you'll be saying that again."

And she was like music, just like music.

About the Author

Dave Diotalevi began his career working on atomic submarines then moved on to doing calculations for power plants. His writing includes poems, articles, a nonfiction book called *God's Questions*, and a trademarked and licensed tattoo language system.

His knowledge and experience of religion and mysticism form an underlying current in *Miracle Myx*.

He is the happily single father of one daughter, Kristin. They live in a central Massachusetts town, one very much like Miracle.

Miracle Myx is his debut novel.

KÜNATI

MADicine
■ **Derek Armstrong**

What happens when an engineered virus, meant to virally lobotomize psychopathic patients, is let loose on the world? Only Bane and his new partner, Doctor Ada Kenner, can stop this virus of rage.

■ "In his follow-up to the excellent *The Game*.... Armstrong blends comedy, parody, and adventure in genuinely innovative ways." *The Last Troubadour* —*Booklist*

■ "Tongue-in-cheek thriller." *The Game* —*Library Journal*

US$ 24.95 | Pages 352, cloth hardcover
ISBN 978-1-60164-017-8 | EAN: 9781601640178

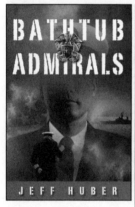

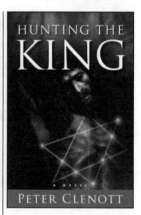

Bathtub Admirals
■ **Jeff Huber**

Are the armed forces of the world's only superpower really run by self-serving "Bathtub Admirals"? Based on a true story of military incompetence.

■ "Witty, wacky, wildly outrageous...A remarkably accomplished book, striking just the right balance between ridicule and insight." —*Booklist*

US$ 24.95
Pages 320, cloth hardcover
ISBN 978-1-60164-019-2
EAN 9781601640192

Belly of the Whale
■ **Linda Merlino**

Terrorized by a gunman, a woman with cancer vows to survive and regains her hope and the will to live.

■ "A riveting story, both powerful and poignant in its telling. Merlino's immense talent shines on every page." —*Howard Roughan, Bestselling Author*

US$ 19.95
Pages 208, cloth hardcover
ISBN 978-1-60164-018-5
EAN 9781601640185

Hunting the King
■ **Peter Clenott**

An intellectual thriller about the most coveted archeological find of all time: the tomb of Jesus.

■ "Fans of intellectual thrillers and historical fiction will find a worthy new voice in Clenott... Given such an auspicious start, the sequel can't come too soon." —*ForeWord*

US$ 24.95
Pages 384, cloth hardcover
ISBN 978-1-60164-148-9
EAN 9781601641489

KÜNATI

Callous
■ T K Kenyon

A routine missing person call turns the town of New Canaan, Texas, inside out as claims of Satanism, child abuse and serial killers clash, and a radical church prepares for Armageddon and the Rapture. Part thriller, part crime novel, *Callous* is a dark and funny page-turner.

■ "Kenyon is definitely a keeper." *Rabid*, STARRED REVIEW, —*Booklist*

■ "Impressive." *Rabid*, —*Publishers Weekly*

US$ 24.95 | Pages 384, cloth hardcover
ISBN 978-1-60164-022-2 | EAN: 9781601640222

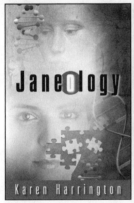

Janeology
■ Karen Harrington

Tom is certain he is living the American dream. Until one day in June, the police tell him the unthinkable—his wife has drowned their toddler son.

■ "Harrington begins with a fascinating premise and develops it fully. Tom and his wife emerge as compelling, complexly developed individuals." —*Booklist*

US$ 24.95
Pages 256, cloth hardcover
ISBN 978-1-60164-020-8
EAN 9781601640208

Miracle MYX
■ Dave Diotalevi

For an unblinking forty-two hours, Myx's synesthetic brain probes a lot of dirty secrets in Miracle before arriving at the truth.

■ "What a treat to be in the mind of Myx Amens, the clever, capable, twice-dead protagonist who is full of surprises." —*Robert Fate*, *Academy Award winner*

US$ 24.95
Pages 288, cloth hardcover
ISBN 978-1-60164-155-7
EAN 9781601641557

Unholy Domain
■ Dan Ronco

A fast-paced techno-thriller depicts a world of violent extremes, where religious terrorists and visionaries of technology fight for supreme power.

■ "A solid futuristic thriller." —*Booklist*

■ "Unholy Domain...top rate adventure, sparkling with ideas." —*Piers Anthony*

US$ 24.95
Pages 352, cloth hardcover
ISBN 978-1-60164-021-5
EAN 9781601640215

Provocative. Bold. Controversial.

Kunati hot titles

Available at your favorite bookseller

www.kunati.com

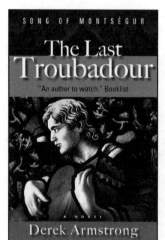

The Last Troubadour
Historical fiction by Derek Armstrong

Against the flames of a rising medieval Inquisition, a heretic, an atheist and a pagan are the last hope to save the holiest Christian relic from a sainted king and crusading pope. Based on true events.

■ "... brilliance in which Armstrong blends comedy, parody, and adventure in genuinely innovative ways." *Booklist*

US$ 24.95 | Pages 384, cloth hardcover
ISBN-13: 978-1-60164-010-9
ISBN-10: 1-60164-010-2
EAN: 9781601640109

Recycling Jimmy
A cheeky, outrageous novel by Andy Tilley

Two Manchester lads mine a local hospital ward for "clients" as they launch Quitters, their suicide-for-profit venture in this off-the-wall look at death and modern life.

■ "Energetic, imaginative, relentlessly and unabashedly vulgar." *Booklist*
■ "Darkly comic story unwinds with plenty of surprises." *ForeWord*

US$ 24.95 | Pages 256, cloth hardcover
ISBN-13: 978-1-60164-013-0
ISBN-10: 1-60164-013-7
EAN 9781601640130

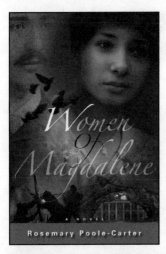

Women Of Magdalene
A hauntingly tragic tale of the old South by Rosemary Poole-Carter

An idealistic young doctor in the post-Civil War South exposes the greed and cruelty at the heart of the Magdalene Ladies' Asylum in this elegant, richly detailed and moving story of love and sacrifice.

■ "A fine mix of thriller, historical fiction, and Southern Gothic." *Booklist*
■ "A brilliant example of the best historical fiction can do." *ForeWord*

US$ 24.95 | Pages 288, cloth hardcover
ISBN-13: 978-1-60164-014-7
ISBN-10: 1-60164-014-5 | EAN: 9781601640147

On Ice
A road story like no other, by Red Evans

The sudden death of a sad old fiddle player brings new happiness and hope to those who loved him in this charming, earthy, hilarious coming-of-age tale.

■ "Evans' humor is broad but infectious ... Evans uses offbeat humor to both entertain and move his readers." *Booklist*

US$ 19.95 | Pages 208, cloth hardcover
ISBN-13: 978-1-60164-015-4
ISBN-10: 1-60164-015-3
EAN: 9781601640154

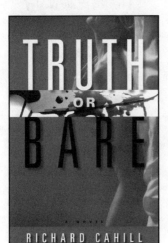

Truth Or Bare
Offbeat, stylish crime novel by Richard Cahill

The characters throb with vitality, the prose sizzles in this darkly comic page-turner set in the sleazy world of murderous sex workers, the justice system, and the rich who will stop at nothing to get what they want.

■ "Cahill has introduced an enticing character ... Let's hope this debut novel isn't the last we hear from him." *Booklist*

US$ 24.95 | Pages 304, cloth hardcover
ISBN-13: 978-1-60164-016-1
ISBN-10: 1-60164-016-1
EAN: 9781601640161

Provocative. Bold. Controversial.

The Game
A thriller by Derek Armstrong

Reality television becomes too real when a killer stalks the cast on America's number one live-broadcast reality show.
■ "A series to watch ... Armstrong injects the trope with new vigor." *Booklist*

US$ 24.95 | Pages 352, cloth hardcover
ISBN 978-1-60164-001-7 | EAN: 9781601640017
LCCN 2006930183

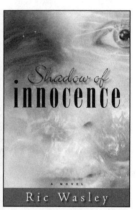

bang BANG
A novel by Lynn Hoffman

In Lynn Hoffman's wickedly funny *bang-BANG*, a waitress crime victim takes on America's obsession with guns and transforms herself in the process. Read along as Paula becomes national hero and villain, enforcer and outlaw, lover and leader. Don't miss Paula Sherman's one-woman quest to change America.
■ "Brilliant"
STARRED REVIEW, *Booklist*
US$ 19.95
Pages 176, cloth hardcover
ISBN 978-1-60164-000-0
EAN 9781601640000
LCCN 2006930182

Whale Song
A novel by Cheryl Kaye Tardif

Whale Song is a haunting tale of change and choice. Cheryl Kaye Tardif's beloved novel—a "wonderful novel that will make a wonderful movie" according to *Writer's Digest*—asks the difficult question, which is the higher morality, love or law?
■ "Crowd-pleasing ... a big hit." *Booklist*
US$ 12.95
Pages 208, UNA trade paper
ISBN 978-1-60164-007-9
EAN 9781601640079
LCCN 2006930188

Shadow of Innocence
A mystery by Ric Wasley

The Thin Man meets *Pulp Fiction* in a unique mystery set amid the drugs-and-music scene of the sixties that touches on all our societal taboos. *Shadow of Innocence* has it all: adventure, sleuthing, drugs, sex, music and a perverse shadowy secret that threatens to tear apart a posh New England town.
US$ 24.95
Pages 304, cloth hardcover
ISBN 978-1-60164-006-2
EAN 9781601640062
LCCN 2006930187

The Secret Ever Keeps
A novel by Art Tirrell

An aging Godfather-like billionaire tycoon regrets a decades-long life of "shady dealings" and seeks reconciliation with a granddaughter who doesn't even know he exists. A sweeping adventure across decades—from Prohibition to today—exploring themes of guilt, greed and forgiveness.
■ "Riveting ... Rhapsodic ... Accomplished." *ForeWord*
US$ 24.95
Pages 352, cloth hardcover
ISBN 978-1-60164-004-8
EAN 9781601640048
LCCN 2006930185

Toonamint of Champions
A wickedly allegorical comedy by Todd Sentell

Todd Sentell pulls out all the stops in his hilarious spoof of the manners and mores of America's most prestigious golf club. A cast of unforgettable characters, speaking a language only a true son of the South could pull off, reveal that behind the gates of fancy private golf clubs lurk some mighty influential freaks.
■ "Bubbly imagination and wacky humor." *ForeWord*
US$ 19.95
Pages 192, cloth hardcover
ISBN 978-1-60164-005-5
EAN 9781601640055
LCCN 2006930186

Mothering Mother
A daughter's humorous and heartbreaking memoir.
Carol D. O'Dell

Mothering Mother is an authentic, "in-the-room" view of a daughter's struggle to care for a dying parent. It will touch you and never leave you.
■ "Beautiful, told with humor... and much love." *Booklist*
■ "I not only loved it, I lived it. I laughed, I smiled and shuddered reading this book." Judith H. Wright, author of over 20 books.
US$ 19.95
Pages 208, cloth hardcover
ISBN 978-1-60164-003-1
EAN 9781601640031
LCCN 2006930184

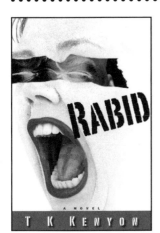

Rabid
A novel by T K Kenyon

A sexy, savvy, darkly funny tale of ambition, scandal, forbidden love and murder. Nothing is sacred. The graduate student, her professor, his wife, her priest: four brilliantly realized characters spin out of control in a world where science and religion are in constant conflict.
■ "Kenyon is definitely a keeper." STARRED REVIEW, *Booklist*
US$ 26.95 I Pages 480, cloth hardcover
ISBN 978-1-60164-002-4 I EAN: 9781601640024
LCCN 2006930189